CUTTING
EDGE

CUTTING EDGE

Jeffrey S. Savage

Covenant Communications, Inc.

Cover photo © 2001 PhotoDisc, Inc.

Cover design copyrighted 2001 by Covenant Communications, Inc.

Published by Covenant Communications, Inc.
American Fork, Utah

Printed in the United States of America
First Printing: August 2001

07 06 05 04 03 02 01 00   10 9 8 7 6 5 4 3 2 1

ISBN 1-57734-844-3

Library of Congress Cataloging-in-Publication Data

Savage, Jeffrey S., 1963-
   Cutting edge / Jeffrey S. Savage
      p. cm.
   ISBN 1-57734-844-3
      1. Computer programmers--Fiction. 2. Mormons--Fiction. I. Title
PS3619.A83 C88 2001
   813'.6--dc21   2001037204
                                        CIP

acknowledgments

A first novel is a constant battle between faith and fear. The fear has been strictly mine, but the faith and support that allowed me to complete this book has come from many wonderful people.

First, a very special thanks to Elder and Sister Savage, of the New Hampshire, Manchester, Mission (and coincidentally my mom and dad) for reading each chapter and giving me the encouragement to write the next one.

Thanks to Kathy Clement, Deanne and Kent Blackhurst, Mark Savage, and Dawn Apsley, for their combined support and great suggestions. It is a much better story because of you.

To Shauna Nelson and everyone at Covenant, thanks for being able to see past all of the rough edges and showing me how to polish them off. Your edits and plot ideas were awesome.

Alan and Cara Black, thanks for the day of fly-fishing on the Provo River. I didn't catch anything, but it was the best stress reliever ever.

And finally, thanks to my family. Erica and Scott, you two are wise beyond your years. Many times you saved me from making mistakes that would have hurt the story, and your enthusiasm was contagious. Jake and Nick, thanks for trying to time your worst diapers for when I wasn't in the middle of a groove. And Jennifer, without whom everything else in the world would just be window dressing, thanks for listening to countless re-readings, and for couching your criticisms in the nicest possible terms. Without your love and patience, this book would never have gotten past the first page. You are the beacon that always helps me see through the foggiest days.

Prologue

"I assume those clicks mean we are on scrambler?"

"As always. So what's important enough to interrupt my Sunday barbecue?"

"There may be a new player."

"What? I thought you said everything was set!"

"It was. This guy's a bluebird—he came out of nowhere."

"I don't believe in coincidences. How did they find him? I thought this stuff was so cutting edge even they didn't know what they were doing."

"He came in off a classified ad. They weren't even looking for . . ."

"Bull! Don't jerk me around here. A classified? I don't believe this for a minute. What are the chances that he's a ringer?"

"I've had a quick background pulled on him. Two years out of college, married, looks pretty clean. And, get this, he's Mormon. I mean, I'm not saying it isn't possible, but . . . would you pull a Mormon kid into this if you were them?"

"For this kind of money I'd pull the Pope in if I thought it would buy me a month or two." After a drawn-out silence, "Has he accepted? I thought that Mormons all stayed in Utah and had babies."

"Hasn't even interviewed yet, but the top guys are really hot on his background."

"Yeah, all right. So do we have someone to put on him? I'm not willing to have things screwed up at this point."

"I'll make some calls."

"OK. But watch him close. If it looks like he's getting in over his head, pull him out quick. If he gets too deep we won't be able to move in without blowing our cover. And I'm not going to blow this one."

"Will do. Get back to your barbecue."

"I think you just ruined my appetite."

CHAPTER 1

For the first few miles, the asphalt bike path appeared deceivingly flat. Skirting the riverside picnic areas, now snow covered and closed for the winter, there was no single point where a runner could say to himself, *Now I am really starting to climb.* But if the increasing ache in his legs wasn't enough to convince Travis that he was running steadily uphill, all he had to do was turn his head and watch the white water next to him rushing madly down the canyon.

Not that he needed convincing. As a college freshman on a full-ride track scholarship, he had raced along this trail beneath the shadows of the Wasatch Mountains more times than he could count. There had been plenty of other places to train, of course. He had definitely spent more hours than he cared to remember sweating through laps around the BYU track, with Coach Westman shouting out split times. But something about the sound of the stiff mountain wind rushing through the leaves of the cottonwoods and elms, playing an understated counterpoint to the roar of the fast-moving water, had allowed him the tranquility to work things out in his head when things got tough.

In the past two years, since his graduation, this trail had become less of a companion though, and more of a demon, reminding him how out of shape he was getting. He had thought that graduating from college would give him more free time. But between the long hours at work, his church responsibilities, and the seemingly infinite number of relatives that had adopted him the day he married, he had found it increasingly difficult to make it up here. And at over 4500 feet in elevation, the thin air was unforgiving to anyone who tried to fit a week's worth of workouts into a single Saturday morning.

Then almost two months ago, Jim Hammond, the president of Exasoft, had called him into his office and informed him that, effective immediately, the company would no longer require his programming skills. Even before telling his wife Lisa, he had pulled on his shorts and running shoes and headed up here to mull over his options. The severance package had been more than generous. With their savings, they could easily last five or six months before things got tight. And, although it was disappointing, it hadn't exactly come as a big surprise to him.

Three months earlier, Exasoft had been purchased by a medical-technologies firm out of Minnesota. It had probably been a good move for the company, but for everyone except the most senior employees, it had been a financial bust. Exasoft had issued so many shares that employees' stock was almost worthless—less than a thousand dollars in Travis's case. And it had quickly become obvious that the new ownership was only interested in the customer base of the small Utah software company. His group, which had been doing some interesting work with Intelligent Assistants, hadn't been the first to be laid off and he was sure they wouldn't be the last. At least, he thought with a smile, it had given him a chance to get back into shape again.

Passing the concrete drinking fountains that would be surrounded by cyclists, runners, and rollerbladers in another few months, he peeled back his glove and checked his pace. The icy winter air met the heat from his body and condensed on the face of the black sports watch strapped to his wrist. But not before he read the elapsed time of nineteen minutes, thirty-three seconds. He needed to push it if he was going to keep his pace under six and half minutes per mile.

Halfway up the canyon, the trail crossed over the river and began to get noticeably steeper. Shortening his stride a little to compensate, Travis reminded himself to relax his arms and hands. On the other side of the bridge he passed by two women bundled from head to foot in heavy winter clothes. He heard one of them mutter something about "skimpy shorts" and the other woman said something that sounded like "indecent exposure."

Turning, Travis backpedaled up the trail and waved. "You should come out here in the evenings. I run in the nude then." He could see their faces turning red and one of them placed her hand on her chest as though the very idea made her grow faint. Laughing, he turned and continued up the trail before they could reply. He could imagine them going home and telling their families about the pervert stalking innocent women in the canyon.

Of course, with my luck, he thought, they'll end up being Lisa's visiting teachers. They'll come to the door with a plate of cookies and a refrigerator magnet that says something like "Modesty Fills our Hearts with Gladness." He would have to apologize on the way back. Besides, he would hate to see them leave this beautiful trail to slog endless loops around one of the local tracks just because of him.

Following the twisting trail into the darkness where it passed beneath Highway 189, he listened to the hum of cars and trucks heading toward Robert Redford's Sundance ski resort and the Heber Valley. Emerging from the frigid concrete tunnel, he increased his pace as he passed by a small gravel parking lot and up the last steep rise of his run. Now, above the sound of his shoes slapping against the asphalt-paved trail, he could hear the deeper sound of a waterfall ahead.

Just over three miles from the west entrance of the Provo Canyon, located about forty miles south of Salt Lake City, Bridal Veil Falls cascades over 600 vertical feet before crashing to the rocks below, where it joins the Provo river and eventually flows into Utah Lake. In the winter, the waterfall freezes, drawing hundreds of ice climbers, who use ropes and picks to scale the treacherous frozen water. And, until an avalanche destroyed the popular tourist attraction, it was also the site of the world's steepest aerial tramway.

To Travis though, it was just the turnaround point of his run. After sweating through five miles of almost continual uphill terrain, it was the point where he could open up his stride and let gravity carry him back down to his car. Sucking the icy air in huge gulps, he picked up his pace over the last two hundred yards and prepared to press the lap timer button on his watch as he came into view of the pool at the bottom of the falls.

"Yes! Thirty-two minutes exactly." He doubled over, resting his hands on his upper thighs, and relished the feeling of the cold mountain breeze against his sweaty face as he caught his breath. Although sunrise had been hours earlier, the rays were just beginning to peek

over the steep cliffs on the east side of the canyon. Straightening, he
left the trail and wandered closer to the river. The warming weather
over the last few days had melted much of the snow on the side of the
trail, and the subfreezing night had formed a thick crust of ice that
crunched under his weight as he walked across it.

Shading his eyes with one hand, Travis studied the slower-moving
water at the edge of the river for signs of the brown, German, and
cutthroat trout that lurked just below the surface of the water, waiting
for a meal to float past them. His father-in-law was an avid flyfish-
erman, stalking the local streams and rivers every chance he got. By
tagging along, Travis had learned the art of choosing just the right fly
and finding the most likely spots to hook the wily river veterans that
could easily exceed twenty inches. But fishing was another thing that
he seemed to have lost time for over the past couple of years.

Watching the rays of sunlight glitter off the sparkling water, he
thought back to the first time he had come here for something other
than a good, quick workout. Only two months after he left his home
in Michigan to start his freshman year of college, his father had called
to tell him that his mother was dead. Although she had left the two of
them when he was only eight years old, and he had seen little of her
since then, the news that she was dead had stunned him. Not even
bothering to change out of his jeans and sweatshirt, he had come here
to run through his confused emotions.

Then, less than six months later, came another call from
Michigan. Only this time, it was his Dad's older bother, Alan. "Travis,
I'm sorry, it's your Dad." The rest of the conversation had seemed to
make no sense, something about a blown tire, and no one's fault, and
then arrangements to fly home. He had found himself agreeing
mechanically, desperate to get off the phone.

He couldn't remember driving to the parking lot a few miles from
the mouth of the canyon. But somehow he had found himself here,
pounding out mile after mile, mentally counting the strike of each of
his steps, until he had finally lost track and started over—knowing
only that the counting would keep his mind occupied, keeping at bay
the pain that threatened to swallow him. He had run until his
normally even breathing had turned ragged and his legs had grown
wobbly with fatigue. Every time his steps had slowed, he had felt

something black and cold bearing down on him, and he had somehow managed to pick up the pace again, until finally, he found himself facedown next to the river, pounding his fists against the rocky bank, and cursing God for leaving him alone.

The next twelve months had gone by in a blur. Word had quickly spread across campus of the double tragedy. But he didn't want sympathy, and he wouldn't stand for talk of greater meanings, or life after death. If he had ever believed in a God before, he didn't then. He simply couldn't credit a being that had the power to create something as majestic as the Wasatch Mountains and yet still allowed innocent people to suffer horrible deaths every day. Mentally burying his head in the advanced math classes he was taking, and running himself to exhaustion at the track every evening, Travis erected an impenetrable shell around himself. He had tried returning to the trail once, but even before he could begin running, his stomach had cramped into a tight hot ball of pain, and he had to stumble back to his car, doubled over and gagging.

* * *

Travis's thoughts shifted. It had been late April, but as the sun disappeared into the clouds to the west, the mountain air had quickly developed a bite to it. Tucking his head low against the cold, Travis was running the last lap of *ladders*, a torturous drill that included three quarter miles, three half miles, three miles, and then back down again. The other runners had all left over an hour before, but he continued, even though the track lights hadn't kicked on yet, and he had to concentrate just to see the lanes in front of him. Sprinting into the final turn, he suddenly realized there was someone else on the track with him, and he'd barely had time to veer over to the next lane as he gasped out the traditional runner's warning that he was passing, "On the right."

As he began to pass, the other runner, who was bundled up in heavy sweatpants and a dark windbreaker, glanced over the wrong shoulder and sidestepped directly into his path. Suddenly, his legs were cut out from under him and he was spinning desperately to the side, trying to keep from falling on top of the other, much smaller person. He had always been naturally athletic, and miraculously he found himself somehow regaining his balance. Then just as he thought he had caught himself, delicately balancing on the tips of his toes, arms windmilling out to his sides, the other runner had crashed down against the backs of his knees, and he collapsed chin-first against the inside rail of the track.

His teeth had snapped violently together, and he was oddly reminded of the sound his cleats made as he clapped them against each other to clear out rocks and dirt after a long workout. As he pushed himself groggily to his knees, the metallic taste of blood filled his mouth. He spit onto the grass and turned angrily to confront the person who could easily have injured them both.

"What did you think . . ." His growl cut off abruptly as he got his first good look at the woman, now sitting cross-legged in the middle of the track. The hood of her windbreaker had fallen back, and long black hair covered her right shoulder and fell across her face, hiding one of her eyes behind its satiny curtain. Her other eye, though, was opened impossibly wide and her mouth formed a perfect "O" that instantly reminded him of the Far Side cartoons drawn by Gary Larson. She was holding her right foot in her left hand. To Travis she looked like a yogi who had just seen a ghost. Unable to help himself, he burst into his first real laughter since the death of his father.

His laughter seemed to break her trance. Her eye narrowed and her mouth finally finished the word it had started to form. "Ow!" she hollered, with surprising volume for someone her size.

Over the following months, Travis and Lisa Whitcomb had become almost inseparable. Like Jack Spratt and his wife, they were complete opposites who were thoroughly compatible. As an only child, he was introverted and uncomfortable in large groups. She made up for this by sharing her nine brothers and sisters with him, and carrying the conversation when he stumbled over his words. Where she was always picked last for the kickball team as a child and was apt to stumble and fall at the worst times, he was almost unnaturally graceful, and always caught her before she could hit the ground.

But they had one difference that threatened to become a major problem. It first came up on their way back from the track that night.

"What ward do you attend?" she had asked as he walked her back to her dorm.

Only a year earlier, he would have been dumbfounded by such a question, but after two years of attending BYU, he felt like he had taken a crash course in Mormon jargon. Ward, he knew, was the term Mormons used for their congregations.

"I'm not a Latter-day Saint." He used the formal name for her religion, trying to make a good impression. Even though he had only just met her, he found that he really did want to make a good impression on her.

"Oh." Her dark eyes were impenetrable, but he had been through this many times before. Here it comes, he thought. Now she will either find a quick excuse to leave, or she'll try to convert me.

But her next words caught him completely off guard. "Do you like steak?"

She had invited him home for the weekend, and her family had welcomed him like one of their own. Her father, a Heber cattle rancher with hands the size of T-bones, immediately put him to work tossing bales of hay down from the loft of the barn.

Although the closest he had ever been to a cattle ranch was a brief stint flipping hamburgers at McDonalds, he enjoyed working up a sweat, and soon he felt like he fit right in. Her brothers showed him the ropes, and Chris, six years old and the youngest of the children, latched on to him, following him around all evening like a lost calf.

But later that night, after a dinner that could have fed a small army, a large calloused hand had dropped onto his shoulder, and Mr. Whitcomb suggested that the two of them walk out and have a look at the stars. From the look on Lisa's face, this might have been a euphemism for the firing squad.

After pointing out several constellations, the conversation had settled into a long pause that made Travis feel both comfortable and yet nervous at the same time. Larry Whitcomb was a man who seemed completely at one with his surroundings. With one toe of his worn boot he pushed down on the barbed wire strung between wooden posts that stretched out as far as the eye could see. He seemed to be considering his words carefully before speaking.

"Lisa tells me you are not of our faith." His words carried neither accusation nor acceptance but rather the same open-faced honesty of the man who spoke them. And yet Travis instantly felt defensive. How dare he judge him or what he believed?

"Not only am I not of your faith, I'm not of any faith." Travis knew he should stop there, but he couldn't. "I could never believe in a God that would let people suffer the kind of pain that I can read about in the paper any day of the week."

He steeled himself for the rebuke that he was sure he had earned. But the big man merely nodded as though Travis had just commented on the weather. "What *do* you believe in son?"

That question had stopped him. At first he had started to answer something glib like *Death and taxes*, but he somehow knew that the man before him would see through that. He rubbed the ball of his thumb lightly over one of the sharp barbs on the fence wire, trying to collect his thoughts. "When I was little, my Dad used to come to all of my competitions. It didn't matter whether it was a baseball game or a track meet; before the event started he would pull me aside and say 'Travis, remember, I believe in you.'" The sound of his own voice saying those words sounded so much like his father's voice that he had to swallow several times before he could continue. "I could always believe in him. And knowing that he was there, I always believed in myself. But, since he died, I'm not sure that I believe in anything anymore."

In the silence of the evening, he could hear the crickets chirping, and the sharp, distant cry of some large bird of prey looking for its dinner. For a moment he had almost forgotten that he was not alone, and the sound of the other man's voice startled him into pricking his thumb.

"A person who doesn't believe in anything is no good to himself, or anyone else. One way or another, you need to find something to believe in."

* * *

The next few months had been difficult for him. The more time he spent with Lisa and her family, the more he had come to respect and admire them. He was around the house so often that Lisa's mother, Annette, had added his name to the chore chart. A sure sign of acceptance, Lisa assured him. He even took part in their family home evenings, making refreshments, leading the music, refereeing the crazy games that her twin ten-year-old brother and sister came up with, and joining the kneeling family as they prayed. But the one thing that he refused to do, felt completely unable to do, was pray himself.

"I just don't understand why you won't even try," Lisa said. They were standing in the field behind the barn. It had been cold enough over the last few weeks to turn the leaves beautiful shades of gold and crimson, but today the warm sun directly overhead made it feel almost like summer.

Travis picked up a rock and threw it at the side of the barn, the noise echoing in the still air. "It would be like . . ." He paused, trying to think of the right words. "Like *you* taking the Lord's name in vain."

Lisa shook her head. "I don't understand that at all."

"Lisa, how can I pray to someone I don't believe even exists? I might as well set up a pile of stones and pray to that, or worship that barn over there."

"You don't need to be sacrilegious." Travis could tell from the set of her jaw that he was upsetting her, but he didn't know what else he could do.

"That's just it. If I prayed now it would be a sacrilege. I hate the idea that an all-powerful, all-knowing God would let His children suffer like they do. I could no more accept a God like that than I could accept a parent that would knowingly let their child step out in front of a moving car."

"But that's what free agency is all about."

"I know, I know. I've listened to the missionary discussions so many times I could teach them myself, and *you* made sure that I read the Book of Mormon. But until I can honestly say that I have the least bit of faith that someone is really listening to me, I won't pray. I can't."

"But how will you ever know if God exists if you won't ask Him?"

"I don't know."

And so, once again he had returned to the canyon. Watching the multicolored leaves skittering across the gravel and asphalt trail in the crisp autumn air, he had felt like Tevye in *Fiddler on the Roof.* "On the one hand, I love her and her family. But on the other hand . . ." Until he was sure there couldn't be any hands left.

Then one afternoon, while hiking along the cliffs far above the canyon, he stopped to watch a pair of red-tailed hawks circling the valley floor in search of a meal. One of them dropped rapidly through the trees, then reappeared with some small rodent clutched in its talons. The creature struggled for a minute, seeming almost to break free and then, as the hawk clamped down its claws, stopped moving.

As he watched the hawks head back up the valley with their meal, Travis felt as though something clicked into place inside his head. Silently he stared into the canyon below, trying to understand what had just happened. Afraid to even breathe for fear it would break his concentration, he replayed the picture in his mind over and over, looking for some meaning. He wasn't sure he could articulate it and didn't think he would ever want to try. But somehow looking down on a life-and-death struggle from this height had given him a different perspective. It was as though for a brief moment he had been able to view everything below him as pieces in a much larger puzzle. Just as the water flowing below was a necessary part of the land that it divided, maybe pain and suffering were necessary parts of happiness.

He sat down heavily on the ground, unmindful of the sharp rocks that cut against his palms. Could it be that he had been so wrapped up in his own needs that he couldn't see the rest of the world clearly? Tossing pebbles down the slope below, he played with the idea in his mind.

Losing his father had been the hardest thing he had ever gone through. But was it possible that it had somehow helped him too? If it hadn't been for the pain he was going through he might never have met Lisa.

Had that been random, a simple toss of the dice that brought her to him when he was sure that he just wanted to be alone? He didn't think that it had. But if it wasn't chance that brought them together then what was it? Like the tiniest break in a bank of thick gray clouds, a crack that allowed a single golden ray of sunlight to slip through, he felt something in his heart soften and the words that he thought he could never utter filled his mouth.

"Are You there?"

Slowly, a grin spread across his face. It was a huge leap from accepting the possible existence of a God to joining an organized religion, but for now it was enough. Without completely understanding how it had happened, he realized that he did believe in something, and suddenly he wanted nothing more than to be with Lisa. He raced back down the trail to find her and tell her that somehow he had found the faith that he had thought would always elude him.

Almost a year to the day later, dressed all in white, he had followed Lisa's father into the baptismal font and listened as the man he had come to think of as a second father raised his hand to the square and said the words that would change Travis's life forever. Later as he had been confirmed and given the gift of the Holy Ghost, he thought that it was the happiest he could ever feel.

Six months after that as he sat with Lisa on a granite outcropping, her younger brothers and sisters in the park below filling the night air with the sound of laughter and excited shouts, he had asked her to marry him. When she had instantly accepted his stuttering proposal, he realized her words could make him feel even happier if that were possible.

* * *

The sound of a group of runners approaching broke his reverie, and he turned to watch two men and a woman continue up past the falls and disappear behind a stand of trees. Crunching his way back to the trail, he looked up the canyon and briefly considered continuing further along the path. He felt like he could easily do twelve or thirteen miles before running out of steam. But Lisa's brother had taken the day off work so he and his wife could move from their apartment into their new house this morning, and he had promised Lisa that he would help. The thought of carrying furniture almost made him change his mind. It seemed, no matter how many other people there were, he always ended up on one end of the piano. But after a few quick stretches he restarted his watch with a sigh and headed back down the hill. If he pushed himself, he thought maybe he could make it back to the car in under twenty-eight minutes.

* * *

Travis pulled the old Ford Escort that he had driven since starting college into the driveway, gathered his damp gloves and shirt off the passenger seat, and jogged down the steps to the front door of their basement apartment. His watch read 9:55, and he had promised Lisa that they would be to her brother's by 10:00. Opening the front door as stealthily as possible, he tiptoed toward the bedroom, hoping he could get in and out of the shower before she realized he was late.

"Travis?" Lisa called out from the kitchen. She sounded annoyed.

"I'll be ready to head out the door in two minutes." He had already kicked off his shoes in the general direction of the closet, and was stripping out of his shorts as he headed into the bathroom.

She came through the bedroom door, wearing a pair of jeans with the cuffs rolled up and one of his sweatshirts. In one hand she carried a half-eaten slice of peanut butter toast, and in the other, she held a piece of paper from the to-do list that hung on the refrigerator. "You got a call this morning."

"Your brother saying that he wouldn't need us today after all?" he half joked. He stepped into the shower and turned the water to full. For a moment the cold stream caused him to back away from the shower head as goose bumps raised on the backs of his arms, then it began to warm up and he stuck his head under the powerful spray.

"No, it wasn't." She deliberately pushed down the handle on the toilet and grinned mischievously as he danced back out of the water that had suddenly turned scalding hot.

"Aaugh! I hate it when you do that." Although he had introduced her to that particular form of bathroom torture, she'd quickly adopted it as her own. He angled the spray to the right and splashed it over the shower door at her, but she had anticipated him and backed into the bedroom doorway.

"It was from a company calling about a job." Although this was good news, she still sounded annoyed. And something about the way she stood with both arms folded above the belly that was now beginning to show signs of the child that was growing inside her, her head cocked to the side, and her lips pursed, told him that she was holding back some important piece of information.

"It wasn't that guy from the ward who's been trying to sign us up on one of those multilevel marketing plans was it?" Travis stepped out of the shower, rubbing a towel over his head and wiping at the steamy mirror with one hand. In the sun, his short clipped hair was nearly red, but when it was damp like it was now it turned so dark it looked black. He debated for a moment on whether or not he needed to shave and decided it was his brawn that would be in demand today, not his good looks.

"No it was a software company . . ." she held the slip stiffly away from her body as though it had some foul substance on it. "From San Jose."

"Oh shoot." This had been a sore subject since he had first begun talking to recruiters during his junior year in college.

"We agreed that we would stay in Utah at least until the baby is older." He recognized the look in her eyes and knew that this was a battle that he stood little chance of winning. "A little girl should be spoiled by her grandmother, and a little boy should play catch with his grandfather."

And when this baby has a little brother or sister? he almost asked, and then thought better of it. The truth was, he liked living in Utah as much as she did. And although he was a little overwhelmed by her large outgoing family at times, he envied her childhood, and he wanted his children to have what he had missed.

"Don't worry. I'll let them know we aren't interested. I only e-mailed my resume to them because I liked their ad anyway. 'Great benefits and all the Pepsi you can drink.' I wrote back 'Does that go for caffeine-free too?'" He laughed, but she still looked dubious.

"Give me the number. I'll call them right now."

She handed him the slip, and hugged him. "I love you."

"Yeah, yeah. *Now,* you love me." He dodged her halfhearted right hook, and was glad to see her smiling again.

As the phone rang on the other end of the line, he checked his watch. He was a little surprised that they had called him this early. It would be a little after nine in California, but programmers tended to keep different hours than most other people. It wasn't unexpected to see someone surrounded by empty soda cans and candy bar wrappers, studying lines of code at two o'clock in the morning. As a result, they often didn't show up at the office until ten or eleven.

"Open Door, come on in!" The voice on the other end of the line sounded perky and energetic.

"I'm not sure I have the right number." For a moment he was confused by her words, and then he remembered it was the company's tag line.

"Who are you looking for?" She seemed unfazed by his initial confusion, as though she was used to the response her greeting elicited.

"Robert . . . Detweiler" he struggled over the pronunciation of the name on the slip of paper, while Lisa shook her head and smiled.

"And may I ask who's calling?" Apparently she had been able to decipher his slaughtered attempt.

"Travis Edwards. I'm returning . . . " his words were cut off by a woman's voice "The Nimitz is backed up for miles. And you know what that means don't you?" He started to answer before realizing that he was listening to a radio announcer. "Don't plan on being in to work for at least another hour." She continued to enumerate the stalls, rollovers, and spills that had freeways Travis had never heard of running even slower than usual.

A few seconds later the phone was picked up by an energetic-sounding male voice. "Travis, how are you? Thanks for calling me right back. I was just discussing your resume with one of our team leaders. Some very interesting things you've been working on out there. Exciting technologies. *Very* exciting."

Travis was overwhelmed by the barrage. "Well, um, thanks. We really thought it had a lot of potential." From across the room Lisa frowned intently at him, and he remembered why he was calling. "Listen Robert, I really appreciate your looking at my resume, but . . . "

"Call me Rob. Now listen. What I'd like to know is how quickly we can get you out here to interview. I have several people I'd like you to meet. Oh, and can you bring some examples of your code? We are very interested in enhancing the design of our . . . Hey, we don't have you under NDA yet do we? Gotta be careful what I say until we have that signed." His voice was muffled for a minute as though he had put the phone against his chest. "Sheila, can you fax out a copy of our standard nondisclosure?"

"No really, it's not necessary. That's why I was calling." Travis glanced at Lisa who was nodding her head up and down vigorously.

"I know, I know. But you can't be too careful these days. Everybody's trying to knock the other guy off the top. Listen, I was thinking about

Friday morning. What do you normally fly out of Salt Lake? Delta? United?" Again his voice was muffled. "Sheila can you check on what flights come in from SLC on Friday morning? Try for San Jose but go with SFO if you need to. Oh, and he'll need a rental car too."

Realizing that the only way he could get through to this person was by imitating his style of talking, seemingly without stopping to breathe, Travis tried again. "No really, I don't think you understand. I appreciate your call, and I wish that I could come out." He continued over the other man's protests, "But I can't. My wife and I have decided to stay in Utah, so it really wouldn't make any sense to meet with you."

Moving to the edge of the bed, Lisa sat and visibly relaxed as she listened to Travis explain their position. She unconsciously patted her stomach as though emphasizing the need to stay near their family. But as she listened to the conversation, her brow furrowed again, and her arms folded tightly across her chest. His protests were turning into nods and murmurs of "yes" and "that makes sense."

"That would be nice." Travis tried to smile encouragingly at her, but that only seemed to infuriate her even more, and she shook her head vehemently and mouthed the word *No!* "Well, as long as you understand that it really won't make any difference." Lisa stood up suddenly and glared at him.

"All right then. I guess I'll see you Friday." As he listened to the voice on the other end of the phone he covered the mouthpiece and whispered, "It's OK." But she still looked furious. "I am sure she will," he continued.

"No we haven't ever been there," he nodded again. "Well thanks, Rob. Bye."

As Travis hung up the phone, Lisa turned and stormed out of the room.

"It's not what you think," he called, following her as she marched stonily out the front door.

"We're late!" As she yanked open the car door and got into the driver's seat, he could see that she was beginning to cry.

He grabbed the edge of the door and held it open. "They want to fly us both out to spend a three-day weekend in San Francisco. I told them that we wouldn't even consider moving there."

She stared at him as though he were speaking a foreign language.

"You promised!" she shouted and tugged on the door so suddenly that he had to pull his hand back quickly to keep from getting his fingers smashed.

He barely had time to run around to the other side of the car and get in before she accelerated back out of the driveway with the tires squealing against the concrete. And from the look she gave him as he got in, he thought that maybe she wished she had remembered to lock the doors first.

In their two years of marriage they had seldom fought, and the fights they'd had were usually heated but short. But after two hours of helping her brother and his wife move, she was still seething and refused to talk to him. Finally, he found her alone for a moment, sitting on a box in the shade of the garage, and he sat wearily beside her on the floor.

"Lisa, I just thought that it would be nice to take a little vacation before the baby comes. San Francisco should be really nice this time of year. They want to pay for the hotel, meals—everything, even though I told them we wouldn't consider taking a job there. All I have to do is spend a few hours at their offices in San Jose on Friday morning, and then the rest of the weekend we are free to go sightseeing. But if I had known how much this would upset you, I never would have agreed. I'll call them back and cancel as soon as we get home."

Leaning down to wrap her arms around his shoulders, she shook her head. "No, you're right. I'm being a big baby about this. I've never been to San Francisco and I'm sure we'll have a great time. It's just that I thought we had both decided that we were only going to look at jobs around here. I guess this pregnancy just makes me overreact to everything." She struggled to keep from sniffling again.

"Are you sure? Because I will call them and cancel if you want." Even as he said the words though, a part of him was already envisioning what they would do on the trip. As a developer with Exasoft, he had never traveled on business, and the idea of a company thinking so highly of him that they would pay for him and his wife to come to San Francisco was exhilarating.

"No, I'm OK." She wiped the back of one dusty hand over her eyes leaving a raccoon-like smudge across her face, and smiled. "And who knows, maybe I'll like it there so much I'll decide to move there. "

"Really?" He couldn't believe what he was hearing.

"No, not really," she said pulling him tightly toward her with a grin, "but I *will* go." And then she smiled at someone over his shoulder. Just as he started to turn, he heard her brother's voice. "Hey Travis, I think they need someone to help with that piano."

Shaking his head ruefully, he heaved himself to his feet. "And don't worry," he said. "There's not a chance that we would move there."

CHAPTER 2

From the outside, the building looked like little more than a two-story warehouse. Silver-tinted windows were spaced sporadically along the smooth concrete walls. Only an inconspicuous vinyl sign stuck to a window near the entrance identified this as the home of one of the hottest Internet companies in Silicon Valley.

The only other hint of the technology hidden inside was the card scanner mounted on the wall to the left of the double glass doors. Outside of regular business hours, employees would have to place a magnetically encoded card against the reader to enter the building. Now, however, as he approached the doors, they swung open automatically, and a female voice announced his entrance. "Open Door, come on in!" Travis searched for the hidden speakers before deciding that they must be built into the door frame itself.

It took a moment for his eyes to adjust, as he stepped from the bright glare of the sunlight outside to the darker interior, and as they did he stopped and stared, dumbfounded by what he saw.

Inside, the building looked like a strange, high-tech nursery school. Brightly colored inflatable chairs and couches were placed randomly around Internet kiosks the height of coffee tables. Miniature palms and giant ferns growing from the in-ground planters to the right and left of the entrance were adorned with red, gold, and silver cards that said things like "Mike Sweeny's team: 120% growth," and "Kwan Lu's team: 128 straight days up time." Through a doorway to the right, he could see five people sitting on the floor of a hallway. A woman with fiery red hair was standing in front of them, performing what looked like a puppet show, while the others laughed and took notes. From another doorway came the unmistakable sound of video games.

The obvious exception to the festive atmosphere was a huge Asian security guard sitting behind a semicircular reception desk just inside the doorway. Biceps the size of softballs bulged beneath the sleeves of his khaki uniform. He sat half reclined in a high-backed chair, arms folded across his expansive stomach, and stared intently forward as Travis approached him.

Walking up to the front desk, he waited for the guard to acknowledge him, but the man remained frozen in place, his eyes now staring directly at Travis's chest. For a moment he wondered whether the guard might be a mannequin of some kind, like the giant cowboy with the speaker in his hat that took orders in front of the Burger Barn where he and Lisa regularly picked up dinner. He imagined himself shouting into the man's belly, "I'd like a bacon cheeseburger, orange soda, onion rings, and extra fry sauce," and had to struggle to keep from laughing. Instead he said, "I have an appointment with Robert Detweiler."

Without changing his solemn expression, the man leaned forward and slid a pen across the desk. "Sign the book."

As he added his name to the bottom of the guest book, Travis scanned the company names printed on the lines above. A few of the hardware and software companies looked familiar, but most of the names meant nothing to him. His eyes dropped back down to one name that seemed to ring a bell—Cochran Edmonds. Where had he heard about that company before? It sounded like an industry analyst, or maybe a venture capital firm, but he couldn't quite place it.

"Take a seat, please." The guard's voice boomed out at him like a cannon, and Travis quickly dropped the pen back onto the desk and took the guest sticker the man was holding out to him.

"Oh, sure." Peeling the back off the sticker and placing it on the front of his shirt, he wandered over to one of the inflatable chairs. As he lowered himself cautiously into it, he wondered absently if the security guard had ever sat on one of these, and then decided that it would be easier to balance an anvil on a water balloon.

The chair was as uncomfortable as it looked, but he soon found himself caught up in the images on the screen of the kiosk in front of him. Open Door had started out as one of the dozens of web search engines, cataloguing the ever-increasing data published on the Internet and providing a tool for users to find the information they were looking for. But as the competition increased, they had quickly added more features. From what he could see, users could sign up for free e-mail, create personal home pages, chat with other web surfers on a variety of subjects, shop for just about anything, download free software, and do dozens of other things.

He wondered why they were so interested in him. They had a very impressive user interface, but they didn't seem to be using Assistants anywhere. Reaching out to the touch screen, he selected the "About Us" link. According to the company profile, Open Door was a little over three years old—young by most industry standards, but long in the tooth for an Internet company. It was surprising that they hadn't gone public already. Scanning the company press releases, he saw that they had received their third round of venture capital funding, a little more than $100 million, nine months earlier. They had received good reviews from the *Wall Street Journal*, *Wired*, *Red Herring*, and several other publications.

He was playing with a nifty Java application that let shoppers compare different products based on their own preferences, when a man about his age plopped down onto the bright orange sofa across from him.

"Travis?" He cradled a worn leather basketball in his left hand while he pumped Travis's hand with his right. "Rob Detweiler." Rob looked every bit as manic as he had sounded on the phone. Wispy light brown hair shot out from his head in every direction and a thick pair of glasses that looked as though they had been stepped on several times, hung precariously from the end of his nose. Baggy blue shorts hung loosely on his long pale legs and he wore a gray sweatshirt that had apparently gone several weeks too long without a washing.

"Just got done whupping up on some UI guys." He smiled noticing Travis'ss surprise at how he was dressed. "Not that there's a real strict dress code here. In fact I don't know if there *is* a dress code here. Anyway, thanks for coming out. How was your flight? No problem finding us? Is your wife here? Come on, let me show you around."

Travis barely had time to nod yes, and shake his head no. Before he was halfway through explaining that Lisa had taken a cab into the city, Rob was pulling him energetically to his feet.

Rob led him through the hallway to the right, past the group sitting on the floor. "Guys, this is Travis Edwards. He's a real whiz at creating Intelligent Assistants. Travis, this is Mary Kowalski. She is the team leader for our Net Greeter project." The puppet on her hand, he could now see it was a bumblebee, nodded hello, but before he could blurt out a quick "Hi," Rob was leading him out of the hallway and past a row of cubicles.

"Sorry for the crowd. We've been growing so fast lately that conference rooms are a little tough to come by," Rob said. Stopping in front of a huge whiteboard, he pointed to a large red grid. Columns were labeled with headings like time line, objectives, team leader, coach, and status. "As you can see, all of our projects are done on a team basis. Team leaders recruit members for their projects from within the company, and based on the success of the project, they all share in the cash bonuses."

He ran his finger down the grid until he came to Mary's group, and whistled softly. "They are shooting for keeping new users on our site for an extra seven and a half minutes on average. If they can do it . . . " he seemed to be adding numbers up in his head, "that would probably translate to a bonus of 17k per person."

"Seventeen thousand dollars? Each?" Travis wasn't sure that he had heard correctly. "How can you afford that?"

"Can't afford not to. Eyes, stickiness, and revenue, that's what it's all about in this business. How many people you can get to your site, how long you can keep them there, and how much money you can make from them. Besides, it's an incredibly competitive job market out there. If they weren't making it here, they'd be making it somewhere else."

As they turned away from the board, Travis noticed a bank of three cameras aimed at different points around the room. "Pretty high-tech security huh?"

"What, those?" Rob waved at the camera nearest them and then made a face. "Not even connected. It's bad enough that big brother can track every time you scan your ID card. They lock the doors to everything but the bathrooms and the break room at nine P.M. After that you have to use your key just to get around the building. But when they wanted to have surveillance on us twenty-four hours a day, all the programmers threatened to walk out. I think they leave the cameras around just to remind us of what a magnanimous concession they made."

They were walking again, past a large white-tiled room containing dozens of different types of computers. Cables snaked out of each of the computers and disappeared into the floor. Rows of monitors were hooked to switch boxes that let the user track what was running on more than one computer. Most of the systems seemed to be running tests of one sort or another.

"This is the testing department. We test our site on over one hundred different computers, with more than twenty operating systems, and dozens of different browser versions. And that's just in English." He stopped and called out to a heavyset man wearing cutoff jeans and a polo shirt, who was bent over two terminals, pulling a long line of cabling out of a hole in the floor. "Runt, come on over here and meet Travis."

As the man stood up, hitched at his shorts, and turned toward them, Travis was instantly struck by two thoughts. *Geez, he is huge!* and *He's going to come over here and snap me like a twig.* As the man came closer, he wondered where the second thought had come from. True, he stood at least a good six-feet-five, towering over Travis, but his smile seemed warm and genuine, and he was already reaching out to shake hands. It was just that, for a second, when their eyes first met, it had been like looking into the cold black eyes of a shark. It was probably the fluorescent lighting, or maybe he had just been reading too many Robert Ludlum books, he thought.

His hand was swallowed in the other man's grip as he introduced himself. "I'm Travis, good to meet you . . . Runt?" The word sounded ludicrous when referring to this giant, and Travis spoke it hesitantly, hoping he hadn't misheard.

But apparently he hadn't, because Runt was laughing and nodding his head. "I know what you're thinking, but I really was tiny before the hormone treatments."

"Hormone treatments?" To his left, Rob was moaning and rolling his eyes.

"Yup, I was barely four feet tall when I started high school. But then my folks took me to a doctor who specialized in helping smaller kids to start growing again. He set me up with steroid treatments that I took twice a day."

"And it worked?" Travis could hardly believe he had ever been four feet tall, even at birth.

"Dang straight. But there was only one problem; I wasn't allowed to have any dairy products while I was on the treatment. And man that was rough, cause I lo-o-oved milk shakes." He rubbed his stomach at the thought.

"So finally one night, I cracked. I was really getting hungry from the growth hormones, and I must have binged on six chocolate shakes at McDonalds. And a week later three of my toes fell off." He looked down and shook his head sadly as though mourning a lost friend.

"What?" Travis was sure he was being strung along now, but he couldn't resist hearing the end of this.

"Um hum. Found 'em in the toe of my left sneaker. My mom was so mad that she rushed me right down to the doctor's office and slammed his door open, gripping three green toes in her fist and threatening to sue him for everything he had." He grinned mischievously down at one huge boot and waggled it back and forth.

"OK, I'll bite. What happened?"

"Well the doctor said that he had warned me not to have any milk or cheese, and pulled a big stack of reports out of the file cabinet. And there, right on top, was a headline that laid it all out in black and white." He paused significantly. "The headline read 'Milk Drinkers Lacked Toes in Taller Runts.'" He was bursting with laughter before he could even get the words out.

Rob patted Runt on one of his broad shoulders. "We want to hire him, not scare him off." Leaning conspiratorially toward Travis he stage whispered, "He tells that Lactose Intolerant joke to everyone he meets. But I saw his Dad once, and I think maybe he really is the runt of that family."

Runt grinned. "But I make up for my lack of size with my incredible wit." Again, Travis was struck by something in his eyes. With his huge size and "aw, shucks" sense of humor, he should have come across as a great, big, lovable teddy bear, but instead he couldn't shake the feeling that just under the surface was a predator marking his prey.

Rob chuckled and shook his head. "In testing maybe, but then again testers aren't exactly hired for their repartee." Taking Travis by the elbow he turned him away from the lab. "Come on, let's get out of here before he starts in on his Bill Gates jokes."

Rob led him down the hall and up a narrow flight of stairs. As they walked together, he went over the morning's agenda. "To save time, we're going to have you meet with several of the honchos all together. Holly Richards heads up Marketing, David Lee is Natural Language Processing and Machine Learning, Peter Makovitch is Product Management, and I am the humble VP of Engineering and Emerging Technologies. It sounds like a mouthful, but I'm really just a glorified coder."

As they reached the second-floor landing and entered another long hallway, he noticed that this level was almost all offices, with only a few scattered groups of cubicles here and there. The carpet was noticeably deeper here, too, and through the occasional open door he could see that the furniture had gone from cheap and functional to expensive and showy. Along the walls, oil paintings that looked to him like fairly expensive originals shared space with framed reviews and awards. If the floor below had been a nursery school, then this was a high-class law firm.

Stopping to stick his head into one of the offices, Rob whispered to a woman who was talking on the phone and typing furiously on her keyboard. "Holly, Travis is here."

Nodding, she held out one hand with three fingers extended, and mouthed, "Just give me three minutes."

Rob nodded, and they continued down the hall. "When this meeting is over, Keith Spencer, the company president, would like to meet with you individually. Martin Graves, our CEO, is in Germany for the week, so he won't be able to see you today. After you meet with Keith, we'll break out for a series of one-on-ones until lunch, and then the rest of the weekend is yours to enjoy."

Stopping in front of a large, glass-walled conference room, Rob pulled open the door. "Here we are," he said, waving Travis in. A dozen comfortable-looking leather chairs surrounded a long mahogany table. In the middle of the table, an ornate silver tray that held a tall coffee urn and a collection of cups sat next to what looked like a high-tech speakerphone. At the far end of the table, a projector showed a series of colorful balls slowly bouncing across a retractable white screen. On the near wall, a white board was covered with bullet points and diagrams that were only partially erased.

"Take a seat, and I'll run and tell everyone you're here." Rob started to leave and then turned back. "You want a cup of coffee or a soda while you wait?"

"No thanks, I'm fine." In truth, he was suddenly not feeling so fine. The rubbery ham and cheese omelet they had served on the plane were still sitting heavily in his stomach, and, even though he knew he couldn't accept whatever job they might offer him, interviews of any kind always started the butterflies flittering around inside him.

Trying to relax, he settled into a chair toward the end of the table and studied the diagrams on the white board. It looked like whoever was in here last had been discussing Natural Language Processing algorithms. Natural Language Processing, or NLP for short, was the means by which computers were able, or unable, in many cases, to understand language the way people spoke it, rather than in preformatted commands. A computer game, for example, might understand the command "Open treasure chest." But a variation like "Lift the lid on the big wooden box," would leave it completely confused. NLP was designed to parse through the text of any sentence and translate it into commands that the program could use.

At Exasoft, he had incorporated NLP into several of the Assistants he had created. By allowing a surgeon to tell his computer, "Get me all of the files relating to this patient," the company's medical software became not only easier to use, but also more thorough in its searches.

Very little of the code on the board looked familiar to him, but that wasn't surprising, considering how little of the NLP programming he had actually done himself. Mostly he had integrated existing NLP modules into his source code. He found, though, that he could follow the general idea of what the developer who wrote it had been doing. One line of code seemed incongruous with the rest, and he tried to puzzle out what it meant. It looked like someone's name had been inserted into the lines of C++ code. "Orville?" he muttered under his breath.

"At your service!" a male voice called to him.

He spun his chair back toward the table, embarrassed that someone had entered the room without him noticing, and then did a double take when he realized that no one was there. Looking under the table, he called out tentatively, "Hello?"

"Hi, how are you?" The voice sounded amused and somewhat familiar but its southern good-old-boy twang sounded out of place in this high-tech office. He wondered if maybe this was supposed to be some kind of a test. It was impossible to locate the source, because the sound echoed in the small, enclosed room, seeming to come from everywhere and nowhere in particular at once.

Searching for hidden speakers, or maybe even cameras, his eyes stopped on the speakerphone at the center of the table, and he realized his mistake. "I'm fine. And you?" It would have been nice if Rob had thought to mention that someone had already joined the meeting by phone. He was glad he hadn't said anything embarrassing.

"I'm great! Hey, would you like to play a game?"

Suddenly he realized why the voice sounded so familiar. It was a dead ringer for Bill Clinton. But he wasn't sure he had understood it correctly. "A game?"

"Do you like classical music?" the voice on the phone asked. This was not exactly the way he had expected the interview to go.

"I guess so," Travis said.

"See if you can name the composer of this piece." Suddenly the sound of an orchestra filled the room. Either the speakerphone had amazing surround sound or else it was hooked up to an internal speaker system. He listened to the sonata for a minute, wondering if this was a normal part of the hiring process or if he was being singled out for some reason.

"I'm gonna have to say Beethoven." He was glad it hadn't been something harder like Liszt.

"Wow! You're smarter than you look, Pilgrim!" Now the voice on the other end of the phone was a perfect John Wayne. He knew programmers could be weird, but this was just too bizarre. First there was Baby Huey telling bad puns, and now a classical-music-loving, Rich Little wannabe. He was wondering how to respond when the door swung open and Rob walked in with a tall blond man.

"I see you've met Orville." Travis thought the man most resembled a nearsighted St. Bernard. It wasn't so much that he was big, as that everything about him looked slightly rounded and shaggy, except for his eyes, which seemed locked into a perpetual squint.

"I have. He's an interesting guy." Unsure of whether or not they were yanking his chain, he tried to keep his voice noncommittal.

"Yeah, he's not too bad for a lizard." Rob had changed into a pair of khakis and a button-down shirt. Dressy by programmer's standards.

"A what?" Struggling to articulate some appropriate response, Travis realized that they were both looking past the phone to the other end of the room. Following their gaze, he saw that the bouncing balls on the screen had been replaced by a grinning iguana sporting a fancy black and gold cowboy hat with the Open Door insignia on the front.

It took a moment to sink in that he had been conversing with a piece of computer software. The voice quality and intonations were perfect. Not at all like the tinny monotone of digitized speech that he was used to. That it had recognized his speech without any training was equally amazing. He had used several dictation packages with fairly good voice recognition in the past, but they usually required hours of training, and even then, the user had to speak directly into a microphone. Thinking about microphones, he looked more closely at the "speakerphone" and realized that there was no number pad. What he had mistaken for a telephone was actually a multidirectional microphone.

As he looked up from the microphone and back at the iguana, he saw a door appear on the screen next to it. The door swung slowly open, and a small brown mouse seemed to step out of some kind of storybook landscape and onto the screen. She was wearing a blue flowery dress and a matching bonnet. In a perfect, squeaky mouse voice she said, "That sounds like my good friends Peter and Rob. But there is someone new here. What's your name?"

This was getting more and more amazing by the minute. To his left, Rob and Peter grinned at each other, obviously enjoying his surprise. "My name is Travis." Although he had been speaking in a normal voice when he thought he was talking to a real person, he found himself beginning to talk louder as though speaking to someone hard of hearing and then corrected himself. He had done enough work with voice recognition to know that speaking louder than necessary actually made the voice more difficult to process.

"Well, hello Drabis! I'm glad ad ad ad ad ad ad ad. . ." The voice kept repeating the last syllable like a scratched record, and then the screen turned blue and an error message appeared.

Peter instantly stopped grinning, and Rob quickly slid out a recessed keyboard from the far side of the table. But from the doorway, a woman's voice sounded completely unperturbed. "It's a feature!"

"I'm Holly Richards." The VP of marketing wore a sharply tailored, gray business suit, and took Travis'ss hand in a firm hand-shake. "Here's a card, which I see these two bastions of civility have failed to give you. Did they even bother to introduce themselves before they turned Orville the Iguana and Maggie Mouse into mincemeat?"

"I'm Peter." The shaggy blond spoke with a strong Russian accent and looked slightly sheepish as he handed his business card to Travis. But Rob was still hammering on the keyboard as he watched strings of computer code fly by the blue background on the screen.

"Cards? We don't neeeed no steenkin cards roun here Senorita," Rob affected a weak bandito accent. But he reached one hand into his shirt pocket and slid a business card across the table, still typing with the other hand.

The door opened again and a young woman carried in a stack of forms and set them on the table. "Was there anything else you needed, Rob?"

Looking up, Rob glanced around the room and let out a frus-trated sigh. "Only if you can somehow find a way to get David to meetings on time."

"Sorry, I don't think that's listed in my scope of responsibilities," Sheila called out over her shoulder as she left the room.

"Sheila thought she'd finally managed to get him to meetings on time by telling him the start time was a half hour earlier than everyone else." Rob picked up the stack of papers and began sorting through them.

Peter laughed and rebooted the computer that Rob had been using. "He figured that out weeks ago. He says that the first thirty minutes of all meetings are a waste of time. He even wrote a filter that intercepts all his e-mails and moves the time on his appointments to half an hour later, so he can plan on being late."

"Is *that* what we pay him to do? Well, we're just going to have to start without him." Rob glanced at his watch. "I've got 9:45, and that means he won't be here for at least another fifteen minutes."

As everyone took their seats, he went around the table handing a stack of papers to Peter and Lisa and dropping another set, apparently for David, on the table in front of an empty chair. "I've included a copy of Travis'ss resume, the two-way NDA signed by Travis and our attorney, and a list of the projects that Travis was working on at his last company."

Each of them glanced briefly at the documents and then at each other, as though no one was sure who should begin. Holly pulled a sleek black pen out of her planner and tapped the back of it on the resume in front of her before finally speaking. "You've done some pretty impressive work for someone only two years out of college. But if you don't mind my asking, why Intelligent Assistants?"

Travis could feel his stomach muscles beginning to relax. This was more like what he had been expecting. "I've always felt that most software is too hard to use. How can you expect the average user to learn an application that's more complex then the problem it's supposed to be solving? For my senior project I created a genealogy helper assistant that's still being used in two commercial genealogy packages."

Shaking her head as though dismissing his words, Holly continued. "I can see that from your resume. But what do intelligent Assistants have to do with a small medical software company in Utah?"

He smiled. "I guess the company that bought us out had the same question."

Around the table everyone laughed politely, but it sounded forced, and for the first time Travis noticed an undercurrent of tension that appeared to be affecting everyone in the room. Rob and Peter sat next to each other directly across from Holly. Peter's hands were clenched tightly on the table. Rob, slouched back in his chair, looked the most relaxed Travis had seen him all morning, but the fingers of his right hand drummed over and over on the sheets of paper in front of him. Holly, seeming to find the documents in front of her very interesting, was smiling slightly as she underlined something with several black lines. At the end of the table, Travis alternated his gaze between the two factions.

"Did it ever occur to you that your company could have invested the money they were spending on Assistants for something more practical, like increased product functionality?" Holly was driving at something. But her words didn't jibe with the direction that Open Door seemed to be headed.

"Honestly, I don't know why every software company isn't investing heavily in Assistant technology." Everyone at the table was leaning forward. Even Rob had sat up in his chair, and seemed to be listening more closely.

"And why would that be?" Holly was still looking down at the papers, but she had stopped writing.

"I know most people still associate Assistants with the paperclip in Microsoft's office products. Or some of the miserable failures that effectively killed the phrase 'artificial intelligence.'" He paused to see if he had offended any of them. Unable to catch anyone's eye, he continued on. "But in the next three to five years, Assistants are going to be integrated into everything from document management to e-commerce. Five years ago, people thought they had information overload, and now we're exponentially increasing the amount of information available electronically every year. You guys have to be aware that standard search engines aren't going to be able to keep up with all of it."

Without any warning, the room suddenly exploded into a series of accusations and recriminations.

"Where's your data?" Holly was waving her pen around like a light saber.

"Haven't I been telling you? Even he can see it!" Rob was on his feet now, leaning across the table as though he was about vault across it.

Peter was shouting something, but his accent had gotten so thick that Travis couldn't tell whether he was speaking English, Russian, or some combination of the two. Travis could only stare dumbly at the two groups, wondering what he had stepped into.

Just at that moment, the door swung open and a tall, thin Asian man entered the room. One of his arms was loaded down with a stack of spiral-bound notebooks, and the hand of the other clutched the largest computer bag Travis had ever seen. He paused in front of the doorway, obviously taking in the scene before him, and then without a trace of irony asked, "Did I miss something?"

For a second, his words seemed to hang in the air like a cartoon text balloon, and everyone stopped speaking, as if frozen into silence.

Then, just as quickly as they had been at each other's throats, they were all laughing. Like popping the cork on a bottle of champagne, the pressure that had been building in the room was instantly gone. Everyone was smiling, except the newcomer, who shook his head as though dismissing all of them as lunatics while he arranged his notebooks and bag on the table in front of him.

"Obviously, we have a slight internal disagreement on the relative value of Intelligent Assistants." Rob drew his hands from only inches apart out to each side of the table in a gesture that looked to Travis like Moses parting the Red Sea. And from what he could see, it would take an equally great miracle to bring these two sides to agreement. "But that is a decision that has already been made, and it's because of that decision that we have asked you here, Travis."

He paused for a moment as though waiting to see if anyone would disagree with him. When no one did, he turned toward the man who had just entered. He had flipped open one of his many notebooks and appeared to be engrossed in its contents. "David, since you have decided to grace us with your presence, do you have any questions for Travis?"

For several seconds David continued to read, oblivious to everything around him. And then, just when it looked like he either hadn't heard the question or was intentionally ignoring it, he pulled his eyes away from the text with what seemed to be a monumental effort.

"Did you bring any samples of your code to show us?" He ran his fingers through his unruly black hair and raised his eyebrows, as he looked toward the screen rather than at any of the people sitting around the table.

"Yes." Travis pulled a slim, white CD case out of his computer bag and slipped one of the shiny gold disks from its plastic sheath. As he stood, he realized that he hadn't yet seen any computers in this room. Obviously the keyboard and the microphone were connected to a system somewhere nearby, but he hadn't the foggiest idea where it might be hidden. And neither Holly nor David seemed inclined to give him any clues.

Fortunately, Rob came to his rescue. "Here, let me." He took the CD from Travis and motioned for him to take the chair in front of the recessed keyboard. Rob pushed on one of the wall panels to the left of the screen and it swiveled outward to reveal the tall beige case of a PC. After he had inserted the CD, he returned to stand behind Travis and reached over his shoulder to start a virus checker running.

"Sorry, but it's company policy. No software can be run on any company system without first being scanned." Travis wasn't surprised. Computer viruses could be especially nasty on a company network, and the best firewall in the world could only stop infected files coming in from outside.

Once the scan had finished, Travis used the keyboard's built-in mouse to open one of the directories and launch the executable file. As the application started up, he explained what its purpose was. "Even in today's world of medical specialists, doctors have to be able to keep up with what's happening in other fields. Most medical research today is available from one Internet source or another, but sifting through it all to find what you need can be very daunting, not to mention time consuming."

On the screen, a two-dimensional picture of what looked sort of like Einstein on one of his better hair days peered inquisitively out from the screen. Above him, a text bubble contained the question "What can I help you find?" Normally, Travis was extremely proud of his Assistants, but after seeing Orville's earlier demonstration, he felt very self-conscious. "Sorry, no speech synthesis here, and the graphics aren't quite up to par with what you guys have."

He hoped the voice recognition would work OK. He had never tested it with this type of microphone. "Wise Guy, get me all of the information you can find on skin cancer in children under five." In the balloon, the text had changed. The question now read "How long would you like me to search?"

"One minute." It seemed like the microphone was going to work OK after all.

On the screen, a large magnifying glass had appeared in front of one of Wise Guy's eyes, making it seem to take up half of his face. The text balloon had now been replaced by the flashing red text "Thinking."

As Travis waited for the sixty seconds to expire, he tried to come up with something witty to say, but his brain seemed to be stuck in the same thinking loop as the Wise Guy on the screen. It was probably for the best anyway, he thought. He had never been very good at getting up in front of people, and now it felt like his salivary glands had suddenly stopped functioning. If he tried to speak, he was afraid it would come out sounding like a croak.

Fortunately, the wait wasn't long. The word "Thinking" had been replaced by the words "Search complete."

Swallowing dryly, he tried to speak clearly. "Show results." This was the "gee, whiz!" part of his presentation. If they didn't like this, it was going to be a long morning. Or maybe a short one.

On the screen, groups of articles were divided by category, relevance, publication, and date. Behind him he could hear murmurs of approval as he instructed the Assistant to find and summarize various documents. Throughout all of his commands, the application worked flawlessly.

Finally he issued his last command, "Go away, Wise Guy," and turned back to face the group. Peter was whispering something to Rob, who looked like a mother whose son has just won the school spelling bee. And even Holly, who had been scowling skeptically when he started the demonstration, looked impressed.

Of the entire group, only David seemed disinterested. He merely nodded to himself, wrote something in another one of his notebooks, and then looked back up. "Is there any more?"

He had two other Assistants on the CD, and through both of his next two presentations the response was fairly similar. Holly seemed to have lost some of her previous antagonism toward Assistants, and at one point Peter actually stood up and clapped. But if David was impressed, he certainly didn't show it. Occasionally asking a question relating to one piece of code or another, he mostly jotted down notes, or in some cases ignored things completely while he read.

As Travis neared the completion of his last presentation, thankfully sipping one of the sodas that an Assistant had carried in, Rob suddenly jumped to his feet. "Look at the time! I have to get you to Keith's office right away. Thanks, guys I'll recap with you this afternoon. And if any of you are free, we are doing lunch at about 12:30."

Travis put the CD back into its case and gathered his things, while Rob fluttered around him looking at his watch like the White Rabbit from Alice in Wonderland and muttering to himself something about Travis missing his appointment. As soon as Travis had closed his computer bag, Rob grabbed his arm and rushed him down the hallway to an older woman sitting behind a low desk.

"Pam, Travis is here to meet with Keith."

Pam picked up the phone, passed on the message, and after listening a moment, stood and gestured toward the door.

"Mr. Spencer will see you now."

As she led Travis away, Rob pantomimed shivering, and, with a wide grin on his face, stage-whispered, "If you're not back in an hour, we'll just assume he ate you."

As Pam escorted Travis into the office, Keith stood up from behind his desk and gripped Travis's hand in a firm dry shake.

Keith Spencer wore business casual the way other men wore a suit and tie. From his gray-flecked, black hair to his solidly square chin, he was the image of professionalism. On the wall behind him hung a family portrait painted in oils. In the portrait, his wife, an elegant-looking woman, who could have been anywhere between her early forties and late fifties, sat in a high-backed chair, flanked by two beautiful blond daughters. Behind the chair, Keith rested one hand on his wife's shoulder, while on the floor, a golden retriever sat at stiff attention.

Motioning Travis to sit, he turned to his Assistant. "Thanks Pam. When's my next appointment?"

"You have about ten minutes." She lingered in the doorway as though waiting to see whether she would need to change his schedule, but he waved her away.

"That should be plenty of time for a couple of hard-working businessmen to come to an agreement, don't you think?" He flashed a smile at Travis that left no room for disagreement.

"Sure." Travis could understand why they had brought this man in to take the company public. He looked like he could woo investors and drive competitors to their knees. And, apparently, all before lunch.

As the door swung closed, Keith returned to the chair behind his desk and silently studied Travis. With so little time, he had assumed that Keith would want to start talking right away. But as the seconds ticked by, the president simply stared intently at him over steepled fingers. Travis shifted uncomfortably under his gaze. What was he waiting for? Was this another test? And if so, what did he need to do to pass it? He opened his mouth, not sure what he was going to say, and then shut it again. What could he say? "Nice company you have here." Or, "Say, those are a couple of mighty cute daughters you have there, not that the dog isn't nice, and well, your wife . . ."

What he really wanted to do was ask, "Why did you bother to fly me here when you know very well that I'm not going to take a job in California?" But he sensed that anything he might say right now could only make him more vulnerable. He remembered a TV documentary on lions. The narrator had pointed out that lions looked for prey that seemed sick or injured. No, he would just sit there silently for the full ten minutes if he had to.

After what felt like an eternity, the man smiled ever so slightly and lowered his hands to the desk in front of him. "Let's get right to the point. I have a company that is going public in sixty-one days, and I have investors that are screaming for a killer application. Now, with barely two months until I hold my throat bare to the public and wait to see whether they slit it or not, my people are telling me we may have a problem."

Suddenly he remembered where he had seen the name on the sign-in book—Cochran Edmonds. One of the business magazines he had been reading on the plane had published a story about the new millionaires being created every day by the Internet stock boom. Cochran Edmonds had been quoted as one of the top investment banks that had acted as lead underwriter in several recent public offerings. If they were underwriting Open Door's IPO, it had to be big. With no idea of how to respond, Travis merely nodded.

"I have some of the cutest, cuddliest, and most likable Internet characters you ever met. I assume you have already met some of them yourself." If it was a question, he didn't wait for an answer. "Unfortunately, my VP of Marketing tells me that they don't actually do anything very useful. And people who had better know what they're talking about for the money I pay them, tell me that you can fix that."

Again Travis had no idea how to respond, so he continued to sit quietly as the president pinned him to the back of his chair with his intense gaze.

"So the only real question for me is, what will it take to get you here?"

Travis coughed into his hand, trying to decide how best to respond. This was even more direct than he had expected.

"I'm really honored that you value my skills so highly, and I have to say that I am really impressed with your company. But I think I made it clear to Rob the first time we talked that I can't move to California. I guess I could consider telecommuting, but my wife is pregnant and I don't want to be on the road a lot." He knew that he was starting to babble and stopped himself before it got any worse.

During his response, Keith never changed expression. Not even with so much as a nod, or a shake of his head. Instead he asked a question that left Travis speechless for a moment.

"What if I offered you a million dollars right now to come to work for me?"

Suddenly swallowing had become very hard. "Are you offering me a million dollars?"

"Just yes or no. Would you take the offer?"

For a moment Travis pictured Lisa's face if he agreed to move out of Utah. But even here, in the excesses of Silicon Valley, they weren't about to offer him that kind of money unless he could hit Jerry Rice with a sixty-yard touchdown bomb, or slam-dunk over seven-foot centers. Feeling that he was on fairly safe ground, he agreed. "Sure, for a million dollars, I'm here."

"OK then, what if I offered you my position as president of Open Door?"

With this one he felt even safer. "You bet." He wasn't sure where they were going with this discussion, but the rest of the day hadn't gone as he had planned so why should this be any different?

"Good. Then we've established the fact that you *can* move to California. It's just a question of making you the right offer."

Travis struggled to come up with the right response, but the other man was already on his feet and coming around the desk.

"It's been a pleasure meeting you Travis, a real pleasure."

As he walked back out the door, Travis tried to understand what had just happened. They had just been talking generalities. No one had even tried to make him an offer. And he certainly hadn't agreed to anything. Had he?

* * *

From the journal of Lisa Edwards

Friday, Feb. 25

Wow, I am exhausted from the top of my head to each of my swollen toes. I really haven't felt like a pregnant woman until today. Gee, couldn't be because I spent the entire day on my feet could it? But, oh, it was worth it! I had no idea how good really fresh seafood could taste, and it felt like we tasted all of it today. I thought that at any minute I would grow whiskers and start barking like the sea lions we saw next to Pier 39. (If I keep eating like this, I'll probably start walking like them too!)

While Travis was in San Jose, I was the brave young adventurer, exploring San Francisco on my own. I told the cabbie I wanted to take a cable car to Fisherman's Wharf, so he dropped me off at the end of the line. The hills didn't really affect me on the way up, (What do you expect? I live next to the Wasatch Mountains) but when we crested the top of the hill and started going straight down, I thought I was about to lose my breakfast. I think it was only the idea of spending the rest of the day wandering around the city in vomit-covered Reeboks that stopped me. Once we got past the steepest part, I felt much better. And then, a block or two before we got to Fisherman's Wharf, I smelled the most heavenly scent. Ghirardelli Square, a chocoholic's paradise! The only exploring I did for the next hour was up one candy aisle and down another. If they don't have chocolate in heaven, then I'm looking into the alternatives. (Ha, ha.)

Once the baby was full, (I'm sure I couldn't have eaten that much sugar on my own!) I explored Fisherman's Wharf and spent far too much money on souvenirs. At first it was too foggy to see the Golden Gate Bridge, but by 11:00, the sun burned through the fog, and it actually got so warm I had to take off my sweater. Can you believe it? Here it is, still February, and I am walking around in shirtsleeves. Won't my friends back in Provo be jealous?

I was thinking about taking a boat ride out to Alcatraz, but then I saw a bus go by with a Macy's ad on the side. Hmmm . . . exploring a cold empty prison, or lunch and window-shopping at Macy's? Let's just say that this was NOT a difficult decision. After lunch I headed back to the hotel to take a nap until Travis got in.

Speaking of the hotel, this place is amazing. I thought the hotel in Hawaii where we stayed on our honeymoon was nice but this place makes it look like Motel 6. "Aloha, we'll leave the light on for you." Every room has its own stereo, complete with CD player and CDs. The bathroom has more bottles of lotion, shampoo, conditioner, mouthwash, and you name it, than some drug stores. And the extremely soft, king-size bed is to die for. I opened the sliding door that led to a small balcony so I could enjoy the afternoon breeze, and was just about to start my nap when there was a knock at the door. I thought that Travis was back early, but instead it was a bellboy with a vase of flowers and, guess what? More Ghirardelli chocolate! Pardon the smudges.

On top of the chocolate was a nice note from the company that Travis was interviewing with. Inside the note were two tickets to tomorrow night's showing of Miss Saigon. I still hate the idea that they think they can talk us into moving out of Utah, but it's hard to despise someone who sends you flowers, candy, and orchestra level theater tickets. (Not to mention paying for this whole weekend!)

I'm really too tired to write any more about today, but suffice it to say that "a good time was had by all."

PS The only really weird thing about today was when I asked Travis how his meetings had gone. He went on and on about their "killer apps" and "awesome technology." But when I pressed him on whether or not he was clear with them that we were not leaving Utah, he said that they hadn't even tried to make him an offer. Then he muttered something about a million-dollar salary and being company president. When I asked him what he was talking about, he just laughed and said that everyone in California was strange, even the iguanas. Oh well, I'll see if I can get more out of him tomorrow.

Saturday, Feb. 26

The show was great.
The food was sublime.
Saw a lot.
Had a wonderful time.
Barely awake.
Tired poet.

Going to sleep?
You know it!

Sunday, Feb. 27

We are on the plane back home and I am so mad I could spit!
Travis knows it, too, and he keeps saying things like, "We don't have
to take their offer. Really." Like I am going to be the one responsible
for turning down all that money! But I'm getting things all out of
order here. It's just that I am SO angry! Why couldn't they make a
nice normal offer that we could politely refuse?

It all started this morning when Travis was in the shower and
there was a knock at the door. I thought it was housekeeping and I
kept telling them to come back later. Finally, I realized that the
woman outside was saying, "room service," and I thought, "Oh, how
sweet, he ordered us breakfast in bed." I pulled on my robe, opened
the door, and she wheeled in a cart covered with at least a dozen
plates. She just kept pulling off one silver lid after another, and,
although I knew we would never be able to eat it all, it looked
yummy. Belgian waffles, ham, southwestern omelets, strawberries and
cream . . . and then I saw the envelope, and my heart just dropped. It
had the Open Door logo in the upper left-hand corner and it was
addressed to both of us.

I tried to tell myself that it was just a thank-you note, but deep
down I knew it wasn't that at all. I even thought about tearing it up
and throwing it away before Travis got out of the shower. (I could
hear him singing in there at the top of his lungs.) I only thought
about it for a second, but was it ever tempting! But instead, I just sat
on the bed with the letter and waited for him to turn off the shower
and come out of the bathroom. I guess he hadn't heard the door,
because he looked as surprised as if I had magically summoned all the
food from thin air.

He was actually halfway through a Belgian waffle and was stuffing
a fork full of omelet into his mouth before he realized I wasn't eating
anything. When he saw the letter, I could see that he was trying to
hide the excitement in his eyes, but he pretended not to know what it
was. I am trying very hard to believe him when he says he had no idea

what was inside, but I just feel like I have been used. It's like Pinocchio having fun and games at Pleasure Island, and then finding out that they plan on turning him into a donkey and sending him to work in the mines.

I am not sure I understand all of the details of the offer, but the relevant points are these: If Travis agrees to work for Open Door for a minimum of one year, starting a week from tomorrow, we get stock options that could be worth anywhere from $200,000 to $500,000 at the end of that time. They are also offering a base salary that is more than twice what we were making at Exasoft, plus performance and signing bonuses. Of course, they will be happy to cover all moving expenses, and their benefits package will cover my pregnancy (like that somehow makes it all better.)

I'm afraid to pray about it, because I just know if I do, Heavenly Father will tell me that it's the right thing for us. The money's great, and this is a once-in-a-lifetime opportunity for Travis. But how can leaving my family and all the friends we've made in Utah be right? It just seems completely unfair that something I know will make Travis so happy is making me so miserable.

I'm going to stop now because Travis is trying to unobtrusively glance over my shoulder. I've been managing to keep up a brave front about this so far, but if I keep writing I am sure that I'll start bawling.

CHAPTER 3

Except for the faint thrumming of the tires on the empty Nevada highway and the occasional spatter of an unfortunate insect impacting on the windshield, the night was utterly silent. In the passenger seat of their new Jeep Grand Cherokee, Lisa lay burrowed beneath a pink-and-white, hand-knitted afghan. On the dashboard, the glowing green digits read 3:15, more than three hours after Travis had hoped to be sleeping soundly in a hotel room. For a moment the numbers seemed to move in and out of focus, then double before his eyes. Rolling down the window, he forced his face out into the biting desert air, allowing the cold to shock him completely awake.

It was Friday night, actually Saturday morning now, and they needed to be climbing the pass into California by nine o'clock to have any hope of picking up their apartment keys before the rental office closed at four o'clock. Their belongings wouldn't actually be arriving until Monday morning, and he would have been happy to wait until then, but Lisa wanted to explore their new apartment over the weekend.

"If we have to choose our new home sight-unseen, then the least they can do is give me at least twenty-four hours before the movers show up, to decide where we are going to put everything," she had insisted when he suggested that they sleep in, then spend the weekend somewhere fun like Monterey.

He felt bad that there hadn't been time for a house-hunting trip, but the human resources department at Open Door had been considerate enough to send out a relocation packet that included a list of rentals in the area. They were hoping to rent a house, but one look at the prices had quickly convinced them that an apartment would have to do for now.

Fortunately there had been a really great deal on a two-bedroom, two-bath that, according to the brochure, included a fireplace, full gym, year-round pool, and sauna. And best of all, it was right across the street from a bike path that passed within two blocks of Open Door's offices. If he wanted to, he could bike or maybe even run to work and never have to deal with the nightmare traffic. Stapled to the front of the brochure was a bright yellow coupon offering a rate that was almost four hundred dollars less than the published price.

It seemed too good to refuse, and so despite the fact that they had never actually seen the apartments, they called the number on the brochure and after checking with her manager, the girl in the rental office had signed them up for a twelve-month lease.

The plan was to stay in a Nevada hotel tonight, reach San Jose by mid-afternoon and spend the rest of Saturday and Sunday at one of the guest suites that the company reserved for out-of-town employees and other visitors. Lisa had tracked down the chapel location and meeting times of their new ward, and they had packed dress clothes so they could attend services on Sunday. And if the members were anything like the ones in their past wards, he thought that they would probably beat the movers to the apartment on Monday, delivering foil-covered casseroles and offering to help unpack boxes.

In the distance, a silver corona of light was just beginning to penetrate the star filled, black sky. That would be Reno, home of the $8.99 steak and lobster dinner and the $29.95 hotel room. Now just under sixty miles away, according to the last highway sign they had passed.

But the distant light could also be symbolic—the bright future awaiting them to the west, a heavenly spotlight pointing the way to new opportunities. Like the star of Bethlehem leading the Wise Men toward . . . no, that was stretching the analogy too far. He glanced over at Lisa and smiled, imagining her response if he woke her up to share *that* image.

He wasn't sure what had brought on this mood anyway. Ever since the movers had come and packed up their belongings under Lisa's watchful eye, he had felt an itch to be on the road west. Surely many of the people in the valley they had left behind would have likened it to their pioneer forefathers leaving their homes in the east and following the wagon trail westward to Salt Lake. But he felt more like one of the forty-niners loaded down with picks and shovels, and flush with the fever of gold, heading to California to stake his claim and prove that he was the best.

That was another analogy that he thought would be better left unsaid right now. While this opportunity might be an exciting adventure to him, he knew that it was one of the most difficult things that Lisa had ever done. That was one of the reasons they had gotten out on the road so late. Two days earlier they had turned in their house keys to Mrs. Hanson, the gray-haired widow from upstairs. She had given them each a long, teary-eyed hug, told them to "Take good care of that baby, now, and send me a picture," and pressed a huge plate of marshmallow brownies on them as "good traveling food."

Then yesterday, all of the relatives had gathered together at the Heber ranch for a going-away party. The day had been a time of conflicting emotions. More than once, he had watched Lisa wandering aimlessly around the ranch as if trying to memorize all of the places and things that she would be leaving behind. He had been hesitant to interfere, afraid that he might be intruding, until her father had come up behind him and reached out to lay a hand on his shoulder.

"Go talk to her."

"But I don't want to make things any worse for her. I mean it's my fault that . . . " Larry halted him by placing a thick-knuckled finger to his lips.

"Did the two of you pray about it?" he asked.

"Yes of course, but . . . "

"Then it's no one's fault." Larry had leaned against the windowsill and stared out at his daughter with the same look that Travis had seen in Lisa's eyes all day. "I think this will be a harder transition than either one of you anticipate, but she's a fighter. Always has been since I could hold her in the palm of my hand. And you two will need each other out there." Although the words had been spoken so softly they were almost inaudible, Travis had felt them burn inside him, and for some reason, goose bumps had broken out on the back of his arms and neck.

"Now go out there and be with her. Talk to her. But most of all just let her know how much you care for her."

As he had stepped off the back porch and crunched through the snow toward the stables where Lisa was brushing down the horse she had owned since she was ten, Travis had tried to decide what he could say to her. This wasn't just about the money. He knew that he could find another job here that might not pay as well, but certainly well enough to meet their needs. And there were plenty of other software companies that would give him stock options, too.

But for Travis, it wasn't about compensation, it was about recognition. After more than twenty years of competing in every sport he could sign up for, and struggling to be at the top of his class in high school, and then college, he had found himself stuck doing a job that meant almost nothing to the rest of the company, and even less to the rest of the world.

Then this opportunity had come along, and he knew that it was his chance to prove himself. Silicon Valley was where some of the best programmers in the world competed head-to-head to create the newest technology breakthroughs. If he could play an important part in a hot Internet start-up, it would be like striding into the OK Corral to face the best gunslingers in the West and living to tell the tale. Then, with the money and the credibility, they could come back to Utah and maybe start up a company of their own. It was as if losing his job at Exasoft had been a blessing, Heavenly Father's way of forcing him to find a job where he could make a real impact.

But as he had watched Lisa stroking the back of the horse she had grown up riding, he had felt guilt welling up inside of him that was stronger than anything good he could possibly get from any job. No matter how he might try to explain things, he would come out sounding selfish and egotistical. So instead, he had simply walked up behind her and wrapped his arms around her, burying his face in the back of her neck.

"Travis." Lisa had turned in his arms and tilted her head to look up into his eyes. "How are you doing? I know this is hard on you."

"Hard on *me*?" This wasn't at all what he had expected her to say. "You're the one I'm worried about. I know how tough it is leaving your family and your best friends and everything."

"Sweetheart, you are my family *and* my best friend. So as long as we're together, I'll be fine." She had taken his hands in hers and squeezed them. "I am going to miss all this, and leaving it hurts even more than I thought it would. But we decided on this together. We prayed about it together. And we're going to do it together." She had pulled him down onto a bale of hay in the stable and sneezed at the clouds of dust that floated up as they sat down.

Laying her head in his lap, she had looked up at him and then squeezed her eyes shut, unable to see, as Travis could, how her chin had trembled as she said. "Now tell me again about how great this job is going to be and about all the things we can do when we move back here in a year."

* * *

Even on the most somber of occasions, the Whitcomb family could not be together long before everyone was laughing and having a good time. And by two-thirty that afternoon, after everyone had eaten as much steak, ribs, and spuds as they could without popping, and the babies had been put down for their naps in various bedrooms, the family members had broken out into their own activities. A few of the older brothers and sisters had gone riding with some of their cousins. The younger boys and girls were down by the barn playing some kind of complicated capture-the-flag game with lots of flying snowballs. Travis could occasionally see them slipping around the sides of the outbuildings or peering stealthily up from the knee-high snow forts they were hiding in. In the dining room, most of the aunts and uncles were involved in a hotly contested game of Scrabble, with much debate and dictionary checking going on.

Travis and Lisa were sitting on the couch watching the cedar logs in the fireplace crack and sizzle as the fire slowly ate away at them. On the rug next to them, Fidget and Mischief, the collies that thought they ruled the ranch, lay soaking up the warmth. He was thinking how much he would miss all of this, while simultaneously wondering how soon he could suggest that they get going, when Lisa's mother, Annette, walked in carrying two slices of strawberry-rhubarb pie.

Sticky red liquid filled the bottom of each of the saucers, and a single drop threatened to fall from one of them onto the floor. Sensing food, the two dogs jumped up and sidled against Annette's legs. Shooing them away with the hand that wasn't holding the plates, she slid onto the couch on the other side of Travis and offered each of them a plate. They both made noises about being too full and not eating another bite, but somehow they each found themselves holding a fork and swallowing bites of her tart red pie as she watched approvingly.

"I know that you two need to be leaving soon," she said.

"Oh, no, we've got lots of time." Lisa was talking to her mother, but her eyes darted toward Travis, daring him to disagree.

"Absolutely. We're in no rush at all." Travis nodded emphatically.

"Well, I don't want you kids out on the road too late. I know you're planning to drive all the way to Reno tonight, even though you know you're more than welcome to stay here and leave first thing in the morning." She paused as though waiting to see if they would give in on that point, and then continued. "Are you sure you have everything? Did you pick up snow chains?"

"Mom, everything's fine." Lisa set her pie plate down on the floor, where the dogs instantly lapped up the remaining juices and crust. She reached across Travis and took her mother's hands in hers. "Is that really what you came in to talk about, snow chains?"

Annette shook her head. "I never have been able to beat around the bush with you. Even when I was trying to teach you about the birds and the bees, you had to get right to the point."

"Mom!" Lisa pretended to be embarrassed, but it was Travis whose cheeks were slowly turning scarlet.

"Well, that's not what I came in to talk to you about either." In the distance the shouts of the playing children carried through the still air, and she turned away to look out the window at the running figures. "You probably won't understand this until you have children, but even when your kids are grown up and married, you still worry about them. You know you can't make their decisions for them anymore, but you hope you've raised them to make the right decisions on their own."

Lisa looked near tears. "Mom, are you saying you don't think we should go?"

"No, it's not that at all," Annette said. "It's more a question of what you'll do once you are there."

"I don't understand." Lisa no longer looked like she was going to cry, but her face was still pale and her voice sounded high and strained.

"It's just that you've lived such a sheltered life here. I'll bet you still don't even lock your front door at night." Lisa and Travis looked at each other guiltily. On hot nights, they usually left the front door open to get more air flowing through their apartment.

"And it's not just that." Now she turned toward Travis. "Money can change people. You haven't told us what they are paying you, and it's none of our business anyway. But I know you wouldn't be leaving if they weren't making you a very good offer. And that shiny, new four-wheel drive out there must have cost you dearly."

She paused for a moment as if she was afraid she had gone too far, but then seemed to make up her mind and hurried on. "Just remember that *things* don't make you happy. Your father and I had some of our best times back when we had to struggle just to afford the basics every month. And if you ever find that things out there aren't working out exactly the way you had planned, well, I just want you to know you can come back and stay with us any time you want."

This was more than Travis had ever heard her say at one stretch, and he was deciding how to respond when Lisa finally did burst into tears. "I love you, Mom." She pushed past Travis to pull her mother into a tight embrace, and he could only lean back and try to keep from being crushed.

Once most of the kids had returned to within shouting distance, and the day's Scrabble Queen had been crowned, Larry called everyone together into the big living room. Waving one open palm downward, signaling everyone to silence, he nodded toward the big picture window where the late afternoon sun was now rapidly disappearing behind the mountaintops.

"Well, these kids have got to get on their way if they don't want to fall asleep somewhere out in the middle of the desert. Assuming, that is, they don't want to spend one more night here." He glanced at Annette for approval, and then on the sly winked at Lisa and Travis. "But before they go, I wanted to get everyone together and offer a word of prayer for their safe journey."

Parents hushed children, and everyone bowed their heads as he began to speak. His deep timbered voice was much softer when he prayed, and everyone listened quietly as he asked Heavenly Father to watch over and protect his children until they returned again safely to their family. Every time Travis listened to him pray he was struck by how comfortable he sounded. It was as though he was talking to an old friend instead of Deity. He had asked Lisa about it once, and she said that her father had told her, "When you've gone through enough good times and bad times with someone, you kind of get on a first-name basis."

After the prayer, it had taken them another half hour to complete all the rounds of hugs, kisses, and last-minute advice, as they made their way out to the car. When they were finally in their seats, Larry had leaned through the passenger's window and kissed Lisa on the top of her head. "You two drive real careful, now. If anything happened to you two because I didn't talk you into staying the night, your mother would plant one of her boots so hard on my rear, I'd be walking funny for a month." Although he was smiling, tears had slowly traveled down the deep creases in his leathery brown cheeks.

Lisa had put her hands up to either side of his face and wiped away the tears. Travis had watched her struggling to keep from crying herself, and then she had rubbed her own eyes and tried to smile. "Dad, after all the time you've spent on a horse, you walk funny all the time."

As they had pulled away from the ranch, waving to the group assembled around the gravel driveway, her smile had trembled, and then disappeared completely. She had buried her face in the afghan her mother had crocheted for them as a going-away present and curled into the position that she was in now. She had wakened briefly when they stopped for gas, but other than that she had slept the entire drive. He knew that she had gotten very little rest the night before, and he had tried to drive as carefully as possible to keep from disturbing her.

Now, as he pulled off the freeway and onto Reno's main drag, she woke up and stared out the front window groggily. The brightly colored neon lights of the casinos flashed an ever-changing pattern on her face, making her look like some kind of sad circus clown. He reached across to squeeze her hand and she smiled weakly.

"Let's find an all-night buffet," she said. "I'm starving."

He grinned. She was going to be OK. "I think I can do that."

* * *

Thick gray clouds leaked relentlessly down onto the tile roof of the church, as though torn by the steeple that jutted up toward them. Rain puddled on the black asphalt behind the building. At five minutes to nine a constant stream of cars and minivans turned off of Hacienda Blvd. and pulled into the white-lined spaces of the parking lot. People with bags, purses, lesson manuals, and the occasional umbrella held protectively above their heads called out quick hellos to one another as they hurried their families into the building.

Inside, the hallways buzzed with activity. Teachers seeking chalk, erasers, and pictures for their classes crowded around the library entrance. Children begged for a stop at the drinking fountain as their parents herded them toward the chapel. Groups of teenage boys and girls eyed each other as they caught up on who had gone where and with whom on Saturday night. From the chapel doors, the sound of organ music blended with the voices of members greeting one another as they slid into their pews.

Lisa and Travis hurried up the hallway toward the chapel, noting the pictures of ward activities tacked to the bulletin board and the world map with colored lengths of yarn indicating where missionaries were serving. Beads of water dripped down Lisa's long hair and disappeared into the dark blue cotton of her jumper. As they passed through the sea of white shirts and ties and Sunday dresses, curious glances followed them. New faces always attracted attention. *Who was that nice-looking young couple? Visitors, new move-ins, or maybe even nonmember investigators?*

As they walked from the foyer into the chapel, a round-faced man in a dark wool suit handed them a bulletin and offered his hand. "Hello, are you two visiting today?"

"No. We're the Edwardses. We just moved into the Waterford apartments on Madison." Lisa slipped the bulletin into the front of her scriptures.

"Great! Welcome to the ward." His pink cheeks rose in a smile as he pumped both of their hands vigorously, and he seemed almost to beam at them. "I'm Bishop Johnson. Do you need any help getting moved in?"

"No, the movers will be unloading everything tomorrow." Travis thought that there must be a Bishop class somewhere that taught "How to Welcome in New Members 101." It seemed to be the same everywhere. By this afternoon phones would be ringing off the hook, setting up meals, assigning visiting teachers from the Relief Society and home teachers from the priesthood. It was comforting to know that Lisa wouldn't be sitting home alone while he plunged into his new job, but he sometimes felt a little suffocated by it all.

"Well, it's good to have you in the ward. I'll have someone get you a ward directory, and we'll get Brother Black to send for your records," he said.

They chose one of the padded benches toward the back of the chapel, and Lisa elbowed Travis and pointed to the program. Next to the phone number of each of the ward and auxiliary leaders was their e-mail address. "Only in Silicon Valley," she whispered, smiling.

In Sunday School, a tall woman wearing owlish brown glasses asked all of the visitors to stand and introduce themselves. When they said they had just moved into the ward, dozens of faces craned around to see the new members. Travis's eyes were instantly drawn to one person in particular. Among the dozens of clean-cut faces, his shoulder-length hair and full beard stood out like a grizzly bear in a field full of sheep. Probably a programmer, Travis thought. They're always looking to break out of the mold.

After the class, Lisa joined the rest of the women heading to Relief Society, and Travis sat through the priesthood opening exercises and then followed some of the other men into elders quorum. Before starting his lesson, the class instructor, an angular man in a loose-fitting gray suit coat, again introduced Travis. "Maybe you could take a few minutes and tell us a little more about yourself. Where you moved from, what you do, what brings you to San Jose?"

Even in church Travis was still uncomfortable speaking in front of people, and he cleared his throat nervously. "Well, I work for an Internet company, called Open Door. I moved here from Provo, Utah with my wife, Lisa. And we're expecting our first child in about three months."

"It's nice to see someone moving here from Utah instead of the other way around," a tall man with a Mickey Mouse tie called out, and everyone laughed. Travis understood the joke well. Although there were Mormons living all over the world, they always seemed on the verge of moving back to Utah. He had once heard a joke that went "Question: What is Mormon wine? Answer: 'I want to move back to Utah.'"

"Well, we'll be living here for at least a year," he said. "But after that I can't make any promises."

"What do you do at Open Door?" It was the bearded man he had seen in Sunday School. Their eyes met for a moment, and Travis thought he saw a flash of recognition. Had he met him before somewhere? He didn't think so, but he wasn't sure.

"I'm a programmer. I'll be working on a new product that could really change the way that people use the Internet. Assistants will . . . " suddenly the class instructor's hand closed around his elbow.

"I hate to cut you off, Travis, but we have a really long lesson today. Maybe we can talk later." The man squeezed his arm twice as if trying to signal something and then turned Travis back toward his seat.

What was that all about? If he'd needed so much time for his lesson, why had he asked him to get up and speak in the first place? The more Travis thought about it, as the instructor began reading from the manual, the angrier he got. It wasn't as though his lesson was so awe-inspiring that he couldn't have spared another minute or two. Maybe Californians thought they were so busy they had to rush everyone else along too. If this was the way people here acted, it was going to be a long twelve months. He stewed all through the class, unable to concentrate on the teacher without getting mad all over again, and as soon as the closing prayer had ended, he quickly grabbed his scriptures and lesson manual and walked out the door.

At the end of the hall, he stopped to take a drink and get himself together. Maybe he was overreacting. There was no point in blaming the whole state for one inconsiderate person's behavior. After all, hadn't there been a few strange people in his last ward? He remembered the guy who always snored so loudly through Sunday School that the teacher had to send someone to wake him up. Compared to him, this guy really wasn't too bad.

As he straightened up from the drinking fountain, the subject of his thoughts was standing right behind him. Travis tried to turn and walk away from him, but the man continued by his side, matching him step for step. "Travis, can I talk to you for a second?"

"I'm really kind of busy right now. Maybe we can find time to talk later." He tried to keep the sarcasm out of his voice.

"That's what I wanted to talk to you about. I just wanted to explain."

He motioned toward a classroom that was temporarily unoccupied.

"No really, there's nothing to explain. You have a lesson to teach; that's your job." The last thing he wanted was to get into an argument with the Elder's Quorum instructor on his first Sunday in the ward, but he found himself turning into the classroom anyway.

"First of all, Travis, let me apologize for what I did in there. I know how that must have looked to you. By the way, my name's Mike Reynolds." He held out his hand.

Travis shook it stiffly. "Mike, apology accepted, but I really have to . . . "

Mike interrupted him. "Travis, would you tell your competitors what you were just about to say in there?"

Travis thought about it for a moment. "Well, no. But these aren't . . . "

"Then don't say it here." He stared levelly into Travis's eyes. "Listen, I would trust any one of those men to take care of my family if I was hit by a car tomorrow. But nearly all of them work for one technology company or another. Do you understand what I'm saying?"

Travis nodded slowly, the impact of his words sinking in.

"No matter, where you are, no matter who you are with, you have to assume that your competitor is listening. This valley is full of stories of guys who discussed an idea over a supposedly private lunch only to see it on the front page of the Technology section in the Mercury News the next week."

He hadn't had any idea it could be like this. In Utah, it had been like one big family. Sooner or later everyone knew what everyone else was doing. Even the stuff that was supposed to be top secret was usually spilled within a week, tops, over shakes at the Burger Barn or standing around in the parking lot after church. Maybe Lisa's mom was right after all. Maybe this wasn't going to be the piece of cake he thought it would be.

"Anyway, I just wanted to say I was sorry," Mike said. "I hope that we can still be friends."

"Absolutely." Travis shook his hand more firmly now. "And thanks for the advice. I'll try to remember it."

* * *

By Tuesday, the weekend's overcast skies had finally cleared, but the weather was still cold. Travis shifted his box of "toys," and tried to fish his wallet out of his back pocket. Because it was only seven forty-five, the main entrance of the Open Door building wouldn't unlock for another fifteen minutes, so he would need to scan his ID card to get inside. He balanced the box precariously between his chest and left arm as he reached back to pull out his wallet. The contents suddenly shifted and he had to lean up against the doors to keep everything from spilling out onto the concrete walkway.

Rebalancing the box in his arms, he tried to back up against the plastic panel. He wasn't sure if the magnetic scanner was powerful enough to read the card through his jeans and wallet, but it would save him from having to set the box down. Besides, now he was curious. Looking at the white rectangle just behind him, he could see that he was just a little too far to the left. As he moved his back pocket to the front of the plate, he heard a metallic click and the light on the panel changed from red to green. The doors swung open and the voice that he had learned was the subject of numerous company inside jokes, greeted him, "Welcome to Open Door, come on in!"

Entering the lobby, he turned back to watch the doors click closed. How would you unlock the doors from the inside? He couldn't see a card scanner anywhere, and there didn't appear to be any kind of mechanical lever on the inside of the door. As he walked back to the entrance to take a closer look, his question was answered. The red light turned green and once again the voice of the "Door Goddess" spoke. "Thank you for visiting Open Door." Now he could see the electronic sensor. It looked like the kind of device that most grocery stores used to open the doors automatically for their customers. His curiosity satisfied, he headed back down the hallway to get settled in.

Programmers tended to have their own ideas about interior decorating. They seemed to follow the adage of a bumper sticker he had once seen on the back of a silver BMW—"Whoever dies with the most stuff wins." Some of them leaned toward a single theme, like Star Wars characters or Disney memorabilia. Others, like him, had more eclectic tastes.

As he walked along the rows of cubicles, he had to admire the creativity that seemed to strike most developers during the hours when normal people were sound asleep. One of the cubes was completely lined with soda cans duct taped into a strange sort of space-pod look. Several people had attached inflatable doors to their cube entrances, creating semiprivate *offices*. But the most unusual one had a dome created entirely of colored plastic storage crates, complete with a dangling mirrored disco ball at the top.

Reaching his space, Travis set down the box and slowly rotated 360 degrees, like an artist examining his canvas. One by one, he removed items from his box, considered them for moment, and then returned them to try something else. Finally he chose his "gun rack." Bright yellow plastic, with black rubber hooks, it held seven different types of Nerf guns. He hung each of his guns on the rack, starting with an orange and blue chain gun and finishing with a black crossbow.

Next he arranged what he thought of as his gadget and gizmo collection. Gadgets tended to be older, often antique, items that he and Lisa had found while foraging through garage sales. These included a 1940s typewriter, complete with instruction manual, a World War I army canteen, and a replica sabre-toothed tiger skull. Gizmos, on the other hand, were newer and usually electronic or magnetic. A Darth Vader bank that spoke and moved when you dropped a coin into it, a device that launched tiny green helicopters up to thirty feet, a horizontal magnetic top that would spin in midair for almost ten minutes, and a twelve-inch-long car that would drive around the floor, occasionally stopping while the tiny woman in the passenger seat raised a miniature camera to her eye and took a picture.

The final touch was the pictures, posters, and other hanging things. On one wall of the cube he hung a painted tin picture of Popeye the Sailor Man exclaiming, "Well, blow me down!" On the other wall, Captain Picard of the Starship Enterprise warned that resistance would be futile.

As he stood back to admire the effect, a voice called out from behind him. "*Muy chevere.*" Startled, he spun around and nearly poked out his eye on a set of bicycle handlebars.

"Easy, easy." A dark-haired man with a mountain bike balanced on his shoulder, stepped back out of the way and put out a hand to steady him. "Are you OK?"

"Yeah. You just scared me a little." Travis smiled. "All right, you actually scared me a lot."

"Sorry. I'm usually the only one here at this time of the morning; maybe I'll need to put one of those little bells on my bike now that there are two of us early birds," he laughed, his wide, brown eyes flashing. Although he was only about five and a half feet tall, he was very trim and muscular. His strong legs bulged beneath his spandex bike shorts and he held the bike in one hand as though it was weightless.

"Yeah, it doesn't look like there are a lot of morning people here." Travis admired the bike. With its alloy frame and heavy-duty shock package, it must cost have two to three thousand dollars easily. He and Lisa had priced good mountain bikes in Utah, but decided that they probably couldn't afford them. But with this new job, he thought maybe he would check them out again.

"Not unless you're talking about one in the morning. Then the place is really hopping." His cubicle, the last in this row, was one down from Travis. He leaned his bike against the wall and called over the divider, "By the way, my name is Ricky Chavez."

"I'm Travis." He was tall enough to be able to look over the cube wall, and he watched Ricky slip on a pair of Walkman headphones as he rolled his chair forward and pulled the keyboard out toward him. He put a CD into his computer, and Travis could just make out the fast-paced rhythm of Latino music coming from the headphones.

"Yeah, I know." Ricky said. "Rob told us you'd be starting this week. I hope you're as good as he says. I'm on your team, and we're going to get a big bonus from this project if marketing doesn't torpedo it." He turned toward the monitor and began scanning through the results of a compile that he'd apparently started the night before.

Ricky's cube looked like something out of *Sports Illustrated*. Every inch of wall space was covered with ribbons and pictures of sporting events. Scattered around his desk, Travis counted at least ten trophies. Although two of them had bike riders on the top, most seemed to be for rock climbing. On the floor in the corner, he could see several coiled climbing ropes and a couple of nylon harnesses.

Travis smiled and sat down at his computer. He liked this guy already. Some programmers seemed to be constantly looking for any excuse to goof off. They would talk your ear off if you let them. Others had no social skills at all and seemed unable to function if they weren't in front of a terminal. It was nice to see someone who looked like he knew how to have fun, but was able to plant himself in his chair and get his work done.

Rob had taken him out to lunch the day before and clarified what projects he would be working on for the next couple of weeks. In some ways, it was the same thing he had been doing at Exasoft. The plan was to combine the searching and compiling skills of his Assistants with the existing Assistant technology that the Open Door developers had written. The hope was that these new Internet helpers would be the "killer app" that pushed Open Door's stock into the heady stratosphere of companies like e-Bay and AOL.

But Travis couldn't help wondering about what Ricky had said. He knew that Holly wasn't convinced that the Assistants were going to be the success that Rob and Peter thought they were. But surely she wouldn't try to undermine the program. With less than eight weeks until the planned IPO, the company would never recover. He shook his head and inserted one of his CDs. It was probably just a little paranoia on Ricky's part.

It took a few hours of playing with code for him to get a feel for the Assistant tools, but once he got them figured out it was a lot of fun to see how quickly he could create new characters. The little demonstration that he had seen upstairs in the conference room was only the beginning. By linking into multiple interfaces, Assistants could respond to voice, mouse, and even video gestures. With a wave of the hand or a pointed finger a user could start an application or browse through a complex web site. That explained why all of the computers here had tiny video cameras attached to the tops of their monitors.

It would be easy to set up an Assistant that could monitor everything you did on the computer and figure out which web sites you would like the most. They could even filter ads and only send you the ones that you might be interested in. It would be like a TV that suggested what movies and shows you would be most likely to enjoy, and then only gave you commercials for things that you liked. And the great thing was that the advertisers would want it as much or more than the viewers. They wouldn't waste their money pushing beer ads to teetotalers, or trying to sell vacation packages to people who never traveled.

It wasn't until his stomach started growling out loud that Travis glanced at his watch and realized that it was nearly one o'clock. He leaned back in his chair and raised his arms above his head. His back and neck muscles creaked painfully as he stretched. It had been too long since he had spent this much time sitting in front of a computer. It would take him a few days to get used to it again. Rubbing at his eyes, he called out over the wall. "Ricky, you want to go get something to eat?"

As he listened for a response, he realized that he could no longer hear the muted sound of Ricky's music coming from the other side of the divider.

"Hey, anybody home?" He knocked on the wall.

It seemed strange that Ricky would have left without saying anything. And he would have had to pass Travis's cube as he walked by. Travis stood up from his chair and looked over the wall. The headphones were hooked over the back of his chair. The bike was still leaning against the wall, but Ricky was gone.

I must have been zoning pretty good, he thought to himself. Well, he would just have to forage for lunch alone today. He saved his work, and then walked back toward the lobby. Although he had never actually been there yet, he had been told that two buildings down was a cafeteria that was shared by the three companies in this complex. Lunch was free for all employees from noon until three. After that, the break room contained a major stash of candy, snacks, and dozens of cases of soda.

Just as he was stepping out from the row of cubes and into the hallway, he remembered that he had left his wallet sitting on the desk. He always took it out of his pocket when he was coding; otherwise, it could be pretty uncomfortable. He would need his ID card if he wanted to get lunch. He jogged back to his cubicle, picked up his wallet and slipped it into his back pocket. As he turned to leave, he paused for a moment. Something seemed slightly off, but he couldn't place what it was. It was like those pictures where you have to find the ten differences between the one on the left and the one on the right.

Everything in his cube was just the way he had left it, but something had changed. It wasn't anything he could see. It was . . . the music. From the next cubicle he could hear Ricky's music playing again. But he had just walked to the end of the row and back. There was no way that Ricky could have gone back to his cube without passing Travis on the way out. He walked out of his cube and around to Ricky's, sure that he would see the headphones still hanging on the back of the chair. But instead, he saw Ricky typing on his keyboard, and tapping his right foot against the base of his chair in time with the music.

He must have seen Travis's reflection in his monitor, because just then he spun around, slipped off his headphones and looked up. "Did you need something?"

"No. I was just wondering . . . " he almost asked Ricky how he had gotten back to his cubicle and then decided not to.

You almost never came across a really good mystery outside of books and movies, and although he was sure there would be a perfectly ordinary explanation, at the moment it completely evaded him. Whatever Ricky's secret was, Travis wanted to solve it on his own.

"I was just wondering if you wanted to go get some lunch with me."

CHAPTER 4

From the journal of Lisa Edwards

Wednesday, Mar. 22

Well that's it, the last box unpacked and put away. Hooray! I would send Travis out for chocolate shakes to celebrate, but he's conked out on the living-room floor again. What lousy timing. They've been pushing him really hard at work to get his products out to the testing group. So he's too tired to do anything but eat dinner and fall asleep, just when my hormones are going crazy and I always seem to feel like I need a hug.

Speaking of hormones, Marty Amsted, one of my visiting teachers tells me that I am having a boy for sure. She and Sherrie Benson came by and helped me unpack and sort books for a couple of hours this afternoon. She saw the rash I've had on the inside of my elbows for the last couple of weeks and swears that she got the same rash with all of her boys, but not with her girls.

They are really funny. Marty is in her late fifties and has to wear thick glasses to be able to see at all. She is thick, but not fat. "Good pioneer stock," as my father would say. She sort of looks like Tyne Daly, that actress who used to be on Cagney and Lacey and is now back on the new legal show. She has raised six children (you can't call them kids around her or she will tell you her "I raised a little billy goat" poem) and is more than willing to give you advice on everything from what foods to eat during which trimesters, to how the Bible predicts that the Democrats will be the downfall of America.

Sherrie is probably close to forty, based on what she told me about her past, but she doesn't look any older than twenty-eight. She is an illustrator for children's books, corporate brochures, and things like that, and she works out of her home. She's been divorced for almost ten years, and is always joking about God accidentally putting her Mr. Right in the wrong hemisphere.

She is a tiny thing, probably couldn't get the scale to break 100 even if she filled her pockets with rocks. She has close-cropped blond hair, and as soon as I complimented her on it, she said, "I'll pass your compliments on to L'Oréal. That's another one of God's mistakes. Somehow He got the impression I was supposed to be a brunette with early streaks of gray."

I think Marty finds her a little irreverent. But even she can't keep from laughing when Sherrie gets on a roll. We were putting away Travis's science fiction paperbacks and Marty found one with a picture of a busty blond heroine on the cover. She was barely covered in a couple of tattered rags, and holding a bloody sword above her head. I think what Marty really wanted to do was throw it into the trash. But she asked me where to put it, with her hand strategically covering most of the picture. I was embarrassed, but when Sherrie saw the cover she hooted and held the book out in front of her. She said, "Now this is a woman who really knows how to accessorize."

That was funny enough, but then she jumped up and ran out of the room. I thought maybe she had decided to throw the book away after all, but then she came back in with a dishtowel draped across the front of her blouse and a butcher knife held over her head. "What do you think," she said, striking a very statuesque pose, "did I miss my true calling?" Marty laughed so hard, I thought she would have a heart attack right there.

When they were leaving, Sherrie took Marty's hand to help her down the stairs. I said something about the blond leading the blind and they both cracked up again. They said they would need to put that on their business cards.

We also met our home teachers last night. They are not nearly as funny, but very sweet. I guess that Travis knows one of them from elders quorum. He looks like something out of a Grizzly Adams movie. He has a long reddish-gray beard and shoulder-length red hair. I could see him living off of grubs and berries in the wilderness. His name is Dave Halloran. His companion looks kind of like one of my old boyfriends (in this case that is NOT a compliment) but seems like a nice enough person. I think his name is something Adams, but I may just be stuck on the Grizzly Adams theme again. Anyway they left a card with their names and phone numbers and said to call them anytime, day or night, if we need anything.

Afterwards, Travis said that he had a weird feeling about Grizzly, (that's our nickname for him). Something about him seemed too nosey. I'm sure they were just trying to be friendly. Sometimes Travis can be so antisocial. Maybe it has something to do with being an only child.

Speaking of Travis, I'm going to go drag the human potato into bed and dream of chocolate shakes so thick you have to eat them with a spoon.

* * *

Travis stood silently in his cubicle, patiently watching over the divider and waiting for Ricky to reappear. He wasn't sure what he was looking for, but he knew that something had to happen soon. After two weeks of the "amazing, disappearing programmer" act, he wouldn't have been surprised to see him suddenly materialize in his chair like something out of Star Trek.

The routine was predictable, but as of yet, completely unexplainable. Sometime between 11:50 and 12:10, Ricky disappeared. He didn't leave his cubicle, or Travis would have seen him walk by. Yet there was no place inside for him to hide. He had even gone so far as to look in the two-drawer filing cabinet under Ricky's desk, though it would have been physically impossible for anyone but an infant to fit inside of it. Once or twice, he thought he had heard the sound of distant music, but he had never been able to track it down. Then, forty-five minutes to an hour later, without any more notice than when he'd disappeared, Ricky would suddenly be back in his chair.

Travis had tried everything, short of asking him outright, to figure out what his secret was. He had once even spent the entire hour searching the building, and the local restaurants where tech employees usually hung out. But he hadn't been able to find Ricky anywhere.

He didn't know why the disappearances intrigued him so much. It wasn't like Ricky was shirking his work or anything. He was almost always the first one in the office in the morning and he was usually there when Travis left for the night. But solving this mystery had become like an itch that he couldn't quite reach. One night he had even dreamed about it. Like the old Disney movie *Tron*, Ricky had turned into a combination of bits and bytes, disappeared into his computer, and gone skulking around inside the network.

So, today he had gone on stakeout. Beginning at about a quarter to twelve, he had started making excuses to go over to Ricky's cube or to ask him a question every few minutes. At 12:02 he had carried over a printout to ask about a line of code and he was gone. Since then, Travis had been standing against the dividing wall, watching the empty space intently. He was afraid that if he so much as blinked, he would suddenly find Ricky back in his chair. He massaged his neck with his left hand, and glanced at his watch. He had been standing, chest pressed against the nubby fabric of the cube for almost an hour now, and his neck and chin felt raw and itchy from the constant friction.

Placing both hands on the top of the wall, be lifted himself onto the balls of his feet and bounced up and down, trying to stretch out his cramping calves. He glanced briefly at his watch again. What would he say if someone walked up behind him right now? What if Ricky were to tap him on the shoulder and ask to know why he was spying on his cubicle? As soon as he allowed that picture into his mind, he actually began to feel the unshakable sensation of someone's eyes boring into the center of his back. Was there really someone watching him? How long had they been there? How could he explain what he was doing? "It's just that I think my coworker here is a shape-shifting, computer-entering alien, sir."

How far could he turn his head and still watch Ricky's chair? He slowly began to rotate his head, shifting his peripheral vision from left to right, and back again. Just as he began to spin around completely, he caught some small movement out of the corner of his eye. Turning back to the wall he searched for what had drawn his attention. At first it seemed that nothing had changed. Ricky hadn't magically reappeared. Then he saw the movement again, and he was suddenly transfixed.

As he watched, a two-foot by two-foot section of the tile floor slowly began to rise. Once it had reached a height of about twelve inches, it began to move to the right, and now he could see Ricky's face in the dark space below. Confused questions arose in his mind. Why would Ricky want to disappear? What was down there? Was it a secret, and would he be upset if he knew that Travis had seen him? Before he could decide whether or not to duck back out of sight, Ricky turned his head and saw him standing there.

"Hey, um . . . " Travis's mind seemed stuck in a recurring loop of unanswered questions. He was sure that there must be dozens of excuses he could give for standing there staring over the cubicle wall like a slack-jawed idiot, but at the moment he couldn't seem to think of any of them.

Ricky seemed completely unfazed. He set down the tile and lifted himself up out of the space below. "Hey Travis, you ready to go grab some lunch?"

Over the past few weeks he had played out dozens of scenarios in his mind. Ricky was a magician. He was a spy. He had a secret passageway in the back of his cube. He was using his rock-climbing skills to scale the wall like a giant spider. When he realized that his secret had been uncovered he would run. He would be incensed. He would swear Travis to secrecy. But in his imagination, the scenario had never played out like this.

"Is everything all right?" With one foot Ricky slid the tile across the floor until it dropped back into place, and then stretched his arms above his head.

"Yeah, everything's fine." he said. "It's just not every day that you see a programmer pop out of the floor."

Ricky's eyes widened in surprise. "You mean no one told you?"

"Told me what?"

"About my siestas."

"Your siestas?" For a moment Ricky's words seemed to make no sense. He might as well have asked if anyone had told Travis about his *eggplants*. Then the meaning of his words clicked into place. "You mean you sleep down there?"

Ricky reached over the wall and tapped him playfully on the head. "You know, you keep making these brilliant deductions and you're going to be running this company in no time. Yes, I sleep down there."

"But, why?"

"Why do I sleep, or why down there?"

"Both, I guess."

"Actually I'm surprised that an athlete like you has never heard of the benefits of the afternoon nap for the body and mind. You should read up on it." He rummaged through the shelf above his desk and tossed a thin book over the divider.

Travis glanced at the cover *The Art of Napping* by Bill Anthony. "I thought that was mostly a South American thing."

Ricky shook his head, "Not unless Churchill, da Vinci, Napoleon, Edison, and JFK were all from South America. No, my North American friend, napping is the secret to success. I take a siesta every afternoon, and I have more energy for the rest of the day than I know what to do with."

Travis thumbed through the pages of the book glancing at the chapter titles. "OK, I guess I can accept that. But why down there? Isn't it all musty, and full of cobwebs and spiders?"

"Not at all. This building was originally built to house mainframes. Those beasts had bundles of cables thicker around than your waist. This entire floor is actually elevated nearly three feet above the concrete foundation to allow space for running cables. It's completely ventilated, just like the rest of the building. Now they mostly use it to run the network cables and for storage. Come on around and take a look."

As Travis walked around to the other cubicle, Ricky pried up the tile again. Through the dark opening, he could just make out an air mattress covered by a nylon sleeping bag. On top of the sleeping bag was a set of headphones plugged into a portable CD player. That explained the mysterious music he had heard. A large blue flashlight and a sports bottle lay on the concrete floor next to the mattress. Leaning closer, he could see that Ricky was right; there were no cobwebs or scuttling insects anywhere in sight

"So that's where you've been all this time." Seeing it all laid out in front of him, Travis felt a little let down somehow. Like having the magician take you behind the stage and show you that the exciting tricks were all done with smoke and mirrors. In a way he wished that he had been unable to figure it out, that the miraculous disappearances were still a mystery.

"Yep, that's it. Come on let's go get some lunch, I'm starving." Ricky lowered the tile and started back down the hallway. "Hey, by the way, have I ever told you about Power Yoga?"

* * *

Travis stared at the lines of code on the screen in front of him. For some reason the second variable in the record was resetting itself. Obviously something was wrong with the order that they were being read into the table. Maybe if he switched the second variable with the first? As he leaned forward to change the code, he felt a strong wave of déja vu wash over him. At this time of night it always felt a little like he was typing the same lines over and over, but now he was almost sure he had tried this combination before. Glancing at his scribbled notes on the legal pad in front of his keyboard, he realized why.

He leaned back in his chair and buried his face in his hands. It wasn't the second time that he had reversed those variables in exactly the same way—it was the third. His head throbbed and his mouth felt like he had been sucking on sweat socks. If he hadn't committed to get this out to the guys in testing by tomorrow, he would have given up and gone home hours ago. He grabbed a couple of aspirin from the open bottle on the shelf above his monitor and washed them down with a flat root beer.

He should probably call Lisa again, so she wouldn't worry. Checking the clock in the corner of his screen though, he decided that he would only succeed in waking her up. When he had talked to her at 11:00, she was getting ready to go to bed. He was startled to see that nearly three hours had passed since then. Even if she had waited up and read for a while, she would have given up and gone to sleep long before now. The thought of her lying in bed made his eyelids start to droop, and he rubbed at them fiercely.

Quickly Travis stood up from his chair, and tried doing some deep-knee bends. If he could just stay awake, he knew that he could have this done in less than an hour. He would do fifty knee bends and then sit back down and knock this thing out. Resting his hands on his hips, he counted each bend out loud. At least he could close his eyes, while he was exercising. The repetition of it was actually very relaxing, up and down three, up and down four. He had never understood the attraction of counting sheep to fall asleep. But now he could not only understand it, he could actually see the sheep jumping over the fence with him as he moved up and down. It was like he was riding them over the fence. He could lay his head down against their fluffy white backs and just let them do the jumping.

His head dropped back against the top of the cube wall with a solid bang. Grabbing the back of his chair to steady himself, he thought of just quitting for the night and picking it up again in the morning. But that would throw the whole team off schedule, and Rob had made it clear that nothing was allowed to mess with the schedule at crunch time. He picked up the can of soda and tilted his head back, swallowing its lukewarm contents. If he could just get a few minutes rest, he knew he would be fine. His eyes fell on the thin, yellow paperback lying facedown on his filing cabinet, and he remembered Ricky's hideaway. It wouldn't be right to borrow someone else's sleeping bag, but right now he was sure he could fall asleep on bare concrete with no problem at all.

Kneeling down by his desk, he tried to pry one of the tiles out of the floor. They seemed to be locked into place. But if that was true, how had Ricky opened his? What he needed was something to pry with, like a small, thin screwdriver. He reached into his pocket and pulled out his key ring. The Jeep's ignition key looked about the right length and width. Sliding it firmly down into the crack between the two tiles, he tried pushing—gently at first, and then harder as he felt something starting to move. Just as he was afraid that the key was going to bend, the side of the tile popped up with a high-pitched squeal.

He looked down into the dark hole and nearly changed his mind. Although it still looked clean, and there was no sign of bugs or other creatures, just the thought of going down there made his skin begin to itch. But then another wave of exhaustion swept over him and he knew he would never be able to get anything done if he didn't get some sleep. The thought of a few minutes rest with no bright fluorescent lights or computer monitors won out over his worries about creepy-crawlies, and he slipped his legs down into the hole.

The opening was narrow, and the concrete was much colder than he had expected, but the sweet feeling of being horizontal more than made up for any other discomforts. He set the alarm on his watch for twenty-five minutes, sat up halfway and slid the tile back down into place. With the square of light gone, total darkness enveloped him and he lay back down onto the cold slab and instantly slipped into sleep with a grateful sigh.

He dreamed that he was back in Utah. He was in the basement apartment, and he was under the gun to finish writing a program, but he couldn't find his computer. The power must have gone out, because it was pitch black, and none of the lights seemed to work. The air in the apartment was frigid, sucking the heat from his arms and legs and he wondered absently if they had forgotten to pay the electric bill. He started walking toward the back bedroom that they used as an office, but someone had switched around all of the furniture, and he kept stumbling over things until he had completely lost his sense of direction. Although he knew that the entire apartment was less than a thousand square feet, it felt like a labyrinth with dead ends everywhere he turned.

As he stood trembling in the dark, afraid to move, he heard the quiet whisper of shuffled footsteps behind him. At first he thought it was Lisa and he almost called out to her, but the footsteps stopped and were replaced by the harsh deep gasps of someone breathing heavily. He couldn't tell if it was a man or a woman, but he knew that it wasn't his wife. He turned slowly toward the sound, but it disappeared for a moment and then he heard the click of a door off to his left. Spinning in that direction, he heard the security alarm on his laptop beginning to beep.

Whoever was in here with him was trying to steal his computer. If they got away with it he would never be able to finish writing his program. He lunged toward the sound of the beeping, and tripped over something that skittered across the floor. His forehead banged against some sharp piece of furniture and he could feel blood running down his cheek. The sound was moving away from him and he rose groggily to his feet and tried to chase after it. If he could just get to the computer and turn off the alarm then everything would be OK, but he was completely disoriented and his legs would barely move.

He jerked awake, and for a moment he thought that he was still in his dream. Everything was dark, and his body was cold and stiff.

He instinctively pushed the alarm button on the side of his watch and the shrill beeping stopped. With his eyes adjusted to the dark, he could see that it wasn't completely black, and he remembered where he was. Occasional cracks of white light interrupted the darkness where the floor tiles didn't fit together perfectly anymore. His neck ached, and his legs were freezing, but at least the overpowering sleepiness had left him and he felt sure that he could finish with this last bug in his application.

As he started to sit up, he heard voices almost directly above him. The sound carried perfectly, and he mentally made a note to keep his voice down when Ricky was taking his siestas. It sounded like there were two different people talking. One voice was unmistakably Runt's. As the head of the testing department, he and Travis had spoken regularly over the last few weeks. He wasn't sure about the other voice though. It might be someone else from testing, but it was hard to make out any words. They had probably come to see if he had finished the latest Assistant. He smiled, thinking how surprised they would be when he popped out of the floor directly under their feet.

In the dark, he reached up to touch the bottom of the tile, and Runt spoke again. He sounded loud and a little angry. "I told you he's not here. His car isn't in the parking lot and I checked the break room and the bathrooms."

The second voice spoke again and Travis realized that the reason he hadn't been able to make out any words was because whoever was with Runt was whispering. At first, all he could make out was a series of sharp hisses, but he found that by putting one ear against the bottom of the tile and covering his other ear with the palm of his hand, he could just make out the words of the whisperer. "Just keep your voice down and stay out of sight. He's been working late a lot lately."

He touched the keys in his pocket, wondering why they hadn't seen his car in the lot. Then he remembered that he had run to work this morning. Though he had biked to work several times over the last two weeks, this was the first time that he had stuffed his work clothes into a backpack and run all the way to the office. Then another thought occurred to him. If they thought he was gone already, then what were they doing here?

"Copy all the files in all these directories, and don't forget the libraries. We can sort through it all later." It was impossible to tell whether the second voice was that of a man or a woman; the sibilant tones rendered the voice into an androgynous monotone. Beneath the sound of the voices, Travis could just make out the soft clicks of someone typing on a keyboard.

It sounded like they were copying files off of his hard drive, but that didn't make any sense. Whenever he completed a new Assistant, he sent all of the files directly to testing. Why would Runt want to copy files that he would be giving them tomorrow morning? Unless they were looking for something else . . .

Then, an even more disturbing thought hit him. When he had climbed beneath the tiles, he had left his computer on, but the screen saver would have started after five minutes of inactivity. Without his password, no one should be able to see anything more than a series of geometrical shapes on the screen. Even if his computer was reset, they would still have to enter his boot password, or the computer wouldn't even access the hard drive. It was a security precaution that every employee in the company was required to use. If they were copying files off of his hard drive, either Runt or the person with him had to know one or both of his passwords.

From above came the sound of Runt's voice again. "OK, I've got everything downloaded."

"Make sure you leave everything on the computer just as you found it. I don't want him to suspect anything," the whisperer said.

"I'm not an idiot." Chair wheels squeaked across the floor tiles as Runt presumably slid away from the computer. Footsteps thudded directly overhead and then faded as they moved away. Travis pressed the light on his watch and checked the time. It was 2:50. He would wait until 3:00 just to make sure they weren't coming back before he climbed up into his cubicle. He didn't know why they were copying files from his computer, but if they were being this careful to make sure he didn't know they had been there, then he didn't think it would be a good idea to bump into them tonight.

As he waited silently in the dark, he thought about what he had heard. Runt and someone else had obviously been copying files from his computer. But what could they have been looking for? As head of testing, Runt would eventually end up with all of the files that Travis was working on anyway. And he couldn't imagine that there was anything else on his computer that would be of any interest to him.

Unable to come up with even a guess as to what they would want his files for, Travis turned his thoughts to the second voice. It had been impossible to tell anything about his or her voice from what little he had been able to hear. But there were some other interesting clues nonetheless.

It was obvious that they knew what files they were looking for, and whoever was with Runt had been telling him what files to copy. That meant that whoever it was must have been either a programmer or someone very knowledgeable about programming. Anyone walking around the building at this time of night was almost sure to be an employee. And anyone in a position to order the head of the testing department around would most likely be at a director's level or above.

He tried to approach it from another angle. Who would know his code well enough to instantly recognize what files to copy? Rob? But as Travis's team leader he could just as easily have openly asked him for any files that he wanted. Why go to all of this trouble, unless he thought that Travis was holding something back. Would Rob break into his computer just to double-check his work? He tried to remember if he had given Rob any reason to doubt him, but couldn't think of anything. What if another team leader was trying to steal his work to get a bigger bonus for their team? It was possible, but he hadn't heard of any other teams working on Assistants.

Maybe it wasn't a "he" at all. Hadn't Rob told him that Holly had nearly left the company over the plan to make Assistants their key differentiator? She had been convinced they should spend their money on a huge marketing blitz spread across the country. When the president shot down her plan, she had stormed out of the conference room and disappeared for the rest of the week. Maybe she was hoping that by sabotaging the Assistants, she could regain her credibility.

Pressing the light button on his watch, he saw that it was exactly three A.M. He reached his hands up through the darkness until they pressed against the tile, then gently pushed upward. If there was anyone still around, he didn't want them to hear any noise as he lifted the tile. Prying it up before must have loosened things, because it came up so easily that he almost lost control of it. For a moment it threatened to slide off his fingertips and crash onto the floor, and he felt his throat tighten until he got the tile back under control again.

Setting the tile softly onto the floor, he wriggled up out of the crawl space and into his cubicle. He lowered the tile back into place and then, still on his hands and knees, edged just far enough out to see that there was no one in sight down the walkway. On his desk, the monitor had returned to its familiar geometrical screen saver and nothing looked out of place. Rising to his feet, he peered over the top of the wall. Everything seemed quiet.

He reached under the desk and pulled out his backpack. He took out his running shoes and switched them with the loafers that he wore in the office. At this time of night it was cold enough that he could run back to the apartment in his jeans and polo shirt. He started to zip his pack shut and then picked up his CD case and dropped it inside. They hadn't had time to go through all the files on his CDs, so that probably meant that they didn't know that he still kept many of his files there instead of copying everything to his hard drive. But after this, he wasn't about to leave any of his work unguarded.

On his way out, he stopped in front of the testing lab. The doors were shut, but he could see light shining from the half-inch space at the floor. He hadn't paid enough attention in the past to know whether that was normal or not. With his pulse racing, he pressed his ear against the wood veneer, but if there was anyone on the other side he couldn't hear them. There was no point trying to open the doors. After nine P.M. all of the building's doors locked automatically, and his card wasn't authorized to unlock these. And even if he had been able to open them, he wasn't sure he would have dared. Although he worked with him every day, there was still something about Runt that bothered him. He was always cracking jokes and smiling, but even while he was roaring with laughter, his eyes seemed to be studying the people around him like a predator gauging the strength of his prey.

He left through the back door, hoping that he would be less likely to run into anyone on the way out. He peered cautiously around each corner before entering. He knew that he had every right to be there, but somehow *he* felt like the intruder, sneaking through the building until he was out into the back parking lot. Shouldering his pack, he cut into a growth of oleander bushes and jogged through to the sidewalk. From here it was only a couple of blocks to the bike trail. As he stepped out of the bushes, a set of headlights turned on in the front parking lot and shot directly into his face, blinding him momentarily. He shielded his eyes with one hand and instinctively stepped back into the bushes.

He recognized Runt's red GMC pickup as it pulled out into the street in front of him. Although he knew that the bushes hid him completely, he still held his breath as the truck drove slowly by. He didn't think he had been seen. He'd barely been out of the bushes when the lights had come on, and even if he had been seen stepping back into the oleanders, it was unlikely he had been recognized. Still, he found himself looking over his shoulder every time a car drove past him until he got home.

CHAPTER 5

Travis woke to the sound of AM 620, "The Talk of the Town." Apparently a sports car had lost control in the early morning drizzle and ended up jammed beneath a gravel truck, backing up traffic for miles. *Big surprise*, he thought as he fumbled in the dim morning light to turn off the clock radio. Next to him Lisa groaned something indecipherable and rolled over.

Burying his head back into the comfortable darkness of the pillows, he tried to go back to sleep, but he already knew that it would only be a matter of minutes before he got up and had breakfast. It had been that way since they got married. Lisa needed at least nine hours of sleep, and could fall back to sleep instantly if she hadn't gotten it. But Travis had never been able to master the trick of shutting off his internal alarm clock. No matter how late he got to bed, he was always awake by six-thirty.

As he climbed out of bed, he saw that Lisa had rolled out from under the blankets some time during the night. She was curled up in a ball on her side of the sheets, her blue and white silk pajamas making her look like a striped pill bug. He pulled the quilt over her and she mumbled something that might have been "thanks" as she drew it tightly up to her chin. Outside he could hear the rain splattering against the windowpane, and the occasional swish of cars driving past on the wet road.

In the bathroom, he pulled a clean towel from the stack under the sink and twisted the hot water knob in the shower up to full. This was one of the "low flow" shower heads that California had begun requiring years earlier, and even turned up all the way it took him nearly ten minutes just to wash his hair. As he watched the lather swirl down the drain, he thought about what had happened the night before. Now in the safety of his apartment, with the thick plumes of steam diffusing under the bathroom lights, the night's events took on an almost surreal quality. It was as though he had watched it all in a spy movie. The hero slips beneath the false floor just in time to overhear the evil secret agent and foil his diabolical plans. Then just as he thinks he has escaped their clutches, he finds the villains waiting for him as he exits the steamy jungle.

Looking back on it in the light of day, there were probably dozens of reasons why Runt might have needed to get into his files last night, not the least of which was the pressure that everyone was under to get Assistants out to the marketing department so they could begin creating content. And the network administrators had every employee's passwords on file. If Runt thought that he had gone home already, he could easily have contacted whoever was on call and asked them to log him on to Travis's system. As groggy as he had been, it would have been easy to take things out of context and completely misinterpret what was going on. When he got into the office, Runt would probably explain everything to him.

He walked into the kitchen and began searching for the packets of instant oatmeal. Although Lisa had adjusted to her new kitchen by the second day, he still found himself going through three or four drawers before he remembered which one held the spoons. After finally managing to track down the breakfast food cupboard, the stack of bowls, and searching the same four drawers for spoons, he added water to the apple-cinnamon mixture in his bowl and stuck it in the microwave to cook. While he waited for it to heat up, he opened the front door and brought in the morning paper.

In the past, he had always progressed from Sports to the Comics and then finished by scanning the headlines. But since moving to San Jose, he always went straight to the Business section first. The Business section of the Mercury News was the heartbeat of Silicon Valley and as a result it was a pretty good indicator of the technology sector as a whole. He was fascinated by the IPO watch that appeared every Monday, listing which companies had gone public, and how their stocks had fared. Today though, he was scanning the articles looking for a mention of Open Door. At lunch yesterday, he had overheard one of the marketing guys saying that there was supposed to be a story on local Internet portal companies in this morning's issue.

The lead story was about unusual things that people were putting up for auction on the Internet. First it had been guns, and then drugs. A few months earlier there had been a spate of people selling human organs. No one knew for sure whether they had been intended as hoaxes or not, but it had caused a pretty major uproar. Now the trend seemed to be offering famous landmarks for sale. The bidding for Mt. Rushmore had reached twenty-five million dollars before the company shut it down. Laughing quietly to himself, he flipped to the next page.

"What's so funny?" At the unexpected sound of Lisa's voice, he jerked his arm back and nearly knocked his bowl off of the table.

"Geez, you scared the heck out of me." He licked off the oatmeal that had splashed onto the back of his hand.

"A little high-strung are we?" She leaned over his shoulder and wrapped her arms around his neck. "I missed you last night. What time did you get in anyway?"

"Oh I don't know, sometime after two." His long hours had been a bone of contention between the two of them lately, and he knew that if she found out he hadn't gotten in until almost four, she would try to make him go back to bed.

She leaned further over his shoulder to look him in the eyes and he could feel the swell of her stomach against his side. "What would you say if I told you that I heard you come in?"

He watched her face, trying to judge how serious she was. In the past he would have just laughed it off, but lately he seemed to always be misjudging her moods. As if sensing what he was trying to do, she kept a perfect poker face. Finally she smiled just a little. "Caught you Mr. *Some time after two*. And just for the record, I *was* bluffing."

Before he could respond, she looked down and pointed at the paper that had fallen open when he dropped it onto the table. "Hey look, isn't that your company president?"

He lifted the paper, and instantly recognized Keith Spencer's toothpaste-commercial smile. He was posing behind what looked like the wheel of an early 1900s clipper ship, one hand shading his eyes, the other pointing toward the camera. Anyone else would have come off looking like a tacky politician pulling a publicity stunt, but the Open Door president somehow managed to look like a cross between Tom Hanks and Clint Eastwood—trustworthy yet determined. The headline read, "Internet Portals Test Choppy IPO Waters."

Lisa slipped into the chair next to him and sipped at his orange juice as she read over his shoulder. The article began by pointing out the high number of Internet companies that had gone public over the last six months. A graph showed how the increasing number of companies was diluting the value of their offerings, and the writer theorized that the window of opportunity for huge profits by Internet startups might have passed. As an example it listed three Internet portals, including Open Door, that would be going public within the next two months. Each of the companies offered fairly similar features, and had a comparable number of users. Some analysts were predicting that shares in these companies would be lucky just to maintain their offering price.

An adjoining sidebar listed brief capsules of each of the companies and the backgrounds of their management teams. Open Door based in San Jose, Telescope.com based in Sunnyvale, and a San Francisco start up called NetSailor. He skimmed the rest of the article until he reached the last paragraph.

"Although all of the companies are in the required silent period before they go public, recently floated rumors indicate that at least one of the portals, and possibly all three, are scrambling to offer something new that will catch investors' eyes. Proving that they will be able to stand out from the competition may mean the difference between a company valuation in the millions of dollars and a valuation in the billions."

Rereading the last sentence, Travis could feel his heart rate increasing as adrenaline jacked through his veins. It was how he had always felt gearing himself up for the beginning of a track meet. The newspaper columnist might not know it, but he was talking about Travis and the rest of his team. It was no wonder that everyone was acting crazy at the office. The stakes in this game were huge. More money than he had ever dreamed of was riding on who released a breakthrough product first.

The second- and third-place finishers not only lost potential billions, but it sounded like they might not even be able to go public at all. He folded the paper and slapped it down on the table. This was huge. His Assistants could be the difference that pushed his company to the front of the pack, and the whole world would be there to see the race.

Sensing his excitement, Lisa rubbed his arm and kissed him on the cheek. "That's really great, honey."

But he barely heard her as he stood up and grabbed his backpack. "I'll call you later." He kissed her absently on the top of the head and walked down the front hallway, lost in his own thoughts.

* * *

As soon as he entered his cube, Travis saw the lime-green sticky note on the front of his monitor. He recognized Rob's printing instantly, its block lettering almost draftsman-like in its uniformity. "Eight-thirty meeting in HERETICS. Be prepared to provide updates on all projects." Following a recent Silicon Valley trend, Open Door had come up with nicknames for each of their conference rooms. Possibly in recognition of the meetings that at times seemed almost interminable, the names had been chosen from the nine circles of Hell in Dante's *Inferno*.

Checking the time, he saw that he had just under twenty minutes until the meeting started. On his run into work, he had been mulling over the bug that had caused him so much trouble only hours before, and he thought that he could have it fixed in time for the meeting if he hurried.

With fresh eyes, it was easy to track down the faulty section of code, and he had just finished compiling the source files into a test-worthy executable file when Ricky walked past his cube. His wet black hair was pasted against his scalp, and water dripped from his face and chin.

"Man, it really started coming down out there in the last few minutes. I'm going to go grab a quick shower and change clothes."

"That should be entertaining for everyone else in the team meeting." Travis inserted a recordable CD into his computer and began copying his files onto the disk.

"What team meeting? No one told me anything about a meeting this morning." Ricky set his bike down against the wall.

"Check your monitor. Somebody must have put a burr under Rob's saddle." Travis said.

He heard Ricky quietly reading the twin of his note. "No kidding! Rob never gets here before ten at the earliest. And why HERETICS? Isn't that a little big for only four people?"

"One way to find out. " Travis ejected the CD and tucked it into his portfolio.

Ricky joined him as he started down the hallway. He had changed into a new shirt and was toweling off his hair with the old one as they walked. A gray leather binder sprouting several pens and a stack of jumbled papers was tucked under his left arm. "Did you see the story in the paper this morning?"

"You mean that one in the cooking section about making zucchini muffins?" Travis grinned.

"I'll tell you where you can put your muffins." Ricky flipped the wet shirt at him. "You know what I think?"

"Hmm?" They turned into the stairway, and climbed the steps two at a time.

"I think we ought to be getting a bigger bonus for this project. According to that writer, we're making these guys billions."

"Hey, I wouldn't turn up my nose at more money, but that's nothing compared to what this can really do for us." Travis said.

"How do you figure?" They hurried along the hallway toward the far end of the building. As they walked, Travis noticed an unusually large number of people heading in the same direction they were and he dropped his voice to a whisper.

"Recognition. How much clout do you think it's gonna add to your resume if you can say that you were part of the team that made Open Door an Internet megabeast? Adding a few thousand dollars to your bonus will be the least of your concerns."

Just then they rounded the corner and were shocked to see that HERETICS, the second largest of the conference rooms, was packed with people.

"Team meeting, my foot. That looks like half the company in there." Ricky raked his fingers through his hair trying to push it into some semblance of neatness and looked for a place to discard his dripping shirt.

"Hey guys, I hope you've got your act together." Rob walked up behind them and placed a hand on each of their shoulders. Although he was smiling, it looked forced to Travis, as though it were held in place with invisible strips of masking tape.

"What is all this?" Travis asked. As they stood in the hallway, another four people walked past them and into the conference room.

"Don't know; some kind of dog and pony show. But Spencer called for it, and when the President wants a show everyone brings their ponies." He squeezed their shoulders and grimaced in what Travis assumed was supposed to be a smile. "So how is our show looking?"

Travis had never seen Rob look so tense. Ordinarily he was the one who calmed everyone else down. He hadn't thought about it before, but Rob must have put his neck on the line to directly oppose the VP of Marketing, and maybe others, on an issue that could decide the fate of the company. Now that things were coming down to the wire, he must be getting a lot of heat from above.

"Well? Is everything on track?"

"What?" Travis was still lost in his thoughts.

"The Assistants, the Assistants." Rob looked more anxious then Travis had ever seen him before. "Are we on schedule?"

"Yes, absolutely. I just fixed the last bug in the Shopping Assistant this morning." Travis handed him the CD.

Rob tucked the disk into his binder and then gave Travis and Ricky an odd look. "You guys keep all these files on your work computers, right?"

Travis felt something jump in his stomach. "What do you mean?"

Rob shook his head as though he wished he hadn't brought it up. "I just mean that you're not showing this stuff to anyone outside the company or anything, right?"

"What do you think we are, idiots?" Ricky looked like he had just been slapped in the face. "We might not be VPs, but that doesn't mean we're stupid enough to go shooting off our mouths about the bread and butter of our company."

Travis was thinking about what he had almost said at church a couple of weeks earlier. "No way, we haven't said a thing."

"No, I'm sorry. I know you guys wouldn't say anything. It's just that some things are being insinuated, and I just . . ." Rob's voice died out and he shook his head again. Then grinning almost like his normal self, he put his arms around their shoulders and said, "Let's go see how much dog and horse manure we have to wade through."

HERETICS was a rectangular room that ran the entire width of the Open Door building. The concrete wall on that side of the building had been replaced with a floor-to-ceiling window that looked out on the foothills to the west. Designed to hold up to twenty-five people around a highly polished cherry table, it now held upwards of forty with chairs backed up against all of the walls. At the front of the room, Keith Spencer sat in whispered conversation with Martin Graves, the CEO and largest individual investor in the company.

As Travis and Ricky found seats in one of the back corners and Rob took his place at the table, Keith Spencer stood and the room instantly quieted.

"It looks like we have just about outgrown this building. Maybe we ought to start thinking about going public." There was a murmur of polite laughter from everyone except Graves, who seemed to be more interested in the view outside the window.

After waiting for the room to go silent again, he continued. "For those of you who might have lost track, we've got exactly twenty-seven days until we go public. I don't know how the rest of you feel about that, but frankly it scares me to death." Despite his words, Travis thought he looked anything *but* scared.

"As I am sure you are all aware, within days after we filed to go public, two of our biggest competitors also filed. We are undisputedly the front-runner here. We have always been first to introduce new technologies, and despite what some local beat writer might think, we have nearly double the number of unique visitors that NetSailor or Telescope has. So some of you might think that we can coast for these last few weeks." He slowly swept his gaze across each of the employees in the room as though he could identify those who were slacking off merely by looking into their eyes.

Halfway around the room, his eyes met Travis's and his stare stopped and locked in on him. At first Travis was sure that it was just his imagination, that it only felt like he was pausing longer on him than anyone else. But as the stern gray eyes remained unwaveringly tied to his own, he could sense people turning around to see who the president was staring at. He could feel his own eyes beginning to water and the urge to look away became almost unbearable. But with everyone watching him it would look like he had something to hide. Biting viciously at the inside of his cheeks, he struggled to keep staring unflinchingly back.

"Travis, you're one of our newest employees," Keith said. Travis recognized the slightly amused half smile from his interview, which was the last and only time they had spoken to one another. "Would you please stand up?"

His legs felt slightly wobbly under him as he rose to his feet, and he wondered how someone could so easily make him feel guilty even though he had done nothing wrong. He had been putting in more hours than nearly everyone in the room, and yet he found himself searching for excuses. It was like having a police car pull up behind you. Even when you were doing the speed limit, you found yourself slowing down five or ten miles an hour and watching your mirror waiting for the blue and red to begin flashing.

"If I remember correctly, you were something of a high school and college track star weren't you?"

Travis felt like his heart had suddenly started beating again and the relief was so great that he almost dropped back into his seat. In a way he felt grateful that Keith hadn't been blaming him after all, but he couldn't help hating the man a little for intentionally putting him through the wringer. "Yes, I ran track."

"I think that you're being modest. Didn't you actually run a sub-four-minute mile?" Travis felt his cheeks flush as around him people began to "ooh" and "aah." Obviously, the president had been doing some research.

"Twice." Travis answered. He didn't know what this had to do with anything. They hadn't hired him for his running.

"Ever win any races?" He couldn't understand where the president was going. Obviously he knew the answer or he wouldn't have asked. "Some."

"Ever lose any races?"

"Several." Travis's feeling of relief was rapidly disappearing and it was obvious that Keith was enjoying his discomfort.

"Did you ever find yourself in position to win a race only to stumble and fall in the last hundred yards?" Again the half smile. Either he was a lucky guesser or he had been doing a lot more research than Travis had expected.

He nodded his head slowly "Yes."

"When was that?"

Travis felt his hatred blooming. This was going beyond making a point. "The national championships. My sophomore year in high school." The people who had been looking back toward him admiringly before were now looking anywhere *but* at him. The only exception was Martin Graves, whose pale eyes studied him avidly.

Keith continued on as though he couldn't hear the tone of Travis's voice. "And how did you feel?"

This had gone far enough. Whatever point he was trying to make had been made. "It never happened again." Travis sat down. The conversation was over.

Apparently Keith agreed, because he turned his gaze back on the rest of the room. "This meeting is to make sure that the rest of you get to feel what it's like to run a sub-four without knowing what it feels like to stumble in the last hundred yards."

He turned to the man beside him. "Martin would you please take a moment and update us on the current state of our IPO?"

Martin Graves looked to be in his mid-seventies. He sat on the boards of over a dozen technology companies, and was usually in the top one hundred of *Forbe's* list of the five hundred wealthiest people in the world. But despite his wealth, Travis had heard him called Ebenezer Scrooge's stingy brother. Rob, who had been out to dinner with him several times, said that he refused to eat at restaurants that didn't offer senior-citizen discounts, and around the office he often dressed in the same worn jeans and denim shirts for days at a time.

In the past, he had taken a hands-off approach to the companies he invested in, but his last few ventures had been expensive failures, and most insiders felt that he was becoming frustrated with the millions of dollars he was losing on his collection of start-ups.

As he stood, he removed a pair of heavy black-framed reading glasses from his shirt pocket and slid them over his large creased ears. For a moment, he shuffled through his papers, and then cleared his throat and began to read.

"Over the past thirty days, Cochran Edmonds has reported a drop of almost forty percent in the number of brokers that are interested in purchasing large blocks of our stock." He hacked a brittle sounding cough against the back of his hand and continued reading. "Speculation at the end of November was that our per share value would reach at least six times its offering price in the first week of trading. It is now down to a third of that number."

He continued to stare at the sheets in his hand as though reading them silently, and then shuffled to another page and continued. "Sources tell us that NetSailor plans on releasing a series of what they are calling 'Personal Assistants' on their site in three weeks. Coincidentally the same week that we had planned our release." Around him, the room broke into a series of shocked gasps and outraged curses as he continued reading. "These 'Personal Assistants' are being described as animated characters that will assist Internet users in activities that include searching the web, scheduling, and e-commerce, among others."

He folded the papers lengthwise in his right hand, tapped them against his thigh and then turned to look out of the window without saying any more. Travis was stunned. What were the odds of two companies developing exactly the same technologies for release within a week of each other? In the silence that followed, people turned to stare at one another like earthquake survivors. Rob and Peter whispered back and forth animatedly, but behind them Travis noticed Holly smiling smugly at the panic going on around the room. He checked to see how Runt was taking the news, and then turned quickly away when Runt glared back at him. In fact the only person who seemed unmoved one way or the other was David Lee, who, as usual, appeared lost in one of his many notebooks.

When Keith stood again, his face was grim. His words now made his earlier comments look like stand-up comedy in comparison. "We have just had a change in plans. Instead of three weeks, we will be releasing all of our Assistants in twelve days. Each of these Assistants will be completely tested and bug-free. They *will* meet all product specifications, and they *will* have all necessary content on-line." He stared at the people sitting around the room as though daring them to disagree. When none did, he continued.

"Martin and I are leaving now. I don't expect anyone else to leave this room until I am presented with a plan detailing how you will meet this deadline. Anyone who thinks they can't cut it can leave their resignations with my Assistant." He and Martin turned and walked out of the room to stunned silence.

"I told you all this was a big mistake." Holly was on her feet almost before the door had closed. Several people nodded and murmured their assent.

"Oh yeah, we'd be a lot better off if the competition was coming out with Assistants and we matched it with what? Another Super Bowl ad?" Rob pounded his hand on the table. "What I want to know is who tipped NetSailor off to what we were doing? You couldn't possibly have given one of your media contacts a little advance scoop, could you, Holly?"

"Don't blame me." Holly's cheeks were turning bright red as she waved around the room. "It could have been anyone here. It was probably one of your engineers showing off, or even someone from testing for that matter."

Runt jumped out of his chair towering over the rest of the room. "If there has been anyone passing secrets, they weren't in testing. We have the highest security on every file that passes through our department. NetSailor sure didn't see any code from us."

"Everybody just calm down." David Lee had finally looked up from his notes. "First of all, we have absolutely no proof that NetSailor even has a clue that we are creating our own Assistants. And they most certainly could not have seen any of our code. For all we know, they have some kind of search bot that they have made to look like a smiley face." People began sitting back down in their chairs as David continued speaking in a calm voice.

"Did you really think that we were working in a vacuum? Are we the only ones smart enough to think of adding Assistants to our site?" Around the room there was quiet laughter and embarrassed smiles. "We've all got a lot of stock options riding on this IPO, and I for one expect to be shopping for a very nice Beemer in May. Now what we need to do is quit worrying about what NetSailor is doing, and figure out how we are going to get everything out on time."

Peter walked up to the white board, nodding his head. "He's

right. Lets start by working backwards. We have until the twelfth of April, so that means that we have to have everything in to testing no later than what? The ninth?" People pulled out their planners or palmtops and began making suggestions. Everyone seemed caught up in the planning except Rob. He was staring at David with an odd expression, and Travis was just about to ask him what was wrong when Rob seemed to break out of his reverie and smiled at Travis.

"Too much fun, huh?" Then he too pulled out a palmtop and started punching in dates.

The next three hours were complete chaos. A dozen plans were considered and just as quickly rejected. The marketing department said that it was impossible to create content until they could test it with real Assistants. Testing said they needed at least ten days just to guarantee that what they had now was bug-free. Rob said that his team was working as fast as they could and he would need more developers if they were going to get the last two Assistants out in time.

At noon, they sent out for pizzas and continued arguing throughout the rest of the afternoon into the evening. It wasn't until after six that everyone had grudgingly reached consensus on a plan. It all came down to moving bodies around, and everyone working fifteen-to-twenty-hour days over the next two weeks. Peter and his group would join with Rob's team for the first week. Testing and marketing would work in parallel, bug testing and creating content at the same time. At the end of the first week, half of Peter's team would join testing, and mop-up would be done over the last three to four days by whoever had resources available.

Walking back down the hallway, Travis could feel the long hours catching up with him. It felt like a sledgehammer was swinging wildly around inside his head, vibrating off the backs of his eyes. As he reached out to grab the stair railing, he saw that his hand was trembling.

"Hey, guy, you look worse than old Graves. Why don't you go home and call it a day." Rob walked up next to him, and slapped him on the shoulder.

"No, it's OK. I've got too much to do tonight. I need to get started on the Calendar Assistant."

"Don't bother. I'm calling a meeting with Peter's team tomorrow morning at eight A.M. to rework our assignments anyway." He squeezed Travis's shoulder. "Get some rest tonight, because I don't think you'll be getting much over the next two weeks."

Travis started to argue before deciding he really could use the rest. "OK, maybe you're right."

As they started down the stairs, he remembered the incident of the night before for the first time that afternoon. He still wasn't sure of what had happened but he now felt a lot more confident that, whatever was going on, Rob wasn't a part of it. It was even possible that Rob might have an explanation that he had overlooked. He looked back up the stairs to make sure that there was no one close to them and then drew Rob aside.

"Do you have any idea why testing might want to get a copy of my files before I released them?"

"What do you mean?"

He searched for any clue of recognition in Rob's eyes before he continued. If Rob were in on this somehow, Travis would need to backpedal quickly. But finding none, he went on cautiously. "I was just wondering if you could think of any reason that someone like Runt might have for taking one of my Assistants before I gave it to him?"

Rob shook his head. "Runt? Not right off the bat. Why? Did he?"

His mind raced for some way to dance around the question. If he came right out and said that he had seen, or actually heard, Runt copying his files, things could get complicated very quickly. On the other hand he had come this far and it would look strange to back off now. "I'm not sure. It's just that I thought I saw them testing the Shopping Assistant already."

"The one you just gave me this morning?"

He nodded.

Rob seemed lost in thought for a minute. "How would they have gotten it?"

This is where things started to get dicey, and Travis decided that he wasn't yet ready to spill everything that he had heard. "That's just it. I don't know how they could have. To tell you the truth, I might have been mistaken. I haven't been sleeping a lot lately."

Rob nodded slowly and rubbed his hand across one stubbly cheek. "Yeah that's probably it," he said, but he still didn't look convinced. "Maybe I'll check into it a little, though."

Suddenly Travis didn't think that was a good idea at all. He remembered Runt staring at him in the conference room, and felt a chill run up his back. "No listen, don't worry about it. I'll talk to Runt myself. I might even have given him a copy without realizing it."

Rob watched him for several long seconds, and Travis felt sure that Rob could tell that he was lying, but he only nodded. "OK. You go get some rest and we'll figure it out tomorrow."

Travis watched Rob walk slowly away, wondering if he should go after him and try to convince him it was all a joke. But it seemed as though Rob had already turned his thoughts elsewhere, because Travis heard him mutter something about *options* and shake his head as he went back into his office and closed the door.

* * *

That night was a disaster. It started almost as soon as Travis came in the door. The adrenaline from the run home seemed to have cleared up his headache, and he had decided to take Lisa out to dinner to begin making amends for all the nights she had eaten alone lately.

When he told her his idea, Lisa tried to wrap her arms around him, but her growing belly barely allowed her to reach to his shoulders.

"Yeah I was thinking that maybe we could go to Carvers. I know how much you like their spinach salad."

"Oh Travis, that would be . . . " But then something in the sound of his voice or maybe it was the tension in his shoulders made her stop and stare up into his eyes. "What's wrong?"

"Nothing. Can't I just take my wife out to dinner without something being wrong?" He tried to keep his voice noncommittal. But he could feel her eyes boring through his outer calm.

"Is it work? They can't possibly think you aren't putting in enough hours."

"Yes. That's exactly it." In his anxiety over the situation with Rob, he had completely forgotten that he'd be working almost twenty hours a day for the next two weeks. But now that he had remembered, it seemed like the perfect excuse. She would be upset about the additional hours, but at least that was a known problem. The last thing she needed at this point in her pregnancy was to stress out about something that even he couldn't put his finger on. "They moved up the release dates on the Assistants. We've got to get everything out in twelve days."

"Oh, honey, I'm so sorry." She dropped her hands to his waist and nuzzled her head against his chest.

As they got ready to go out, and all through the drive to the restaurant, they lamented the longer hours, but agreed that at least the end was in sight. But when their steaks arrived, he realized that she was staring at him again.

"Hey, do you think you ordered that rare enough? I think I just heard it moo." Travis tried to lighten the mood, but Lisa ignored his attempted joke completely.

"There's something else you're not telling me." Again he could feel her eyes trying to bore into him.

"No. I'm just really tired. And hungry." He stared down at his plate, pretending to concentrate on cutting his meat.

"You've been acting distracted since this morning. What is it that you don't want to tell me?" Lisa asked.

He tried to think of another clever excuse, but he was too tired, and he knew that whatever he came up with, she would see right through it. So he opted for honesty, to a point. "It's just a work thing. I really don't want to bother you with it. So let's just enjoy our dinner." He chewed his steak without tasting it and put another bite into his mouth.

"I can't eat if you're going to keep hiding something from me." She slid her plate away. "If it's got you so worried that you don't think you can tell me about it, then it must be bad."

"Just eat your dinner. It's expensive, and it's going to get cold." He slid her plate back in front of her, trying anything to distract her from the conversation. He wasn't exactly sure why, but he felt strongly that whatever was going on at work was something that he needed to keep to himself. At least for now.

"Is money all you can think about?" Her words stung him like a slap in the face. "Whatever the problem is, it's better if we talk about it. We're a team, remember?"

"Just leave me alone!" He hadn't meant to shout the words and as soon as he said them, he wished that he could take them back. Around the restaurant people were turning in their chairs to see what the commotion was.

For a moment, Lisa just stared at him and then she raised her hand to her mouth and ran from her chair toward the bathroom, her stomach clenching as she rushed through the doors.

They had driven home in silence and eaten cold cereal at the kitchen table without making eye contact. As they knelt across the bed from each other to say their prayers, he had watched her bowed head buried in her folded arms, pouring out her soul silently to the Lord. He had bowed his own head trying to decide what he could say, but he finally gave up and climbed into bed without uttering a word. Neither of them suggested they say their usual couple prayer.

Although they were both exhausted, Travis couldn't fall asleep. And on the other side of the bed he could feel Lisa rolling awkwardly from one side to the other. Finally she moved over next to him and whispered, "I love you."

He pulled her against him, whispering "I love you too," and they both fell asleep almost immediately.

CHAPTER 6

Ricky checked his watch for the third time in the last five minutes, looked across the table at Travis, and shook his head. "One day it's 'rush, rush, rush, everything's got to be done now,' then the next day we sit around the break room for forty-five minutes doing nothing, while Rob and Peter try to get their acts together."

Ajit Ahad, the other member of Rob's team, leaned back in his chair and put his feet up on the table. "I haven't seen Rob all morning. For all we know he's still at home asleep."

Around the table, the five developers who made up Peter's team nodded and laughed. "That's probably where Peter went. I bet he's home in bed dreaming about a sweet little Ukrainian beauty right now," a tall bearded developer, named Randy, ventured and then went back to sipping his cappuccino.

Travis hoped they were right. Nothing would make him happier than to see Rob come slinking into the break room right now with his eyes red and his hair pushed up on one side from sleeping on it. Ever since going home early yesterday, he had been unable to shake the nagging suspicion that he shouldn't have talked to Rob about the copied files. He had tried convincing himself that he was getting all wound up about nothing. Rob had been with Open Door longer than almost everyone else at the company. If anyone could figure out what was going on around here it would be him. And yet, he couldn't get rid of the feeling that talking to him had been a mistake.

At ten minutes to eight, everyone but Rob had gathered in the break room. They had waited until almost a quarter after, joking around and complaining about Rob's possible whereabouts, when their conversation had been interrupted by the ringing of Peter's cell phone. After a brief conversation, he had asked them to wait there, and walked out of the room with no further explanation.

And now almost a half hour later, Travis was sitting here with the other programmers praying that Rob would walk through the door and tell him that all his worries had been for nothing.

"Nice of you to make it back." The tall programmer waved his cup in the direction of the door, and Travis spun around in his chair, hoping that he would see Rob walking sheepishly into the break room. Instead it was Peter. His face looked worried as he carried in a brown cardboard box and set it silently down onto the table. To Travis, he looked like he was about to start crying, but he only slumped down into his chair and blew his bangs back off of his forehead.

"Rob quit this morning."

There was a moment of complete silence. Across the table, Ajit sat up so quickly that he almost fell out of his chair, and then everyone was asking questions at the same time.

Peter shook his head morosely and told them what little he knew. At eight this morning, Mr. Spencer's Assistant Pam had come into the office and found Rob's typed letter of resignation and a box with his keycard and all of his papers and disks on her desk. The letter hadn't gone into any detail, just that he had decided that he didn't need the stress and that he was going on an extended vacation, after which he would come in and pick up his final check. They had tried calling his house, but had only gotten the answering machine.

Everyone was having trouble accepting that one of the company's stalwarts could have abruptly left at such a critical time, but it looked like he had cracked. He wouldn't be the first high-tech employee to throw it all away when things got too tense. They hoped that they could talk him into coming back, but until that happened, Peter would take Rob's place as VP of Engineering. As he spoke, Peter's accent became more and more pronounced, and Travis had the feeling that Peter envied Rob, just a little, and wished that he too could shrug off the heavy load that had just been placed on his shoulders.

The mood through the rest of the meeting was subdued. Peter reviewed the progress of the Assistants and made assignments to each of the developers. He would be relying heavily on Travis and Ricky to help keep all their efforts coordinated. Travis went through the motions of outlining what they would each need to accomplish, but his mind was still on Rob.

It didn't make any sense. Just yesterday Rob had been making plans for the next two weeks. What could suddenly make him do such an about-face? Again Travis's thoughts went back to the files. Was it possible that Rob had discovered something so bad that he had decided he could no longer stay with the company?

But even if that *had* happened, why just drop everything and run? He could have come in for one day, long enough to transition his workload to Peter, and to tell the rest of his team good-bye. At the very least, why hadn't he sent an e-mail or a voice mail to the team giving them some kind of explanation?

Had he checked for messages this morning? Looking back on it now, Travis didn't think that he had. They had all come directly to this morning's meeting.

As soon as the meeting ended, he went back to his cube and checked his computer. There were three new e-mails waiting in his In-box. Two were from Rob and the third was a recap of yesterday's meeting sent to all attendees. The first of Rob's messages had been sent at six P.M. the night before. Glancing at it quickly he saw that it was just a brief note reminding them of this morning's meeting. The second message had been sent at seven A.M. today. With his hands shaking just slightly, Travis clicked on the message.

To: All
Subject: Good-bye Team
This e-mail is to inform you that I have decided to resign from my position with Open Door. After serious consideration, I have come to the conclusion that the company and I would be better served by my leaving. I am sure that Peter will be able to cover everything at the 8:30 team meeting. I am sorry for the abruptness, and I wish you good luck.
Rob

"I don't believe it," Travis whispered under his breath. Would the person who yesterday had been joking about how much dog and horse manure they might have to trudge through, the person who had told him to go home and get some rest, even though he was under the gun to get his products out on time, ever cop out like this? He didn't think so.

He picked up the phone to call Rob's home number and heard the stuttered dial tone that meant he had messages. Punching in his code, he listened to the computer voice informing him that he had two unheard messages. He felt his heart jump as he heard the voice on the first message. Rob's voice sounded slightly out of breath in his ear. The message had been left at ten twenty-one P.M. the night before.

"Hey, guy. I just wanted to let you know that I have been looking into the . . . issue we discussed earlier. I should have more information tomorrow, but for now don't talk to anyone else about what we discussed." He paused for a moment and then continued. "Also, until I tell you differently, don't communicate with me by e-mail. All right. I have to go now. I'll talk to you in the morning."

He listened to the message again, and then one more time. What had happened between ten-thirty last night and seven this morning? He started to hang up the phone and then remembered that he had a second message. It was recorded at two-twenty in the morning and had come from an outside line. He recognized the voice immediately. It was one of the old text-to-speech synthesizers that you could download off the Internet. The computer-read message was brief, and he listened to it three times just to be sure he had understood it correctly. "Mind your own business and don't mess with things that don't concern you."

He slowly lowered the receiver back onto the handset, trying to understand what it all meant. Yesterday evening, Rob had scheduled a meeting for this morning. Later that night he had called to say that he was looking into the "issue" that they had discussed. That could only mean Travis's files. Almost four hours later, someone had made an anonymous . . . what? Threat? That sounded so melodramatic, but what else could it be called? Then, this morning, Rob had turned in his resignation letter.

He thought back to Rob's voice mail. Why had Rob warned him not to communicate by e-mail? E-mail should have been the most secure way to communicate, unless Rob wanted to keep their conversation untraceable or . . . unless someone was tampering with it. He remembered how Runt had gotten past his screen-saver login. If he could get that password, how difficult would it be to get someone's e-mail password as well? And if Runt had access to other people's e-mail passwords, he could not only read their e-mail, he could also send out fake messages with their IDs. That would mean that any company e-mails sent could be suspect. Maybe even Rob's farewell that he had just read? And if that was forged, then was there a possibility that his resignation was also a fake?

He picked up the phone again and scanned the company directory for Peter's extension. Punching in the four digits, he listened as the phone rang in his ear.

"Hello."

"Peter, this is Travis."

"Oh, hey, Travis, what's up?" he sounded relieved, and Travis thought that maybe he had been expecting someone else, like Keith Spencer.

"I just had a quick question."

"Sure, what do you need?"

"Did you actually see Rob's resignation?" He tried to keep his voice casual, as though it were just idle curiosity.

"Yeah, Travis, I did. I'm really sorry."

"OK. Well I was just curious." He waited just long enough to make his next question sound like an offhand throwaway. "Did he handwrite it or print it off the computer?"

"Actually, that was a little weird. It was all printed off of the computer. He didn't even sign it by hand."

Travis could feel his grip tightening on the receiver. "You're sure?"

"Yeah, I remember thinking that it was kind of cold, not signing it at least. Why do you ask?"

"I was just curious, you know, trying to figure out his state of mind and all that."

"Well, for the record, I am really going to miss him. He was one of the best programmers this company has ever had, and a really good friend too."

Travis disconnected the line and dialed the first number on the directory.

"Security." He recognized the deep voice of the guard at the front desk. After more than a month of walking past him every day, Travis still hadn't thought to ask his name.

"Hi, this is Travis Edwards." He listened to the silence on the other end of the phone, and then, remembering their first encounter continued on. "Do you have any way to track when people scan their cards to get in and out of the building?"

He half expected another long silence, and was surprised when the answer came so quickly. "I have a complete list of all cards scanned."

He breathed deeply before continuing. "Could you please tell me what time Rob Detweiler came in this morning?"

"Wait." The sound of a local FM radio station came on the line as the guard placed him on hold. Listening to Britney Spears lamenting her misunderstood emotions, he tried to think clearly about what he was doing. Did he really believe that someone had forged Rob's resignation letter? He pictured someone recording a synthesized message on his voice-mail while he slept, someone tall, broad shouldered, and menacing. With a shiver, he realized that this was exactly what he did believe. And if they had, where did that leave Rob?

The radio station clicked off abruptly, just as a shadow fell across his screen. He turned to look behind him, and the voice of the guard came back on the line. "No scan."

Looking up, it was as if by simply thinking about him, he had somehow magically summoned Runt here like a great, gray golem towering above his chair. He was staring down without a trace of his normal good humor, and Travis found it almost impossible to force his tongue and lips into making words. "No . . . scan?"

On the other end of the line, the voice sounded impossibly far away instead of just across the building. "No scan. Either he never came in or he came in with someone who used their own card."

Travis stared up into Runt's dark eyes. "OK, well thanks. I have to go." The line went dead before he finished speaking and he slowly set the receiver down.

"Did I interrupt anything?" Runt took a step nearer, and Travis found himself craning his neck and leaning back in his chair.

He shook his head. "No."

"I see. Well I just wanted to see if you had anything new, ready for testing."

"No." He felt incapable of uttering anything more complicated than that single syllable.

"Well, when you have something you know where you can find me."

"Yes."

Runt turned to walk away, and Travis found himself breathing for what seemed like the first time in decades. Then he stopped and turned. "Oh, and my condolences."

Travis felt the air rush back out of him. "Condolences?"

"Yeah, I know Rob was a friend of yours."

"He still is."

For the first time, Runt smiled, and Travis instantly wished that he hadn't. "Right. That's what I meant." He turned and walked away.

* * *

Travis tried to concentrate on his work, but after only a few minutes of typing he found himself staring blankly at the keyboard, trying again to understand what was happening. It was like looking at a Rubik's Cube. He felt that all of the pieces were in front of him, if only he could twist and turn them in the right way. If only he could find the pattern, suddenly everything would fall into place.

But where was the pattern that tied the strange events of the last few days together? He was sure that Runt had been stealing his files. But for what purpose? And who inside the company would benefit from making it look like Rob had quit? He thought back to this morning's meeting. Peter had claimed that Keith had called him on his cell phone. And then, an hour later, he had come back with Rob's title. True, it was an interim position, but if he were the one whose team delivered the agents on time, how long would it be before it was permanent?

Was it possible that all along this had been a power play to get Rob out of the way and put Peter in his place? Could he have convinced Runt to steal the files so that he could get the first look at them? Maybe the plan had been to let Peter's team make modifications to the Assistants that Travis was working on and then somehow have testing sabotage the files from Rob's team. Peter's team would come out looking like heroes, which had to be worth a pretty big stock bonus. And obviously there would have to be some payoff to Runt as well.

Travis got up from his desk and headed toward Peter's office. He had to talk to him, gauge his mood. But as he started down the hallway, he nearly collided with Holly, who had just come down the stairs.

"Have you heard?" Her voice was somber, but her eyes gleamed.

"Yes, I've heard." Travis started to walk past her but she grabbed his arm and leaned conspiratorially toward him.

"You can't say I didn't warn you. I only wish that it had happened a long time ago."

"What? Rob quitting?" Travis couldn't believe what he was hearing.

"No." She laughed as though it was all some big joke. "I genuinely liked Rob, even if he was bullheaded. But you can't blame him for leaving can you? I mean it was obvious from yesterday's meeting that Graves and Spencer realized this project would never fly, so they turned up the heat until Rob was forced to admit what the rest of us knew all along. I just wish that they had decided to can the project sooner, so I could get to work on my alternatives."

"But the project is still on." Travis pried her hand from his arm.

She shook her head. "It can't be. Not without Rob. Who would coordinate it?"

"Peter is taking his place. He's been named the interim VP of Engineering."

Holly grabbed his shoulders, her fingers like sharp pincers. "Peter? But why would they . . . I mean he's so . . . Where did you hear that?"

"This morning, from Peter himself."

"I can't believe this." Her fingers pinched even tighter on his arms for a moment and then, visibly fighting to control her emotions, she released him and smiled. "I'm just a little surprised that they would deem someone like Peter ready for a project of this magnitude."

"Well you'd need to take that up with Mr. Spencer. I understand that it came straight from him." Travis brushed past her and continued down the hallway, but she turned and followed him.

"Travis, can we talk for a minute?"

"I think we just did." He turned the corner and crossed to Peter's office. If Holly wanted to continue this conversation, she would need to do it there. But looking through the open door, he saw that the office was empty.

"Please. Just give me five minutes in my office. This is very important."

Travis pressed his palms against his eyes. This was all getting too complicated. Everyone seemed to have their own personal agenda. Holly was right. It did seem like a big leap to place Peter over the project. He had never seemed like a leader. But what choice did they have? And what were these other options she had referred to? He couldn't imagine that she would have forced Rob to quit, but if she was the one conspiring with Runt, he wouldn't put anything past them. Or maybe Rob really had just cracked. He knew how drained *he* had felt after yesterday's meetings. Would he have noticed if Rob was even worse off? Maybe the thought of having to complete such a monumental task had just been too much.

"All right, five minutes. But then I have to get back to work." As he followed Holly back to her office, Travis noticed that the whole building seemed more subdued than he had ever seen it. Whether that was because of the departure of one of their senior executives, or simply because of the time crunch they were now under, he didn't know.

When they entered her office, Holly offered him a chair and then pulled her own chair around so that they were on the same side of the desk.

"What have you heard?" she asked.

"Only what I told you. Rob supposedly quit sometime this morning, and they have replaced him with Peter until they get everything sorted out."

She continued to stare at him as if expecting more and then abruptly asked. "What did the two of you talk about last night?"

How did she know that he and Rob had talked? She was still in the conference room when they had walked down the stairs. "Nothing. He just told me to go home and get some rest."

"That's not what *he* said." It was obvious that she was fishing, but she must have known something to even ask the question.

"What *did* he say?" He could fish as well as she could. But her next words took him by surprise.

"He said that you might have given him a tip on how NetSailor was getting a sneak peak at our files. I thought he was just blowing smoke, but now I'm not so sure." Travis could feel drops of sweat forming on his forehead as she continued to study him. "So give it up. What do you know?"

He thought back to the message on his voice mail, and to what

Runt had said earlier. Rob must have trusted Holly at least a little to have said even that much. Either that, or he was trying to elicit some kind of telling response from her. Either way, Rob was gone, and Travis decided that he would be better off keeping his thoughts to himself until he knew more.

"If I did give him a tip, it must have been accidental, because I don't have a clue what you're talking about. Now I really have to get back to work." He stood and walked out of her office without looking back.

He ran through their conversation again on his way back down to his cubicle. Would Rob have spoken to Holly that soon if he didn't trust her? And yet she had seemed so surprised—no, shocked—that the Assistant project hadn't been canceled outright. Almost as though she had expected it all along. But in truth it seemed that she had expected it to fail on its own. So why would she have gone to all the trouble of sabotaging it?

He wished he knew whom he could trust. What he should really do was set up a meeting with Keith Spencer and let him sort it all out. But until he had some kind of concrete proof, there was no reason for anyone to believe him. But what kind of proof could he get? He could just see himself dusting his keyboard for prints, or extracting DNA evidence from his chair. If only the security cameras were hooked up he could check the tapes and see whether Rob had actually come in this morning. And he could see who had been stealing his files with Runt.

It wasn't until late that night as he was waiting for his files to finish compiling that the thought of the security cameras surfaced again. The perfect solution was to find a way to tape Runt stealing his files, and then take it to the company president. But how could he get Runt on tape? He needed to set up some sort of trap. Leaning back in his chair, his eyes wandered to his computer monitor, down to the keyboard, and then suddenly back to the monitor again.

That was it. He didn't know why he hadn't thought of it earlier. Like nearly every computer in the building, his monitor had a tiny video camera attached to the top. They were only used for teleconferencing now, but it was hoped that eventually they would be used for gesture recognition by the Assistants. Travis started the teleconferencing software running, and clicked on the icon that switched the view to his own camera. There, in a slightly grainy resolution was his own face gawking up at the camera.

Pulling back the zoom, he was able to able to broaden the view to six inches beyond his shoulders. He switched on the microphone, clicked the Record button, and talked into the camera. Then he replayed the clip that he just recorded.

The speakers reproduced his voice. Not in the highest quality, but at least it was understandable. Travis grinned as he listened to the figure on the screen voice its warning. "And the rebellious shall be pierced with much sorrow; for their iniquities shall be spoken upon the housetops, and their secret acts shall be revealed."

It took him another forty-five minutes to get everything set. He wished that he could have moved the camera back another foot or so, just far enough that it would show the full width of his cube. But he knew that if he moved it at all, it would stand out to anyone using his computer. At last, setting the software so that it would start recording as soon as someone touched a key, he rolled his chair back from the desk. The trap was set; now all he needed to do was wait.

"Calling it a night?" The voice next to his head was so unexpected that for a split second Travis stared at his computer screen, sure that somehow it had started up one of his Assistants. He hadn't heard anyone step up behind him, which made it doubly surprising when he turned and saw that it was Peter leaning against the doorway to his cube. Peter had many talents, but cat-like grace had never been one of them.

"Yeah." He fumbled for words, realizing that he had no idea how long Peter might have been watching him. Had he seen what Travis was working on? Even if he had, it would have been almost impossible to tell that it wasn't part of his normal programming. But just to play it safe he covered himself anyway. "I've been testing the Entertainment Assistant for compatibility with the camera."

"I thought we weren't going to implement gesture recognition until later this year." Peter leaned over Travis's shoulder to study the monitor, but just then the screen saver kicked on filling the screen with whirling colors.

"We aren't. But the code still has to be compatible for when we do release that feature." Travis stood up from his chair and stretched.

He yawned and pressed his thumb and forefinger against his eyes, hoping that by pretending to be exhausted he could sidetrack Peter from any further questions about the camera. It wasn't hard to pretend, since it was almost three in the morning. Apparently Peter felt the same way because he covered his mouth with his hand as his jaws cracked into a yawn as well.

"That makes sense." Peter nodded. Travis waited for him to continue, but he remained silent, staring blankly at the moving colors on the monitor as though hypnotized.

"Was there something you wanted?" Travis finally asked.

"What?" Peter tore his gaze away from the screen and then shook his head sheepishly, his hair flopping back and forth over his eyes. "Sorry. Too much to do and too little time. I think I need to go home too." He rubbed his cheeks with both hands for a moment as though trying to wake himself up, and then seemed to remember why he had come.

"Someone said that you and Holly came by my office earlier. What did you want?" Behind his bangs, the eyes that had looked almost dazed a few seconds earlier now darted from Travis to his computer and back again.

Travis had almost forgotten that he had gone looking for Peter, and when he remembered why he had, he felt heat spread across his face. Did he really suspect Peter of trying to get Rob out of the way just to get his job? He had never detected that much ambition in him before.

Peter must have sensed something, because he stepped closer to Travis until they were almost chest to chest, and his eyes narrowed with distrust. "What did she say?"

"She?" It took Travis a moment to realize that Peter was talking about Holly.

"I know what she thinks. I know what they all think." Peter's voice dropped into the heaviest Slavic accent that Travis had ever heard him use. It was almost like he was trying to parody the Boris and Natasha characters from the old Rocky and Bullwinkle cartoons. It would have been funny if he hadn't looked so depressed.

"She doesn't think I can do it. She tells everyone that I'm no good. You two come to tell me that I should let someone else take over. Maybe David Lee."

It took Travis a second to realize that Peter had been asking him a question, and then he shook his head vigorously patting Peter on the shoulder. "No that's not it at all. Maybe Holly does think you're not ready for the VP job. But what does she know? She didn't want to do the Assistants in the first place."

Peter looked up as though gauging his sincerity, and then nodded slowly. "You are right." He made *right* sound as though it had at least three syllables. "What does she know? I can do this job as good as Rob. As good as anyone. Doesn't matter what she thinks, other people know how good I am."

"Sure. You're going to do just fine," Travis agreed. But inside he wasn't so sure. Had all this hostility been there all along? Watching Peter and Rob work together, he never would have suspected that Peter had resented Rob's success, and yet here he was baring his soul with Rob gone less than a day.

Peter seemed to regain some of his composure as he stood and gripped Travis by the arm, his accent once again barely noticeable as he whispered, "There are things going on in this company that you don't know about. Friends have to stick together. I can trust you."

This time it was not a question, and Travis simply nodded at Peter, who turned and walked away. As he gathered his pack and went to the restroom to change into his shorts and running shoes, Travis couldn't help but feel sorry for Peter. He seemed like a nice guy who had just been put in a tough position. Travis had known that there was a lot of discord over the Assistants project, but he'd had no idea until today what kind of a snake pit he had walked into.

Stepping back out into the hallway, his pack slung over his shoulders and bumping lightly against his back as he walked, he wondered who else Peter might be confiding in. He had said that Holly didn't think he could do the job, but other people did. If Holly was against him, and Rob was gone, who was telling him that they thought he was up to the new position? Obviously not David Lee, who seemed as inscrutable as ever.

Out of the corner of his eye Travis saw someone step out of the testing lab, and he ducked behind a cubicle wall just in time to avoid being seen by Runt, who seemed especially cheerful tonight. Turning in the direction of Travis's hiding place, he wore a big grin on his face as he laughed at something someone inside the lab had said. Whoever he had been talking to followed him out of the lab, and for a moment they were obscured by Runt's sheer bulk. And then, as they turned to continue toward the break room, Travis felt a chill rush through him as he saw that it was Peter.

Chapter 7

"Brother Edwards, you look like a man who could use a slice of pecan pie." One of Lisa's visiting teachers (Travis could never remember which one was Sister Amsted and which one was Sister Benson) set a paper plate with a huge wedge of pie on the table in front of him.

"No, I couldn't eat another bite," Travis said, raising one hand to her in surrender. But she had already headed back across the cultural hall to the kitchen.

"It's OK. We'll share." Lisa slid the plate over between them and cut into the gooey confection with the side of her fork.

Deciding that maybe he did have just a tad more room left in his stomach, Travis took a bite as well. Washing it down with the last of his punch that seemed to be a mixture of lemon-lime soda, sherbet, and, for all he knew, eleven secret herbs and spices, he looked around the room realizing that he wasn't sure he knew the name of a single person there.

It wasn't that he hadn't been coming to Church; Lisa made sure that he didn't even consider working on a Sunday. It was just that he hadn't actually engaged with anyone there. They were just faces he passed in the hallways, nodding his head when they commented that Brother and Sister So-and-so had given a nice talk, or reading a scripture when he was asked to in class. This was the first non-Sunday activity he had come to since they had moved in. And it was only because Marketing had fallen behind a day that he was here on a Saturday night at all.

"What happened? Did the guards at Open Door grant you prisoners a furlough? Or did you escape?" Grizzly looked Travis up and down before sitting in the empty chair next to him. "Nope, you aren't wearing one of those bright orange jumpers, so it must have been a furlough."

"Hey," Lisa grinned, "what kind of accomplice would I be if I didn't bring the convict a change of clothes?"

"Good point." Grizzly nodded approvingly at Travis as though admiring Lisa's handiwork. "Although you might want to consider a disguise too. Maybe fake sideburns, and one of those little black goatees."

"Oh no. It would have to be a big full beard like yours. Then if we had to hide out in the mountains we could use it to filter our water." Grizzly and Lisa laughed like old friends.

Travis watched the repartee between the two and then shook his head. "Why don't you just get me a big red nose and a rainbow-colored wig? Then I could blend right in with you two clowns."

"Touché." Grizzly chuckled, slapping Travis lightly on the shoulder. "Seriously though, it's good to see that you two could make it out here tonight. I understand that they've really been working you hard down there."

"Yeah. Well, you know how it is when you've got to get a project out on time."

"Sure. I've been there before myself. But you can endure anything for another ten days, huh?" Grizzly laughed.

"Even if it feels like ten years," Lisa added.

Travis laughed along with them, but something about Grizzly's comments, or maybe just the way he said them, bothered him. Inside his head a warning bell was ringing. Quietly, but persistently nonetheless.

"So how are things going down there at work anyway?" Grizzly interrupted his thoughts.

"OK, I guess," Travis answered distractedly. What was it about Grizzly that always seemed to get on his nerves? He was a nice enough guy, funny and easy to talk to. Maybe a little too nosy at times, but didn't all home teachers seem to get that way occasionally? It was part of the job to know what your families needed and sometimes they were too timid or too proud to come right out and ask. It just seemed that Grizzly was always a little too interested in Travis's work.

He remembered the warning that the elders quorum instructor had given him. *You have to assume that your competitor is listening.* What did he really know about Grizzly? He had assumed that he worked for a technology company, and was probably not a salesman from the looks of him. For all Travis knew, Grizzly could be a spy from one of Open Door's competitors.

Oh yeah, he thought. *The latest trend in corporate espionage. Hire-a-home-teacher. They can get in the door at least once a month if they're good. They can plant bugs as they help paint. They know when your suspect moves in and when he moves out. And best of all, they can deliver a lesson and a hit at the same time. Why wouldn't everyone hire them?* Travis was so caught up in his own internal dialogue that he hadn't been listening to the conversation that Lisa was carrying on with Grizzly until he heard her say, "I think he's got Assistants on the brain. Even when he's awake it's always *voice recognition this and document management . . .* "

"Lisa!" Travis shouted, cutting off anything further that she might have said.

"What?" She jumped in her chair at Travis's shout, looking wildly around her as though a swarm of locusts had just come through the door. Travis would have found it comical if he hadn't been so concerned with keeping her from saying any more about his project.

"It's just . . . " Travis tried to think of a polite way to word it. Finally he blurted out, "It's not something that we should be talking about. It's confidential."

Travis was sure that Lisa would be angry. After all, he had all but said that their home teacher couldn't be trusted. And at first she did look as though she was angry; her eyes narrowed and her cheeks took on a bright-red tinge, high up near her eyes. But instead of the harsh words that he had expected, Lisa burst into loud laughter, spraying crumbs of pie across the white plastic table cloth.

"You don't . . . " she started and then began giggling so hard that she had to take a drink of punch before she could continue. "You don't honestly think that our home teacher is going to spill the beans about your Assistants, do you? Would you like me to pat him down and see if he's wired?" Again she burst into gales of laughter, wrapping her arms around her stomach.

"Maybe Sherrie slipped something into our pie, just to loosen our lips a little," Lisa gasped between bouts of hilarity. Travis glowered at her. Her words were uncomfortably close to what he had been thinking, but coming from her, they did sound ludicrous. Before he could think of a suitable response though, Sherrie Benson herself swooped back over to their table.

"Are you giving away the secrets of my patented lip-loosening pecan pie?" she said in a mock serious tone.

"Not in front of this infamous double agent." Lisa covered her mouth and pretended to whisper as though she was trying to keep Grizzly from overhearing. "We're being discreet."

Now Grizzly looked uncomfortable, although to Travis he also looked like he was trying to hide a smile. "No, Travis is right. Confidentiality is very important in the technology world and if Travis is uncomfortable talking about something then he shouldn't."

Travis slid awkwardly back in his seat. No matter how he responded now it would sound weak. Fortunately Sherrie came to his rescue, leaning conspiratorially toward him as she half-whispered, "Truthfully, if I did have a secret lip loosening recipe, I would have used it on my hunky Tae Kwan Do instructor a long time ago, to make him ask me out."

"Now Sherrie, if I've told you once, I've told you a hundred times. No fraternizing with the guests during working hours." Marty Amsted took Sherrie by the arm and pretended to pull her back toward the kitchen. Seeing that she wasn't going to get her to go anywhere near the stack of dirty pots and pans, she sighed and settled into a chair. "She's incorrigible, you know."

Sherrie opened her eyes wide in feigned surprise, batted her lashes melodramatically and doing a passable Polly Pureheart impression said, "Why Ah deeeclare, Ahm as pure and innocent as a snow whaht bunny rabbit, Ah am."

Grizzly shook his head and stood up from the table. "With those eyes, I don't know why you'd need a potion to get anyone to ask you out."

Sherrie grinned at him. "You talk big, but I haven't noticed you rushing to sign my dance card."

Grizzly, whose face suddenly looked hot behind his red beard scratched his head and said, "I'm scared of you."

Travis, feeling like he was stuck in the middle of either a Monty Python sketch or an Oprah book-of-the-month, took that opportunity to stand.

"Now see," Marty elbowed Sherrie, "you've scared him off. And before we could get him to start folding tables."

"No. I'd really love to stay." Travis tried his best to look sincere. "But if I want to be at Church tomorrow, I've got to get back into the office for a couple more hours tonight."

"Furlough's over," Grizzly said. And Lisa who looked as though she'd much rather stay and chat held out her hand to Travis so that he could pull her up out of her chair.

"See you tomorrow." Sherrie waved as Marty dragged her back toward the kitchen.

As they stepped out of the double glass doors and into the cool evening air, Travis finally remembered what had bothered him about Grizzly's comments. "Lisa, did you tell anyone that I had ten more days until Open Door released the Assistants?"

"I don't think so. Why?"

"It's just that Grizzly said I . . . " He paused, knowing how she would react.

"Oh, Travis. You don't really believe that he would betray a confidence do you? He's our home teacher. It's like . . . " she struggled for the right analogy. "It's like suspecting the school nurse of telling everyone you got a pencil eraser stuck up your nose."

Travis stared at her dumfounded, and then couldn't help snickering. "I'm not even going to ask."

* * *

Travis tugged at his tie as he waited impatiently outside the doors to the Relief Society room. In the time that he had barely managed to learn the names of three or four of the other Elders, Lisa seemed to have become best friends with every woman in the ward. Across the room, she smiled at him and waved, then turned to take the hand of a tiny, elegantly dressed, gray-haired woman.

He leaned back against the wall and twisted the gold wedding band on his left hand. He knew he should be happy that she was making friends, but what he really wanted to do was go home and take a long nap. Behind his eyes, he could feel a headache lurking. He had been in the office until nearly midnight Saturday, and he knew that well before sunrise, he would be back there again.

At last, Lisa weaved her way through the remaining women in the room and poked him in the ribs. "The least you could do is to try to look like you are glad to be here. Then maybe someone would come and play with you too."

He took her books from her and smiled dourly. "I'm glad to see you're feeling so chipper."

She took his hand. "Actually my back really hurts today. I'm glad my doctor's appointment is Tuesday."

As they walked down the hallway, Travis nodded mutely. He had been trying for the last three days to convince her that she should go in to her doctor's appointment early, to no avail.

"Oh, by the way, Grizzly asked if he and Rich Adams could come home teaching next Sunday. I told them I thought you would be home." Squeezing his hand she looked up into his eyes. "You aren't going to let them make you work on Sundays are you?"

His anger and frustration threatened to boil over as they walked out into the parking lot, and he clenched his teeth tightly together. "No. I promised you that I wouldn't, so I won't."

She gave his hand another squeeze, then let it go, and wrapped her arm around his waist. "Thanks, Travis. That means a lot to me."

A moment later, she stopped abruptly and he nearly knocked her over. As she stumbled, he reached forward and grabbed her before she could fall. Holding one of his arms for support she looked past him in the direction they had been walking. "What's wrong with the car?"

Following her gaze, he turned and looked, at first not seeing what she was talking about and then noticing how the front passenger side sagged a good six inches below the rest of the car. Even from this distance he could see the tire flattened against the pavement like a partially eaten doughnut.

"Great! A flat tire, that's just what I need. It looks like I'll be working on the Sabbath after all." He pulled off his suit jacket and began rolling up the sleeves of his white shirt as he walked toward the disabled car. As he got nearer he noticed what looked like a long black grin standing out on the sidewall.

Kneeling on the warm asphalt, he ran his finger along the side of the tire. Except in the movies he had never seen a slashed tire before, but there was no question in his mind that while they had been in church, someone had vandalized their Jeep. He raised his hands to his face and rubbed fiercely at his temples. The headache that had been patiently waiting all through church had come on with a vengeance and he could feel the pounding of his pulse resounding all through his skull.

Behind him, a car engine idled roughly and then died. He jumped to his feet and turned, somehow expecting to see Runt's bright-red pickup parked diagonally behind him. When he saw the rusting blue sedan, he was relieved, but only until he saw the face peering inquisitively out the window. The last thing he needed was a nosy ward member telling everyone that someone had slashed the Edwardses tire, and Grizzly was about as nosy as ward members came.

"Do you need any help?" He opened the door halfway and started to get out.

"No," Travis edged in front of the damaged tire, "I must have run over a nail or something."

Grizzly opened the door the rest of the way and stepped out. His long bushy beard all but hid the red paisley tie that hung slightly askew from his neck. He stepped up next to Travis and scratched his cheek. "I don't think I've ever seen a nail do that before."

"I think that I hit a board on the way into the parking lot."

"Well I guess that might do it." Grizzly ran his finger along the tear. "But it sure looks smooth, almost like someone cut it on purpose." His eyes traveled from the tire to Travis and lingered there.

Now Lisa was kneeling awkwardly by the side of the car, one hand resting on the passenger door. "Wow, it sure does."

Travis was already opening the back of the car to get out the jack and lug wrench, but he grimaced as the would-be Good Samaritan knelt down next to Lisa and inspected the tire just as he had done moments earlier. "Any idea why someone would want to slash your tire?"

Travis took out the tools and began removing the spare as Lisa stood and pressed her hands against the small of her back. "No, we hardly know anyone outside of the ward." She sounded as though she were in pain, and Grizzly helped her to sit on the front seat of his car.

"I'm a little surprised your car alarm didn't go off," Grizzly said, gesturing toward the silver decal on the side window.

"Oh, we almost never remember to turn it on," Lisa said.

Travis tuned out the rest of their conversation, as he worked on jacking up the car and replacing the flat. Although he tried to convince himself that it had been a random act, not aimed at him directly, he had a sick feeling about who might have slashed their tire.

As he struggled to loosen the lug nuts, he was surprised to find that instead of increasing, his headache was actually going away. Maybe he needed a little more physical exertion in his days to offset the mental stress he was facing.

After replacing the tire, he lowered the jack and tightened each of the lugs. Grizzly picked up the flat and carried it to the back of the Jeep. As Travis walked past him, he opened the tailgate and dropped his voice. "*You* have an idea who might have done this, don't you?"

His words stopped Travis, and he turned to stare into the other man's eyes. It was impossible to read the meaning in the hushed monotone of his words, but they had sounded almost like a threat. Was there any chance that he could be in on this? Grizzly could easily have slipped out of the building for a moment, cut their tire, and then returned to the meetings without anyone noticing. Travis rubbed his forehead; the sharp pain behind his eyes was back again.

"No, I don't." He didn't need to start getting paranoid now. Grizzly was their home teacher. Soon he would start suspecting the Avon lady and the guy who cleaned his shirts.

"Hey, what's this?" At the front of the car, Lisa was up on her toes, straining to reach something on the windshield.

Travis and Grizzly met each other's eyes for a second and then hurried around to the front of the car.

As Travis reached her side, Lisa's fingers closed on a folded piece of paper. It had been tucked under the windshield wiper, on the passenger side of the car, right where Lisa would see it first. It looked like a sheet of printer paper folded into quarters, and he knew intuitively that he didn't want anyone else reading what was inside. He reached to snatch it out of her hand, but she pulled it open before he could get to it.

The words were printed in block letters almost two inches high, more than big enough for all three of them to easily read what they said. "Next time it could be *You*."

Lisa dropped the sheet, letting it seesaw its way to the ground and stumbled backward against Travis's chest. "Who would do this?" As she turned to face Travis he could see that she had turned almost as white as the sheet of paper that now stood out against the blacktop. Her wide eyes searched his face as if the answer might be written on his forehead or cheeks.

To his right, Grizzly was also studying his face and something about the knowing look in his eyes set Travis's teeth on edge. He wrapped one arm protectively around Lisa's waist and pulled open the door to the car. "It must be some kind of mistake."

"But, why?" Lisa was resisting his urging to get into the car, but he was going to get them both away from the church if he had to physically lift her into the seat. As soon as he had her in, he locked the door and slammed it closed. Without looking back, he got into the driver's seat and shoved the keys into the ignition.

Cranking the wheel hard to the left to avoid Grizzly's sedan, he gunned the engine and the big car lunged across the parking lot. As he pulled out into the street, he checked the rearview mirror and saw Grizzly leaning over to pick up the paper. Fine, let him have it. He could tack it up on the church bulletin board for all Travis cared.

Without knowing why, he pulled onto Highway 101 and headed south. He didn't know where he was going, only that he needed to get away. To find someplace where no one could expect him to be. Someplace where he could think clearly.

Across the car, Lisa's face had lost its pasty white look. Her cheeks were glowing red and her eyes drilled into him.

"Travis, what is going on?"

He turned back to the road. "I don't know any more than you do."

He felt her sharp nails digging into his arm, but he refused to look her in the eye. "That is a lie. You've been hiding something from me, and I want to know what it is, now."

His mind raced for some kind of story, but she leaned across the center console to take his face in her hands, forcing him to look at her. "We have been married for three years, and to the best of my knowledge you have never lied to me before. Why are you starting now?"

He tried to turn his head back to face forward, but she hung on with surprising strength. "Lisa, you're going to make me drive off the side of the road."

She pulled even harder on his head until they were face to face. She stared directly into his eyes, not sparing so much as a glance to see where they were on the road, and he was uncomfortably aware of the bulge of her seat belt across her stomach. "You are either going to tell me the truth right now or you are going to run this car off the road. You can choose which."

"OK, OK!" She let go of his head, and he turned back to face the road. As she leaned back into her seat he tried to decide where to begin.

As if reading his mind, she folded her arms across her chest and said, "Tell me everything."

As they left San Jose and passed first through the new housing developments of Morgan Hill and then the pungent garlic fields of Gilroy, he told her what he knew. Starting with his nap under the floor and finishing with Rob's resignation. When he got to the part about Rob's final message, he decided to leave out his fears about the legitimacy of Rob's resignation letter and Runt's comments. Until he knew something concrete, there was no point in worrying her more than he already had.

For her part, Lisa sat quietly and listened, occasionally asking a question, but mostly just watching him in silence. To most people she would have appeared to be taking it all in calmly, but Travis had been married to her long enough to recognize the signs of how upset she really was. When she was a little girl, she had developed a habit of nervously twisting her hair between her thumb and forefinger. She thought she had broken herself of it, but he had seen her return to worrying the thin strand of long black hair a few times during their marriage. The last time had been when he had told her about getting fired from Exasoft.

"So you think it was someone from work that slashed our tire today?" She noticed the hair between her fingers and let it drop, only to take it up again a second later.

Briefly he remembered his doubts about Grizzly, and then he nodded his head. "Yeah, I think it was."

"What are we going to do?" That she would instinctively view it as *their* problem made him want to reach over and hug her tightly to his chest, but as he had been talking he had come to understand what he needed to do. And he couldn't do it if there was any possibility that it would put her in danger.

"I want you to go back to Utah until things get sorted out."

He had halfway assumed that she would be happy to go back to

Utah and stay with her family for a while, and so her sudden shout nearly made him lose control of the car. "Don't you ever, *ever* think about sending me away from you!"

"I just thought that . . . "

"Never." She cut him short, both of her hands balled into fists as though she would pummel him if he tried to argue with her any further. He pulled off at the next exit and turned onto the ramp that would take them back north to San Jose. She slid a Tabernacle Choir CD into the stereo and sat rigidly in her seat staring straight ahead. Apparently their discussion was over.

* * *

Travis scanned his card and opened the back door to the office building. Although the sun had yet to rise above the hills to the East, the mornings were getting warmer, and sweat soaked the front and back of his thin gray T-shirt. He would take a long hot shower in a minute, but first he wanted to check the trap he had set on Friday night.

When he had checked his computer Saturday morning, the only thing it had recorded was one of the cleaning crew running a duster over his keyboard and wiping down the monitor. But he had gone out of his way Saturday night to tell Runt that he would be handing off a new set of files to check on Monday morning, and that he would be out of the office all day Sunday. He hoped it had been too good an offer for Runt to pass up.

As he entered the password to get past his screen saver, Travis felt like an angler pulling on his fishing line to see if a lunker had grabbed the bait. Pressing the Enter key, he cleared the screen and saw the small, red camera symbol flashing in the bottom-right corner of the Windows toolbar. Double-clicking on the flashing icon, he saw that twelve minutes of video had been recorded, beginning at three-fifteen Sunday morning.

He clicked on the Play button, and was not surprised at all to see Runt's flushed face staring almost directly into the camera. Runt was copying files from Travis's computer. He would download a set of files, check it off in the notebook he was holding, and then move to the next set. Occasionally Travis thought he could make out a second voice whispering something, and several times, he could just make out the edge of another face leaning toward the screen, but it was never enough to show more than a brief blur of color. After about seven minutes, Runt's face disappeared and the last five minutes were blank until the screen saver restarted, shutting off the camera.

"Gotcha," he whispered, and then restarted the clip from the beginning again. This time he started the CD burner running, creating his first solid proof of what was going on. He was so intent on making the minute adjustments that would give him the best copy, that he nearly jumped out of his chair at the sound of the voice behind him.

"You really are one stupid puppy, aren't you?"

If anything, Runt looked more menacing than he had before, but now, instead of inspiring fear in him, Travis was astonished to find himself enraged. It was like having the playground bully push and push, until finally something snapped and he found himself standing chest to chest with the much bigger man. His hands clenched into fists and he could feel his entire body shaking with tension. "I don't know what you think you've been pulling around here, but it's over. You'll be lucky just to find yourself fired and not in jail, you over-stuffed sack of guts."

Before Travis could move, Runt had pinned his arms to his sides in a crushing grip and he felt his feet lifted off the floor. "You have no idea what you're screwing with."

He might not be able to move his arms, but his legs had always been his greatest strength anyway and as he bent back his knee and prepared to swing forward with all his strength, he thought that maybe Runt wouldn't be walking so well for the next few days. But just as he started to kick his leg forward and down he was dropped abruptly to the ground, and he heard a familiar voice growl from behind him.

"What's going on here?" Ricky stepped up next to them and dropped his bike unnoticed to the floor.

"Just having a friendly little conversation, weren't we, Edwards?" Runt held his hands out to his sides, palm up.

Like a bulldog, Ricky plowed into the man, who was a good foot taller than he was. He put his hands on Runt's chest and pushed him back with so much force that Travis was amazed to see Runt nearly topple over backwards. "You want to have a little conversation with *me?*"

Runt's eyes flew open in surprise and he put one hand forward, whether in defense or aggression it was impossible to say. "Hey, what's the big deal, the two of us were just talking. It has nothing to do with you."

Ricky slapped Runt's hand away like an annoying bug, and grabbed the front of his shirt, bunching it so that it pulled out of the front of his shorts. His biceps bulged under his yellow cycling jersey. "You talk to my friend, you're talking to me. Sabe?"

Runt's mouth curled into a grimace, and for a moment his huge hands closed into massive fists as though he was going to attack. Then he opened them again, and the grimace relaxed into an easygoing smile. "OK, my mistake. I'll just be leaving if you can bring yourself to let go of my shirt."

Ricky gave him a final shake and then stepped back and watched him leave. He turned to Travis. "Man, you look terrible. Are you OK?"

Travis sat weakly down in his chair. Now that the action was over, the extra adrenaline in his body had no release, and he could feel his body shaking violently as he picked up the phone. "I will be, as soon as I make an appointment with Keith Spencer."

CHAPTER 8

From the journal of Lisa Edwards

Tuesday, May 4

I'm really worried about Travis. He looked like a wreck when he got in last night. The circles under his eyes are so dark they look like big purple bruises, and he has started muttering to himself under his breath. I don't think I have ever seen him this upset. He was up early this morning burning copies of CDs and organizing a binder full of papers.

He wouldn't tell me what was going on except that he was meeting with the company president this morning to clear everything up. But after he left, I looked through the copies of everything that he left here on his desk for backup. It looks like he has real proof now that Runt has been breaking into his computer. I hope they throw all of those jerks that are involved in jail forever. People like Travis work their tails off to make the company successful and then these idiots try to ruin it for everyone.

At least his problems at the office kept him from noticing how bad the pain in my back was this morning. I had Travis call Brother Adams last night—he refused to call Grizzly—and they gave me a blessing. I tried not to show it, but after only a few minutes of sitting on one of the kitchen chairs I almost couldn't get up. Then this morning, I really didn't know if I would be able to get out of bed.

I hate to say it, but Travis was right. I should have gone to the doctor earlier. When I went in this morning, I was barely able to talk them out of putting me in the hospital overnight. Dr. Canlas said that I've had a severe kidney infection for at least a week. She is such a funny little thing, "If you ever wait this long again when you have a problem, I'll send you to Nurse Haskins, and she'll keep you in the hospital 'til your little one is two!"

She gave me a prescription for antibiotics, and made me promise that I would stay in bed all day except for those pressing biological functions. (Of course at the rate I am eating and going to the bathroom these days, I could actually be on my feet most of the day!)

The truth is, even if she hadn't made me promise, I don't think that I would exactly be running the New York City marathon anyway. I really feel lousy. I just can't let Travis see how bad I'm feeling, or he'll start in on that sending me back to Utah garbage again. As if I would even consider leaving him out here on his own. Not a chance!

Well, I'm going to take a little rest. Even sitting up in bed is really painful. Travis promised that he'd call as soon as he gets out of his meeting, so I am just going to put down my journal and nap until he calls.

* * *

Travis pressed his wallet against the front of the scanner and again watched the LED next to the door flash red. Shaking his head in exasperation, he removed the gray plastic ID card from its place among his credit cards. It was really poor timing for the reader to go on the fritz. He had specifically scheduled his meeting with Keith Spencer for first thing in the morning so that he could get it over with before most people got into the office. But after waiting to make sure that Lisa got off to her doctor's appointment all right, he had ended up running late. And now less than five minutes before his meeting, he couldn't open the back door.

He shook the card as if that would somehow fix whatever was wrong with it, and tried scanning it again. Once more the red light flashed, and he growled with frustration. Sticking his wallet back into his pocket, he jogged along the white concrete walkway that led around the side of the building to the main entrance. At least the front door would be unlocked at this time of the morning.

As he hurried past the newly planted red and white geraniums in front of the building, he mentally reviewed what he wanted to say in the meeting. "I am not in a position to judge who is guilty of what, but I have come into possession of materials which I have no choice but to present to management." He liked the professional, slightly detached way that the phrase sounded. Let them be the ones who suggested summary firing and criminal prosecution of Runt and anyone who was in on it with him.

Passing through the front doors, he ran his fingers through his sweaty hair and checked his watch. He was barely going to have time to change clothes and run upstairs to Mr. Spencer's office. He didn't notice the guard stepping out from behind his desk, until a beefy hand closed on his upper arm.

"Excuse me, Mr. Edwards."

For a change, Travis was the silent one. This was the first time that he had seen the man speak without being spoken to first, and combined with the firm grip on his arm it left him completely speechless.

"I'm going to have to ask you to return to the front desk."

He allowed himself to be herded gently back into the lobby, unsure of what was going on. Did this have something to do with his faulty ID card? Then he remembered his meeting and pulled his arm free as turned to walk back toward the stairs.

"I have a meeting with Keith Spencer in less than two minutes."

Amazingly the hand was back again, even tighter than before. "Mr. Spencer asked me to escort you up to his office when you arrived." His broad flat lips were pulled down into a grim expression that Travis had never seen before. His eyes glowed like golden-brown opals.

"Escort?" Why would he need an escort, unless he was in danger? He grasped the guard's thick wrist in his own hand. "What's going on?"

The guard reached over the glossy black desk, one hand still tightly locked on Travis, and dialed the phone. "Mr. Spencer, Mr. Edwards is here."

He paused, listening, and then nodded and hung up the phone. "He says to bring you up now."

"Is there some kind of problem?" He tried to pull out of the tight grip, but it was like trying to wriggle out of a steel bracket.

Without even glancing over, the guard pulled him toward the elevator. He realized that he had never been in the elevator before, preferring to walk up the stairs. As he waited for the doors to open, he tried again to get the big man to explain what was going on.

"Why are you holding me? Do you think I'm going to run away? I'm the one who called for this meeting, you know."

"Mr. Spencer's orders."

The doors opened and they both entered the elevator.

He tried to imagine what danger could be so great that the president of the company would require that he be escorted up to his office. As the car slowly rose, he pictured Runt waiting on the floor above, armed with a loaded shotgun. Around him, the mirrored walls seemed to close in, and he thought he understood what it felt like to be claustrophobic. When the metallic ping of the elevator bell sounded, he couldn't help jumping a little, but the man next to him seemed to take no notice.

As they approached the president's office, he was surprised to see that Pam was not at her desk. She always came in early enough to start the executive coffeepot brewing for Mr. Spencer, and the rest of the day she guarded his door like a centurion. He thought the guard would finally release his arm as they walked up to the door, but if anything his gripped tightened a little as he rapped twice against the solid wood.

"Mr. Spencer, I have Mr. Edwards."

I *have* Mr. Edwards? That made it sound like he was some kind of wanted criminal or something. Again he had a sense of things closing in on him, and the hand on his arm began to feel like the steel teeth of a bear trap.

"Send him in, please. Alone." From behind the door, the voice was muted and for a split second he was sure that it would be Runt on the other side and not Keith Spencer at all. Then as the guard swung the door open, finally releasing his grip, he saw that it was Keith after all. Rubbing his upper arm, he walked into the office and saw that the reason Pam hadn't been at her normal spot was because she was inside, sitting just to the right of her boss's desk.

Standing across the room was a man Travis had never met, although he thought he had seen him around the building before. He wore sharply creased, black dress slacks and a matching suit jacket. Hanging from the neck of his white dress shirt was the only tie Travis had ever seen inside the Open Door building. His posture was ramrod straight, as though his shirt and pants had been starched as stiff as a suit of armor.

Acutely aware of his own sweaty T-shirt and shorts, Travis took in the trio in front of him. He was reminded of a group of tense athletes waiting in their blocks for the crack of the starter's gun. Everyone was watching the president, as if awaiting some type of signal. Keith looked completely relaxed though, as he waved Travis to the only available chair in the room, directly across from his desk.

"Travis, please take a seat. We've been waiting for you."

"I'm sorry that I'm running late." He began fishing through his backpack for his CDs and documentation. "My wife had a doctor's appointment, and she's been a little stressed out lately."

The man in the suit jotted something down on a notepad and studied Travis as though he had said something important.

"Yes, I understand." Keith leaned back in his chair and folded his arms across his chest. "Travis, you asked to meet with me this morning."

It came out as a statement, and Travis nodded.

"You scheduled this meeting with my Assistant, yesterday."

"At eight-thirty five." Pam read from her notebook.

"Yes, that sounds about right." Travis said.

"And what was the subject of this meeting, Mr. Edwards?"

It was the first time the president had addressed him as Mr. Edwards, and he tried to respond with equal formality. It was obvious that they were taking this meeting as seriously as he had hoped.

"I hesitated to go into too much detail over the phone, but as I told Pam, I have come into the possession of materials that seem to indicate that someone has been stealing files from my computer." Travis looked to Pam for agreement, but she shifted her eyes away from his gaze.

"That is very interesting. May I assume that the documents you are holding contain information about this—theft?" He had unfolded his arms and now sat forward and steepled his fingers in front of his face.

"Yes they do." Travis looked nervously down at the sheets in his hand.

"Would you please give those to Randall Bennett," he said, indicating the dark-suited man to his left. "He is our corporate attorney."

"Oh, sure." Before he could even stand, the attorney was at his side taking the papers and CD from him. As soon as he had them, he retreated to his previous station and slid everything into a beige file folder that he tucked into his attaché.

"Would you mind telling us how you came by this information?"

Keith continued to stare over his fingers, his eyes dark and unreadable. Randall held an expensive-looking gold pen poised above his notepad.

"All right." Travis licked his lips that suddenly felt like sandpaper and tried to decide where to begin. He looked down at his hands, clenched tightly in his lap, and realized that without his notes it would be hard to keep everything in order.

"Could I get those sheets back for a minute. I have all my notes there." He started to rise, but Keith waved him back to his seat.

"Actually, I'd kind of like to hear everything in your own words first. I think that would prove most enlightening to us all." To his right, the attorney nodded enthusiastically.

Travis looked briefly over at the leather attaché, and then began speaking. "I guess it all started when I noticed Ricky disappearing every afternoon." He told them everything he could remember, trying to make sure that he had all of his dates and times right. At several points the attorney began to ask a question, but Keith silenced him and urged Travis to continue.

When Travis finished speaking, Keith nodded slowly and stared down at his desk for a moment. "And I assume that you have witnesses for these highly unusual occurrences?"

"No." Travis shook his head. "Not unless we can reach Rob Detweiler." This was not the response he was expecting. Instead of being grateful for his information, the people in the office seemed almost accusatory, as though *he* was the one who had done something wrong.

"But I do have the CD and Ricky can . . . "

"No witnesses?" Keith leaned back in his chair and smiled, as he shook his head. "No, I don't imagine that you would."

"I don't understand." Travis felt like he had walked in halfway through a movie and missed some important piece of information that everyone else in the room knew.

"You know Travis, when Rob hired you for your programming skills, he really missed the mark." Keith Spencer sat sharply forward in his chair and, leaning over his desk, pointed a single manicured finger into Travis's face. "With creativity like that, he should have hired you for the marketing department. They could really use a guy who can spin a line of garbage like that with a straight face."

Travis felt a starburst of hot pain in his stomach, as if he had just been sucker punched. He opened his mouth to speak, but he couldn't seem to get enough air to make the words. They didn't believe him. He had spent the last twenty minutes laying out for them what should have been a crystal-clear case of theft, if not worse, by one or more of their employees, and they were acting like he had just said the earth was flat.

"Randall?" Without looking away from Travis, Keith held out his hand toward the attorney, who slapped a folder into his outstretched fingers with the speed of a good surgical nurse.

He opened the folder, leafed through several of the pages, and then snapped it shut. To Travis, his eyes seemed so cold that he could feel them freezing him in place. "Let me get right to the point, Travis. As much as I have enjoyed your little story, I have irrefutable proof that you are a liar and a thief."

Without waiting for a response he continued. "There's been talk about you almost since the day you started here. Minor issues really, misuse of company equipment, stealing office supplies, that kind of thing, and I dismissed it. Not Travis, he's a Bible-reading church boy, honest as the day is long. Then last night, I got this!" He slapped the folder onto the desk.

"But I never . . . " Travis finally found his voice, but he was cut off instantly.

"No! Don't even start with that." Keith slammed his closed fist onto the desk with a hollow bang that echoed throughout the room, and next to him Pam flinched. Travis had never seen him so angry and he sat silently back in his chair, afraid to even move.

"I trusted you. I gave you the chance of a lifetime, and you betrayed me." He pulled a flimsy pink sheet of paper from the desk and waved it in front of him, his face flushed with rage. "What was it, the money? If our offer was too low, couldn't you be a man enough to just say so? They pay off your car, promise you a bunch of stock, and like a coward, you slink off and sell out all of our secrets to the enemy."

At last, Travis understood, and the bitter taste of irony filled his mouth like poison. Runt had somehow gotten here first and convinced them that Travis was the traitor. "You think *I* sold company files to our competitors." He stared at the three grim faces in disbelief.

The president's eyes had turned back to ice chips again as he leaned back into his chair. "No Travis. I don't *think* they paid off the

loan on your brand-new Jeep Cherokee. I don't *think* they deposited
ten thousand dollars into your checking account. I don't *think* you
have been transferring files to an unidentifiable Internet server in
Russia at least twice a week since you started here." He stabbed at the
folder on the desk in front of him with his right index finger.

"I *know* it."

Travis could barely whisper the only words that he could think of.
"No. No. It's not true."

Keith shook his head. "I thought we had hired a competitor, a
winner. But we hired a loser. You make me sick." He turned toward
Randall Bennett.

"Get this over with now."

Like a marionette suddenly called to life by its puppet master, the
attorney sprang forward and spread a series of forms on the desk in
front of Travis.

"Against my judgment, Mr. Spencer is giving you far more than
you deserve. If you sign these forms today, the company will not prosecute you." The attorney held his pen out to Travis.

"Prosecute?" The words rang in his head as he leaned numbly
forward to read the form closest to him. The sentences floated past
his eyes like disjointed accusations. *Admit full guilt. Agree never to
work for any company competing directly or indirectly for five years.
Agree never to disclose . . . relinquish all rights to . . . forgo all communi-
cation with . . .*

He looked up, surprised to see Randall still holding the pen out
toward him, and for the first time that morning Travis felt the first
stirrings of anger. He pushed the attorney's hand away.

"Get that out of my face."

Smirking, Randall slipped the pen back into his jacket. "Good. I
wanted to press charges against you all along."

"Think very carefully Travis." Keith waggled his finger, as if he
was reprimanding a small child. "I don't think prison life would suit
you. Or your sweet little wife."

At the mention of Lisa, the anger stirring inside of Travis
exploded, and he charged out of his chair. Leaning across the desk, his
face only inches from the president's, he spat out words that he would
never have dreamed possible barely an hour earlier. "You pompous

jackass. You wouldn't recognize the truth if I grabbed you by the ears and rubbed your face in it."

It felt like the veins in his temples would explode at any minute. "Against my wife's judgment we moved away from our family and friends, because I trusted you. My sick, pregnant wife has eaten dinner alone almost every night since I started here, because I have been sitting in my cubicle giving everything I have to this company. If you can honestly say that you believe Runt's word over mine, then you don't deserve to be sitting behind that desk."

As he turned and walked to the door, his legs wobbled and threatened to give way beneath him.

"Travis, wait."

He stopped and turned, leaning his back against the door to hide the shaking in his knees.

"This is my final offer. I can't afford to have this leaked. I should call the police right now, but if you come back here and sign these papers I'm prepared to offer you six months' severance."

"*I* can't be bought." Travis turned and walked out the door.

* * *

Travis set the cardboard box full of his belongings on the porch in front of his apartment and fished through his backpack for the keys to the door. Although his arms ached from carrying the box all the way home, he had never even considered calling Lisa to come and pick him up. His mind had been preoccupied, remembering Ricky's eyes as he had watched Travis, security guard in tow, escorted to his cubicle to gather his personal items. The guard had warned everyone in the area that communicating with Travis in the future would be considered grounds for immediate termination.

He had also wrestled with how he would tell Lisa what had just happened. How everything they had gone through over the last month had been for nothing. It didn't matter that he wasn't guilty. He had stumbled when he should have been crossing the finish line, and it was going to cost them both. Travis didn't think that Open Door would really risk the negative press of trying to prosecute him, but just the idea of Lisa opening the door to a pair of blue-uniformed policemen waving an arrest warrant made him feel sick inside.

He remembered the last words he had said to Keith Spencer. *I can't be bought.* But was that really true?

Wasn't this whole move to California one big bribe to your wallet and especially your ego?

Although he hadn't heard that piercing high-pitched voice inside his head for years, he recognized it instantly. It was the inner voice of self-doubt that he had first heard as a child after his mother left him and his father. The voice that suggested it had been his fault that she had deserted them. Maybe if he hadn't sassed her so much, been more obedient, less noisy, or a better student, she would have stayed, and his dad wouldn't have been so sad all the time.

You dragged your wife away from everything she loved because you needed to be a hotshot programmer. You were selfish to come here in the first place, and now you're only getting what you deserve. While a part of him tried to tune it out, another part of him had to listen to it, agreeing with everything it said. Travis tried to convince himself that it was crazy to listen to little voices in his head, but he had a nagging fear that the voice might be the sanest part of him.

So what are you going to do about it? the voice demanded. Travis knew the answer, and the moment he thought it, the voice vanished, as though it had done its job and could disappear back inside his head until it sensed another weakness it could spring on.

"I'll take you back home, Lisa. And everything will be fine," he whispered to himself as he unlocked the door and stepped inside.

The apartment was silent as he walked through the living room and checked the empty kitchen. He couldn't remember the last time he had seen the afternoon sun shining onto the tile counter. He noticed a row of paper cups on the windowsill above the sink, and walked over to see tiny green sprouts emerging from the black soil that filled each of the flowered containers. Lifting one to his face he caught a faint scent of dill. It took him a moment to identify the next one as peppermint. When had Lisa started growing an herb garden? Vaguely, he recalled her mentioning something about a Relief Society project, and was stabbed with guilt at how little attention he had been paying to her lately.

He walked down the hallway, and eased the bedroom door open as quietly as he could. Lisa lay curled on her left side under the quilt. With her dark hair pulled back into a long ponytail and both hands cupped in front of her face, she looked young and vulnerable, like she could be twelve. He sat gently down onto the edge of the bed and lightly ran his fingers over her hair. She moaned softly, and opened her eyes.

"Travis, what are you doing home?" Ordinarily, the words would have seemed perfectly natural at this time of day, but in his current frame of mind they felt like an accusation.

"I missed you," he said, kissing her softly on the cheek.

She sat up and looked at the clock. "That's sweet, but why are you really home? You were supposed to call and tell me how the meeting went. Did they hang Runt from one of those ghastly palm trees in the lobby?"

He couldn't bear to meet her eyes. "What if I said that we are both going to go home?"

He felt her hand on his shoulder. "We *are* home."

"No, I mean it. I brought you here against your will, and we haven't made any real friends. We could be back with your parents by this weekend."

"Travis, what's going on?" He looked at her now, and her brow furrowed with worry.

"I made a big mistake, and now I'm correcting it," he said with a confidence he was far from feeling.

"*You* made a big mistake? *You* dragged me here?" As she sat up, Travis saw her wince in pain, but she pushed his hand away as he reached out to help her. "Do you think that I'm some kind of puppy that follows you blindly wherever you go?"

"No, it's not that at all," he said, anxious to calm her. "It's just that I know you never wanted to come here in the first place."

She grabbed his right hand in her left and squeezed it tightly. "*We* decided to come here together. This was a good opportunity, and *we* took it. Of course I was sad to leave my parents and my brothers and sisters, and I still miss them. But you are my family, and we're here together. And if you'd paid attention, you'd know that I have lots of friends here and so would you if you were ever home long enough to make them."

She pulled his hand toward her. "Tell me what happened at the meeting this morning."

"They fired me." He looked away again. There was no worse feeling than failing the person he loved most in the world.

"What?" She started to get out of bed, and then fell back again, her face pale with pain.

He caught her before she could drop all the way back to the bed, and lowered her onto the sheet. "Are you OK? What did the doctor say?"

"Why would they fire you?" she demanded, determined not to be sidetracked.

"Lisa, just forget the job for a minute. What did the doctor say?"

Shaking her head, she pressed a hand against her back. "I have a stupid kidney infection."

"A kidney infection?" Travis searched his memory for anything about kidney infections, but came up blank. The injuries he was familiar with tended more toward pulled muscles. "Shouldn't you be in the hospital?" he asked.

"No, I'm fine. I just need to stay in bed and take antibiotics." Lisa waved impatiently toward a brown plastic bottle on the table.

"Can I get you anything? A drink or a pill or something?" Travis hovered over her, looking for something to do. He felt completely impotent as a provider and protector.

"You can tell me why Open Door fired their best programmer!" Lisa sounded indignant and angry.

"They think I was selling files to one of their competitors." He barely whispered the words. Even though he knew it wasn't true, the accusation sounded so awful.

"That's crazy!" Again she started to leap out of bed without thinking, but this time he held her back.

"Somehow Runt got there first and convinced them that I was taking money from some other company and downloading files to some Internet server in Russia. They said something about our car loan getting paid off, and someone depositing ten thousand dollars into our bank account." Travis rose from Lisa's side and paced restlessly across the room.

"Oh my gosh, that's what the message was about." Lisa's face paled even further as she raised one hand up to her mouth.

"What message?"

"On the answering machine, when I got back from the doctor's office. It was the loan company asking where we wanted the pink slip for the car sent. But why would someone pay off our car?"

"To make it look like I was being bribed." He ran his fingers through his hair. "No wonder they believe him. He must have been planning this for weeks."

"But, how could he get our account information?"

"It can't be just Runt alone. There's no way he could do something like this by himself. Just the money to pay off the car would be tough for him to come up with, and I think we might find that our account balance is a lot higher than our checkbook register shows." This all sounded so crazy, like something out of a John Grisham novel. In real life, money didn't mysteriously turn up in your bank account. If anything, it was usually the other way around.

Lisa laid her head back onto the pillow and closed her eyes. "This is so crazy. Someone is paying off our car and depositing money in our account just so you'll get fired. Why is it so important to them?"

"I wish I knew." He sat back down on the bed next to her, and pulled the quilt up over her.

"So what are we going to do?"

"There's nothing we *can* do. Whoever they are, they won. We'll get a company to move our things back to Utah now. I'm sure I can find another job there." It was the only choice they really had.

"You just want to quit?" Lisa's eyes flew open again, staring at Travis in surprise.

"What else can we do?" He didn't understand why she seemed so shocked.

"We can fight." She sat halfway up and took the phone book from the top drawer of her nightstand. "First we'll call the police."

"And tell them what? That I just got fired for selling company files? They'd arrest me, not help me."

"OK then, I have another idea." She set the phone book on top of the nightstand and began shuffling through the contents of the drawer. He watched as she pulled out a white three-by-five card with two names and phone numbers on it.

"No, Lisa. This is not the kind of problem you call your home teachers for," he said. But she was already dialing the phone. "At least tell me you're calling Brother Adams and not Grizzly. I still have a weird feeling about him."

"This is *exactly* the kind of problem you call your home teachers for. And Rich Adams is a warehouse manager at a cannery. What's he going to know about technology companies? At least Grizzly is some kind of programmer."

"I'm sure he's still at work."

"It's his cell phone number." She found a pen and scribbled on the card until it started to write.

"Hello Dave, this is Lisa Edwards." She smiled at something he said and then continued. "Well actually, we are having a little problem that I hoped you could help us out with."

She explained that Travis had some problems at work and wondered if, since he had lived in the area for quite a while, he might know a good lawyer they could talk to. She listened to his response, nodding and agreeing occasionally.

"Sure, I can hold." She put one hand over the mouthpiece of the phone and whispered to Travis, "He's calling someone he knows."

"I don't know what good it's going to do," he muttered. He prowled around the room, occasionally stopping to pick something up off the floor and put it away.

"When did you become such a quitter?" She patted a spot beside her on the bed, but he shook his head and kept pacing across the floor.

She could say anything she wanted, but this was his fault and had been from the start. If he hadn't agreed to come out to interview in the first place, all puffed up just because some company was willing to put them up in a fancy San Francisco hotel, none of this would have happened.

You talked to Rob Detweiler and where is he now? He couldn't actually remember his mother's voice, but he thought that it might have sounded a lot like the voice in his head. But that didn't make what it said any less right. *If anything ever happened to Lisa and the baby, that would be your fault too. And I don't think you could ever run far enough to get away from that.*

On the phone, Lisa was repeating an address and writing on the three-by-five card. "This afternoon? That would be great. OK, we'll bring all the information." She nodded, and then wrote something else on the card.

"Yes I will. And thanks Grizzly." Abruptly her face turned red and she laughed nervously. "No, I think you must have misheard. I am sure I called you Dave."

CHAPTER 9

The ringing woke Travis from a series of dark and confused dreams. After hitting the off button on the alarm clock repeatedly, he realized that it was the phone. Raising up on one elbow he saw that it was a little after seven in the morning. Normally he would have been up and showered by now, but he hadn't been able to fall asleep until nearly dawn.

He picked up the white cordless phone and mumbled a hoarse "hello" into it.

"Travis?"

"Yeah. Who's this?"

"It's Ricky. I'm, uh, calling you from a pay phone." He sounded uncomfortable and a little nervous.

Instantly, Travis was awake and out of bed. "Hang on, let me go where I can talk." He looked back at Lisa as he tiptoed through the bedroom door, and was relieved to see that she hadn't budged.

"Ricky, how are you doing? I wanted to call you yesterday, but after everything the guard said, I didn't want to get you in trouble." He sat down on one of the faded vinyl chairs they'd been meaning to replace, and rubbed at his eyes.

"Yeah, well that's probably a good thing. I don't know what Spencer thinks you did, but everybody's been paranoid to even mention your name. It's like they're trying to pretend you never even existed." He sounded tense and slightly out of breath.

"Ricky, I didn't do anything."

"I figured as much. But you know bud, right now I think the less I know, the better."

"It's OK, I understand." The truth though, was that even though he would have suggested the same thing, it hurt to have one of his only real friends outside of Utah suggest that talking to him might be a liability.

"I had to call you though to see if you'd heard the news yet." Ricky seemed hesitant to continue.

"What news?"

"It's about Rob." On the line Ricky's voice sounded soft and flat, and Travis instinctively knew that the news was going to be very bad. The kind of news that you were never really prepared for even when you had been thinking it all along.

"They found him and his wife dead a couple of hours ago."

"How?" His tongue felt thick and rubbery. His wife? He hadn't even known that Rob was married, but somehow that made it seem all the more real.

"Car crash. A couple of fishermen found them at the bottom of an embankment. The police think it's been there for a few days." He paused as though embarrassed to be the one delivering the news. "I just thought you should know before you saw it on TV or something."

Travis sat numbly at the table, trying to understand what it all meant. Suddenly everything around him seemed unreal, insubstantial, as though he could easily drop through the kitchen floor at any moment. He tried to picture Rob as he had seen him on their last day at work together, or dribbling a basketball as he showed Travis around the office, but now all his mind could envision was Rob's broken body entombed in the crushed remains of his car, his eyes staring blankly at Travis in mute accusation.

"Are you OK?" The sound of real concern in Ricky's voice was almost too much for him to handle, and Travis bit sharply down on the inside of his cheek. He had been doing that a lot over the past couple of weeks and he could feel thick tissue forming there, but the pain was still intense enough to force him to concentrate.

"Yeah, I'm all right. And Ricky . . . " he wasn't sure what else he should say.

"Yeah?"

"Thanks for telling me."

"No problem. And when this all cools down let's get together."

"Sure. Well, I'll see you I guess." But as he hung up the phone he wasn't sure that he would ever see Ricky again.

The salty taste of blood filled his mouth and on trembling legs he walked to the kitchen sink and spat pink-tinted saliva into it, then rinsed it down the drain. He tried to make himself believe that Rob's death had been an accident, but everything inside of him screamed that Rob and his wife had been put at the bottom of that cliff by the same people who had manufactured the evidence that got Travis fired.

He knew that later he was going to do a lot of soul searching about how responsible he had been for the Detweilers's deaths, but for the time being he needed to think about the options he had discussed with the attorney the day before. First though, he needed to make sure that no one would find Lisa dead at the bottom of an embankment.

Travis picked up the phone and dialed the 801 area code for Utah, followed by the phone number that he knew by heart. By this time of the morning, everyone at the ranch would have been up for hours. When the voice on the other end of the line answered, it sounded familiar and safe.

"Hi, Mom. Can I talk to Dad?"

Their conversation was brief. It was a little harder than Travis had expected to convince Lisa's father that he had to stay on in San Jose until he could finish a few things, but as he had expected, Mr. Whitcomb quickly understood the need to come and get Lisa. He would leave immediately, and arrive sometime that evening. Travis thanked him and hung up the phone. He knew Lisa would be angry and maybe even feel betrayed, but he couldn't stay and do what he needed to do if she were here. Better to have her angry but safe at home in Heber.

Slumping against the counter, he reminded himself that he was doing the right thing. He could almost hear Lisa's voice asking as she had dozens of times while they were dating and probably hundreds since, *Have you prayed about it?* Dropping to his knees on the cool, blue-flowered linoleum, he shut his eyelids tightly against the growing heat behind them, and, pressing his clenched hands against his forehead, tried to speak. But the words he wanted so much to say wouldn't come.

Straining against whatever bound his tongue, he tried to utter a single word, to call upon the Father and ask for His help. But despite the muscles shivering in his neck and jaws, he remained silent. It felt like his father's death all over again. Every time he tried to speak, he was faced with the image of Rob and the wife Travis had never met, holding hands and crying out for help, begging for mercy, while above them an infinite black sky watched impassively on.

He knew that wasn't true, that God loved His children more than Travis could ever comprehend. He could remember bearing his testimony of that dozens of times, and could picture himself praying and receiving confirmation that his prayers had been heard and answered. And yet now, when he most needed that faith, it had somehow deserted him, leaving him mute. Finally, giving up, he stood and stumbled out of the kitchen.

Back in the bedroom, he changed into a pair of yellow running shorts and a nylon singlet. As he was tying up his shoes, Lisa woke up and turned to watch him.

"Where are you going?" she asked groggily.

He leaned across the bed and kissed her, afraid that she would instantly be able to feel the change in him. "Just out to do a few miles on the trail."

"Are you OK? You were rolling around and moaning in your sleep." Reaching out to take his face between her hands, she stared into his eyes.

"Yeah, I just need to burn off some energy and think a while." Travis turned quickly away, sure that she would be able to sense what he had just done. She must have sensed something, because she waited silently, and when he finally looked back, she seemed to be searching for whatever he was keeping hidden from her. At last though, she shook her head and frowned.

"OK, but don't be gone too long. I'm really worried about you."

"This from the woman who is bedridden and on prescription medication." He tried to coax a smile out of her, but she continued to study him. She obviously knew something was wrong, just not what.

"Just be careful."

"I will." He blew her a kiss as he walked out the door.

Before going down the front steps, he made sure to lock the front door behind him, and tucked his house key into the small pocket in the front of his shorts. The morning air was cool against his exposed arms and legs, but he knew that the sun would quickly burn off the morning haze, and by the end of his run, he would be covered in sweat.

As he leaned against the stucco wall of the apartment building and began his stretching routine, he replayed his meeting with the attorney the day before. Travis had expected to find a Silicon Valley attorney ensconced in one of the tall metal-and-glass office buildings downtown, but the address had been that of a two-story Victorian, at least sixty years old. A young brunette woman, who was wearing a metal knee brace on her right leg, occupied the front desk. She stood awkwardly as he entered.

"Mr. Edwards?"

"Yes, but Travis is fine."

She smiled. "Travis it is then. I'm Kathleen. Mr. Merino will be with you in a few minutes, but first I need you to fill out a few forms." She offered him a clipboard with a ballpoint pen hanging from an attached chain.

He took the clipboard and pointed at her knee. "Skiing accident?"

Kathleen lowered herself slowly back into her chair, being careful not to bend her leg at all. "Originally. But now the doctors say that I'm going to keep injuring it if I don't have surgery." She shook her head. "I just hate going under the knife more often than I have to."

He noticed her developed forearms and muscular legs. She obviously lived an active lifestyle, and he wondered idly what kind of activities made "going under the knife" a regular occurrence for her. Then looking down at the numerous questions on the sheet, he sat on the soft leather couch and began filling out the forms.

Mr. Merino was a middle-aged man with deep brown eyes set in a darkly tanned face, and a narrowly trimmed mustache that showed more gray than black. His clothes were distinctly un-lawyer-like. A silky red shirt with no collar was buttoned all the way to his throat and tucked into a pair of gray tweed pants with cuffs nearly two inches high.

Noticing how Travis took in his appearance, he shrugged without a trace of self-consciousness and smiled. "Never did go in for the three-piece suit and tie."

He liked Merino instantly. He seemed trustworthy, like a person you could really open up to, and Travis soon did, starting with the ad offering all the Pepsi he could drink, and finishing with the call to Grizzly. This time he left nothing out, even mentioning his initial fears that Grizzly might have been a part of it all. Mr. Merino took copious notes, never asking Travis to repeat anything, even though he occasionally got things out of order in his retelling, and had to backtrack.

Merino asked for the documentation Travis had put together and quickly looked through it. Then he put the CD into his computer and played it through twice; once stopping the action and asking Travis if he had any idea who the person just out of the camera's picture might be. Travis thought for a moment about mentioning Holly and then, realizing he had no proof, shook his head. It could have been almost anyone at the company or maybe even someone from the outside.

Humming tunelessly, the attorney leafed through his notes and jotted occasional messages in the margins. Then he flipped his portfolio closed and looked Travis in the eye.

"Well I think we can make a real good case for undelivered soda," he deadpanned.

Travis blinked, confused for a moment, and then burst into laughter.

"I'm sorry, I like to try and lighten up the mood on the first visit," Mr. Merino said.

"No problem." Travis had come into the office tense and worried, but now he felt like he was kidding around with an old friend. He was amazed at how quickly he had warmed to this man. It was completely unlike him to be this comfortable with someone he had just met.

"The fact of the matter is, you've got a lot of circumstantial evidence here. Probably more than enough to convict this Runt fellow if the company were cooperating. But from what you tell me, he must have planted more evidence against you. And with the company taking his side, I'm afraid you don't have much of a case for wrongful termination."

Travis felt his optimism fade completely away. It must have shown because the attorney held out both of his hands expansively.

"Don't give up just yet. I'm not saying we're done for. It's just that we could really use some more solid evidence."

Travis perked up. "What kind of evidence?"

"Well, for one thing, a witness or two would be nice. Can we talk to this Ricky?"

"I don't think so. The company has warned everyone that they'll fire them if they communicate with me at all."

"Nonsense." He waved both of his hands in the air. "We can get past all that without even breathing hard. I'd also like to know who Runt's accomplices in all this are. From what you've told me, I suspect that he's got to have at least one or two people on the inside, plus whoever is buying the information. You never did tell me, by the way. Do you know which of your competitors is buying the files?"

Travis shook his head.

"OK, OK, that's not a real problem. But anything you could dig up would really help." He stood, and extended one well-tanned hand. "I'm going to look this over, make a few calls. Why don't you see what more you can find out? I'd like to move on this quickly. I've got a feeling that we lose a lot of leverage once Open Door goes public."

Grasping the attorney's hand, Travis heaved a sigh of relief. "I have to tell you, Mr. Merino, it's nice having someone on my side. I was really starting to feel outnumbered." Having an attorney on *your* side, he realized, was kind of like owning an attack dog. In his mind he pictured Open Door's corporate black-suited attorney and this man in the red silk shirt slowly circling each other in a litter-strewn alley, growling menacingly. He knew who he'd bet on to win that fight.

"Not a problem. That's what I'm here for." Merino started to get up and then seemed to remember something in his desk. Opening one of the side drawers, he rummaged through a stack of dog-eared folders and pulled out a thin metallic rectangle.

"Stick this to your front window," Mr. Merino said as he handed Travis a decal with the name of an alarm company emblazoned on the front. "If Runt and his pals are half as desperate as they seem to be, they won't think twice about breaking into your apartment. But this sticker should discourage them. This company charges thousands to wire up a place. But all we have to do is convince a potential intruder that your apartment is protected. There are only a handful of pros who could get past this system, and I don't think these guys are on that list."

Travis took the decal, amazed that Mr. Merino would have it in the first place. He wondered what kind of clients regularly came through here that he would need to keep something like that on hand. Seemingly reading his thoughts, the attorney twirled his right index finger next to his head and smiled.

"It's a crazy world out there, Mr. Edwards; divorces, child custody, personal liability. Everybody wants to hire a P.I. to dig up the dirt, and a lot of those investigators don't have a problem with a little breaking and entering if the client is willing to pay enough. With today's technology, they can even place bugs and wiretaps to get the inside scoop."

Not for the first time, Travis wondered what he was getting into. He should probably just hop the next plane back to Utah. But for some reason Merino's talk about bugs and wiretaps brought to mind the Assistants he had been hired to create. Was it possible to use them to somehow do his snooping for him? He felt the beginnings of an idea about how he might be able to do just that.

Now, twenty-four hours later, as he ran swiftly along the bike path, Travis thought he had some ideas about how he might be able to get more evidence. He wasn't sure his plan was legal, wasn't even entirely sure he could pull it off, but it was something to think about.

Easing over to the right, he let a man and a woman on bicycles pass to his left, and watched suspiciously as they both glanced back at him before continuing over a rise. He knew he was overreacting, but it felt like everywhere he went now, people were watching him. From the two muscular guys he had left in the dust a few miles back, to the elderly couple reading the newspaper in the park, he found himself watching everyone's faces, searching for signs of recognition, and checking back over his shoulder to see if their eyes were tracking his passage.

Feeling a little foolish, maybe even paranoid, he returned his eyes to the trail and grimaced at the stretch of asphalt ahead of him. The first few miles of his run meandered through a tree-lined greenbelt and then dropped down into a community park where the path circled around a large duck pond for a quarter mile or so before curving back to this stretch along Highway 85. For the next mile, the trail was bordered by a fourteen-foot-tall cinderblock sound barrier wall on the right and a chain-link fence separating the trail from the freeway on the left.

Between the constant exhaust fumes in his face and the freeway noise echoing off the wall, he always felt like he had accidentally jogged onto the track of the Indy 500 when he reached this point. His only consolation was that he was running almost effortlessly along the trail, while to his left, drivers honked and swore at each other as they jockeyed to get one or two car lengths ahead in the stand-still traffic. Using his arm to wipe the sweat off of his forehead, he tried to decipher the graffiti sprayed all along the wall. He had never been able to understand why someone would go to all the trouble of painting something that no one else could read anyway.

He was almost halfway to the point where the trail dropped back below the freeway and cut off toward the airport, when the explosive bang of a backfiring car split the air. No matter how often it happened, it still made him jump out of his skin, and today he was especially jittery. He had a sneaking suspicion that drivers did it on purpose, grimly taking out their traffic frustrations on the defenseless pedestrians.

Not wanting to give the jerk the satisfaction of a glare back toward him, Travis kept his head facing forward as he ran, and hunched his shoulders, anticipating that the sadist might try a second backfire just for fun. He was prepared for the sound of the next explosion, but almost simultaneous with the bang, something peppered the right side of his face with tiny pieces of rock, making him flinch away from the wall.

His first thought was that someone had thrown a brick or a bottle at him from one of the passing cars, but when he stopped and looked back he saw a round blackened hole in the wall, and chipped brick around it. As his mind finally registered that he was looking at a bullet hole, he was startled by the screeching crunch of tires sliding on gravel. He turned to see a van skid to a stop in the breakdown lane, its rusty, dark blue side panel only inches from the fence. The passenger's window was rolled down, and a man wearing a black baseball cap pulled low over a pair of wraparound sun glasses was grinning maniacally and pointing a huge handgun directly at Travis's head.

For a second Travis could only stand frozen in place, staring into the dark glasses. All he could think was *He's smiling. I'm about to be killed by a man who is grinning like a stuffed pig while he shoots me.* Then the paralysis broke, and he dove to the trail as the man in the van fired another round that hit the wall somewhere above and behind him. He knew he didn't stand a chance of escaping. He couldn't possibly climb the wall, and only the thin wire of the fence stood between him and the shooter. Still, he scrambled forward on his hands and knees, expecting at any moment to feel a bullet plow into his flesh.

Next to him, the driver of the van mirrored his movement along the path and Travis realized that his only chance was to reverse direction, forcing the van to drive against the flow of rush-hour traffic. Dropping to one shoulder, he rolled forward and spun his body around in the opposite direction at the same time. As he jumped to his feet and began sprinting back toward the park, the man in the baseball cap fired another wild shot and yelled something at the driver. He heard the van's transmission grind into reverse, and then the high-pitched whining of the engine as it accelerated backwards after him amid a cacophony of honking horns.

Travis could see the open grass of the park only a few hundred yards away, but before he could reach it, the van shot past him, its side scraping against the fence next to him, shooting sparks and flecks of rusty blue paint through the links. Travis skidded to a stop and ducked, anticipating another shot, but the man in the passenger seat only slid an off-white tube through the fence where it dropped lightly to the trail. Before the tube even hit the ground, the driver of the van dropped the transmission back into drive with a hollow clunk, and shot forward along the breakdown lane, passing dozens of staring motorists. He could see that several of the stunned drivers had their cell phones out, and in the distance he thought he could hear the wail of a siren.

Watching the van slowly disappear back into the flow of traffic in the distance, he felt the surreal nature of the whole situation overwhelm him. He was reminded of the old-fashioned black and white movies where the gangsters and keystone cops fired comically large guns at each other, while chasing each other around in cars that could barely reach twenty miles per hour. Most of the cars had moved on, and now, although a few people continued to crane their necks around to see what was going on, the rest of the commuters seemed to be unaware of what had happened. It was hard to believe that someone had just been shooting real bullets at him. Walking numbly forward, he bent over and picked the tube up off the trail. As he stood staring at it, a pair of cyclists screeched to a stop next to him.

"Are you OK?" It was the couple that had passed him only minutes before. One of them was talking into what looked like an oversized cell phone.

"Yeah, I think so."

"What happened to your knees?"

He looked down and was mildly surprised to see blood running down the front of both his legs. "I guess I must have fallen."

"Did you get the license plate number?" The man on the phone was staring back toward the freeway, but the van was gone.

"No. They must have taken it off." Travis remembered seeing the darker patch of paint where the plate should have been, and something about the image seemed very familiar.

"Let me put something on that." The woman stepped off of her bike and reached into her fanny pack. For a moment Travis was sure that she too had pulled out a gun and he instinctively raised his hands to his face. But it was only a small plastic first-aid kit.

His mind still seemed to be moving at half speed, and Travis shook his head dully. "No. I think I'm just going to go back to the park and sit down."

She looked dubiously down at his legs again, but then the man on the phone whispered something to her, and they both got back on their bikes and raced off in the direction the van had gone.

As he walked back along the trail he checked his watch. According to the chronometer that was still running, the whole incident couldn't have taken more than a minute or two. Dropping onto a shaded bench, Travis tried to remember where he had seen the van. One of the benefits of his growing sense of paranoia was that he had been especially watchful for cars that pulled into parking lots behind him, or followed for more than a turn or two. He thought he remembered the blue two-tone paint job and the gold luggage rack. It had been sometime recently, in the last day or two. He tried vainly to make the memory come into focus, but all he could call up was a vague image of watching it pull out of a parking space and disappear around a corner.

Unable to remember whether he had actually seen that particular van or was just imagining it, he turned his attention back to the tube the men had dropped. It was constructed from a stiff off-white paper wrapped at both ends with transparent sealing tape. Peeling off the tape that held it closed, he unrolled it and saw that it was a manila envelope with his name printed on the front in black blocky letters. He pinched open the metal clasp and slid the loose flap open. Reaching inside, he felt the slick surface of glossy photographs. As he slid them out of the envelope and saw the first picture, he suddenly remembered where he had seen the van before. The photo was a black and white 8x10, showing him walking into Mr. Merino's office. The photographer had been parked across the street and about half a block down, just where he had seen the van pull away when he came out of the office.

The next photograph showed him walking out of the Open Door office building. From the security guard standing at his elbow, he had no question about when it had been taken, and he could imagine Runt smirking as he watched him carrying his cardboard box out the door. He slid the photo back under the stack and wasn't surprised to see that the next one was of him and Lisa walking out of church. They had been following him everywhere. He hadn't been paranoid. In fact, if anything, he hadn't been vigilant enough.

It took him a moment to recognize the last photograph. Someone had drawn a series of concentric black circles on it, probably with the same marker they had used to address the envelope. As he saw what the circles were centered on, and read the message scrawled on the upper-right corner of the photograph, suddenly the awful reality of Rob's death and his own near death caught up with him and he barely leaned over in time to keep from throwing up in his lap. Black waves washed over his vision, and he thought for a minute that he was going to pass out.

He put his head down between his knees and tried to take deep breaths. This wasn't some kind of TV show. There were real people out there who were willing to do whatever it took to protect their secrets. He was lucky he and Lisa weren't dead already. He shoved the pictures back into the envelope and started running for home as fast as he could, forgetting completely about his bloody legs. He had put Lisa into terrible danger, and he had to get her away as soon as possible, no matter what it took. As he raced toward home, he couldn't rid his mind of the last image he had seen.

The photograph had shown Lisa standing behind their car, unloading bags of groceries from a shopping cart, the concentric circles forming a target centered on her distended stomach. The message in the corner, brief and meaningful, echoed over and over in his brain.

"She's next."

* * *

The still night air held most of the day's heat, with jut a touch of humidity, but as Travis reached out to take Lisa's hand, her flesh felt as cold as a corpse. She pulled away from him, and turned to face the other side of the van. He looked to her father for support, but he watched silently on, no emotions visible on his weathered face.

"It's just for a few days. Until things calm down a little," Travis said.

Still she lay silently, wrapped in a thick quilt on the fully reclined back seat of her parents' van with her mother at her side. Travis didn't bother looking to Annette for support. If she had her way, all four of them would be heading east toward Utah already. He hadn't shown her the pictures, like he had her husband, but he sensed that she was equally aware of the danger nonetheless.

"You're sure you don't want to stay the night, and leave in the morning?" he asked. It was hard to believe that a little more than a month ago, they had been asking him the same question.

Larry shook his head. "We've driven across the country in less than three days before; this is nothing. Besides, Mother needs to get back home to the rest of the kids."

Travis thought maybe that was true, but he also thought that they wanted to get their daughter away to safety as soon as possible. Not that he could blame them. He wouldn't be able to sleep himself until they called and told him she was back home.

Travis leaned across to Lisa and kissed one of her flushed cheeks. Although the antibiotics were starting to do their work, she was still feverish most of the time. His lips came away tasting of salt, and, as she squeezed her eyes shut, he saw more tears spill down her face.

"I love you, sweetheart," he said. The only sign that she had heard him was a slight quivering of her chin, and he had to turn away quickly before he began crying, too.

"Well, I guess you better get going then." He reached across the passenger's seat and gripped the older man's hand in his own.

"Take care of her for me," he said.

"I will." Larry squeezed his hand so tightly that he could feel his bones grinding against each other. "And you take care of yourself."

"You understand why I have to do this, don't you?" He studied his father-in-law's eyes, seeking some kind of approval.

Larry released Travis's hand and clamped his thick fingers tightly on his shoulder.

"I believe in you, son." For a moment it was as though his dead father had returned to earth to give him strength, and he felt his eyes begin to well up.

Travis closed the door of the van, and stood in the parking lot, watching until it rounded the corner and disappeared from sight. Then he turned and walked slowly back into the empty apartment, unaware of the tears rolling down his cheeks.

He wandered through the silent rooms, unable to concentrate on anything for more than a minute or two. Walking into the dark bedroom, he sat on the foot of the bed and gathered up the clothes that were scattered across it. Even when it had become apparent that she was going to have to leave, Lisa had refused to pack any of her things, and he had finally been forced to pull items haphazardly from her dresser drawers and stuff them into suitcases.

He carried the pile of clothing to the bureau, intending to put it away, and then stopped and stared at the long silver crack in the mirror. He had known she would be upset, but why did he feel like he had somehow betrayed her? Running his finger along the break in the smooth surface, he tried to convince himself that sending her away had been the right thing to do.

Racing back from the park that morning, his hands shaking so badly that he could barely fit the key into the lock, he had been so worried about her that he had nearly charged into the bedroom still carrying the photographs. Only at the last minute did he remember the envelope, and he had stashed it far up on the top shelf of the linen closet. Even then, he had completely forgotten about the blood that had dried into dark maroon smears down the fronts of his legs and onto his socks and shoes.

As he had entered the room, Lisa sat up and gasped. Sure that she had found out about Rob Detweiler and his wife, maybe even about the gunshots, he had begun trying to babble out an explanation while she was screaming about his legs, until they both stopped, completely confused.

"Get me the first-aid kit," Lisa had ordered. "And then tell me everything."

Sitting next to her, he had started over, describing Ricky's call that morning, and ending with what he had hoped was a believable story about getting cut off in the park by a couple of rollerbladers. He had been sure that once she heard about Rob and his wife she would understand why she needed to leave. Instead, she had seemed all the more determined to stay.

"If we don't prove the truth, then the people who did this are going to get away with it. " She had swabbed gently at his cuts with the damp washcloth that had been cooling her forehead, but her eyes and voice had been fiercely determined.

He had tried to explain how dangerous it would be for her to stay, but the harder he had tried, the more insistent she had become.

"Don't you understand that these people are capable of anything?" He had winced as she sprayed an antibiotic into one of his deeper abrasions, less from the pain than from the stubborn look on her face.

"That's exactly why you need me here. It's going to be too easy for you to get lost in all of this. You need someone to keep you grounded."

The argument had gone on for nearly an hour, finally escalating into shouting before he eventually confessed that he had already called her father to come and get her, and he was on his way.

The look in her eyes had suddenly gone from anger to bewildered shock, seemingly unable to believe what he had just told her. Then she'd reached for the nearest thing she could get her hands on, a vase of slightly wilted flowers, and hurled it across the room where it shattered against the mirror. Collapsing back against the pillows as if that final act had taken the last of her strength, she had closed her eyes and refused to speak or even look at him. Even hours later, when her father and mother had arrived, she had followed them listlessly down to their van without speaking a word to him.

He clutched the pile of her clothes tightly to his face and inhaled deeply, trying to draw some of her essence into him. Beneath the slightly soapy smell of fabric softener, he thought he caught the faintest scent of wild flowers and baby powder. It disappeared almost as soon as he recognized it, and he laid the clothes gently down on the dresser, not sure whether he had actually smelled it or just imagined that he had.

She had said that he needed her to keep him grounded. Walking aimlessly around the bedroom that now seemed like someone else's, he knew she was right. Kneeling on the floor next to the bed, Travis ran his fingers lightly across the spread, remembering how often he had watched Lisa's head bowed there above her clasped hands. He had never felt so completely alone. When his father died, he had lost his closest friend. But now he felt like he had lost a part of himself—the best part.

"Please, please, please." He didn't know that he was going to pray, was even able to pray, until the words were out of his mouth. But as soon as he began to speak, a warm comfort enveloped his body, filling the darkness inside of him with a light so intense that it left no room for self-pity or self-doubt.

He had no idea how long he knelt, but when he finally arose it was with a new sense of determination and purpose. Walking out to the linen closet, he pulled down the stack of black and white pictures. He flipped through the photographs, picked out the one of Lisa, and carried it to his desk. He traced the thick black target with his finger; it looked every bit as dangerous as a coiled rattler, and he thought back to the plan that had been percolating in the back of his mind since his meeting with Mr. Merino.

He had tried to fight back conventionally and had been outmaneuvered at every turn. The thieves had him outnumbered, had more resources, and obviously had more money. If he was going to beat them, it would have to be on his own terms, using the tools that he was the most familiar with. Open Door had hired him for his expertise in creating Intelligent Assistants, and he thought there might be a way to use that expertise against them. He powered up his PC and pulled out the stack of CDs that he had copied from work.

As he waited for the computer to finish booting up, he pulled a pushpin out of the top desk drawer and tacked the photograph to the wall behind the monitor. If his plan was going to work, he would need to get everything set up within the next forty-eight hours. When the familiar Windows desktop appeared, he inserted the CD labeled Voice Recognition and began copying files. He had a lot of work to do before morning, but Open Door had seen to it that he had lots of experience meeting deadlines.

* * *

Travis slid the mouse forward, and on the monitor in front of him the pointer moved to the top of the screen and the menu appeared. He clicked on Compile, and the red hard-drive light flashed as it began processing the code he had spent the night writing. Behind him, the sun had been peeking through the slots of the venetian blinds for almost two hours.

He rolled his chair back from the desk and stood up for the first time since he had started working. His legs moved stiffly as he walked into the kitchen, and he was startled for a moment when he opened the refrigerator and didn't find it stocked full of sodas. It felt strange to finish an all-nighter and walk into his own kitchen instead of the company break room. He opted for a bottle of water and carried it to the table, stopping on the way to sprinkle a few drops into each of the paper cups on the windowsill.

When Lisa woke up she would be glad to see that . . . He stopped in mid-thought, remembering that Lisa was somewhere in Utah with her parents. According to the clock on the microwave oven, they had been driving for a little over twelve hours. They should be getting in anytime now. He reached toward the phone, intending to call and see if anyone at the ranch had heard from them yet, when, as if intuiting his intentions, it began to ring.

"Lisa?" Travis answered, longing for the sound of her voice. But it was her mother that answered.

"Hello, Travis. This is Annette. I hope we didn't wake you, but I just wanted to call and let you know we made it home safely."

"Thanks Mom. I'm glad you did." Although he missed her desperately, it was an incredible weight off his shoulders to know that Lisa was safely out of this mess. "Can I talk to Lisa?"

Travis could hear muted voices, as though Annette had placed her hand over the phone's mouthpiece. But then, instead of handing the phone to Lisa, she was back again, her voice sounding strained. "I'm sorry Travis, but she's feeling a little tired right now. Maybe after she's rested a little."

"She still won't talk to me?" Travis knew that Lisa was angry, but he had been sure that once she was safely back with her parents, she would see that it had been the right thing to do.

"Just give her a little time, Travis. She's been through a lot, but you know that she still loves you." Annette's voice was gentle now, as if talking to a sick child. "You just need to be patient, and she'll come around."

"All right, I will," he agreed, feeling anything but patient. What he wanted to do was get things taken care of out here and get back to her as quickly as possible. Since getting married, they had never been apart for more than a day at a time, and he felt unbearably anxious to be back with her.

"Take care now, Travis."

"OK. Good-bye." He reluctantly hung up the phone and stared at it for a moment, as if it had somehow betrayed him, before turning away.

Walking back to the computer, he saw that the compile was almost halfway done. It had been relatively easy to combine the code he had written at Open Door with some of the more sophisticated algorithms that he had used at Exasoft. With a few changes, he had created an Assistant that he didn't think Open Door would be offering to the general public anytime soon. Although, based on what he had seen of how the company operated, they could probably find dozens of uses for it in-house. He grinned evilly, imagining the press release they could send out.

Internet Portal releases the latest in Intelligent Assistants, Espionage Assistant. Spy on your friends and coworkers. Record their conversations and phone calls, trace their e-mails, even download the most secret contents of their hard drives.

It would definitely attract media attention. Now the only thing left to do was to come up with an animated character for the Assistant he had created. It had to be something that fit in with the other characters that Open Door was already using, while not being an obvious copy of something already in use. It would seem too odd to have another mouse or a different kind of lizard suddenly show up. He paged through his notes to see what character types had been predesigned. He didn't have enough time to create a complete character type from scratch, and even if he did, someone might notice the new framework he would need to create one.

There were birds, rodents, fish, lizards, and even snakes. He shuddered at the idea of a friendly neighborhood cobra curled up in the corner of his desktop. It looked like a fish would be the easiest; he would only need to create a few different angles to move it convincingly around the screen. But what kind of fish to use?

Travis walked to the bookcase that Lisa had made a few months after they were married by tole painting a couple of metal shelf units. Halfway down, he found the book he was looking for. It was called

The Complete Fishing Encyclopedia. Lisa's father had given it to him the first Christmas after he and Lisa began dating.

"If you're going to follow me around every time I go out to the river, you might as well learn what you're doing," he had teased.

He started in the saltwater section, pausing on the sharks and then turning quickly past. Their dead stares reminded him too much of Runt. It couldn't be something vicious-looking, like a barracuda or a pike; that wouldn't fit in with the other "cuddly and cute" characters that Open Door had based their Assistant image on. Although, for that matter, he wasn't sure how any fish was going to look cuddly.

Finally he stopped on the fly-fishing section. Most of the pages here had folded-down corners or were highlighted. He remembered spending weeks studying all the types of flies and memorizing which lure to use when. As he turned to the page showing the different types of trout and their native habitats, his eyes stopped on the perfect fish.

The bright-red line along its lower jaw would be easy to recognize and its face looked almost intelligent in comparison to the bulging eyes of the big-mouth bass, or blunt nose and long whiskers of the catfish. But the thing that clinched it was the name. In all the times he had read about it, and caught it for that matter, he had always associated its name with the bright-red marking. But now its name took on a new meaning, one that seemed to epitomize the insane dog-eat-dog world he had unknowingly walked into.

He tried writing it out on the pad of paper next to his keyboard and enclosed it in a series of concentric circles, unconsciously replicating the target drawn on the photograph tacked to his wall. It would work perfectly.

His new Assistant would be the breed of trout known as Cutthroat.

CHAPTER 10

Standing on the sidewalk in front of the Open Door building, Travis took a deep breath, trying to build up enough confidence to walk through the doors. It was one thing to make bold plans late at night in the relative safety of his apartment, but now in the bright morning sunlight, apprehensively contemplating what was he was about to try, he found his legs threatening to turn and run at any moment.

"Come on, come on. You can do this," he muttered to himself, wrapping his arms across the front of his blue nylon windbreaker as it fluttered in the stiff breeze. If he didn't have enough guts to even walk through the doors, then he might as well pack up his things and go back to Utah now.

"Actually, that's not such a bad idea." He tried to make it sound like a joke, but it came out sounding so much like a concession that it startled him into motion. After making one final check to be sure the item in his backpack was still in place, he took another deep breath, inhaling until it felt like his lungs would pop, and then released it and entered the building.

His first thought was that, despite the number of cars in the parking lot, the lobby seemed unusually quiet. The sounds of explosions and revving engines from the video games in the break room were conspicuously absent, and there were no visitors waiting for their appointments by the Internet kiosks. Before he could take more than a half-dozen steps, the security guard recognized him and instantly got to his feet. He circled around the back of his desk and charged across the lobby, cutting Travis off from any further entry.

"You must leave. You are not allowed here." His elbows jutted out

to the sides of his huge body, straining his canvas uniform as he
planted a meaty fist onto each of his hips.

Stopping before the human roadblock, Travis held his hands out,
palms up, in what he hoped came across as a gesture of surrender.

"I'm here to see Mr. Spencer. He's expecting me." While this
might not *technically* be the truth, he thought Keith Spencer had
probably been expecting Travis to crawl back on his hands and knees
ever since he had fired him.

"He didn't say anything about meeting you." The guard still hulked
in front of him like an NFL lineman protecting his quarterback, but his
expression had changed from hostile to slightly uncertain.

Why don't you call up there and check?" He tried to appear both
confident and harmless at the same time.

For a moment, Travis thought the guard would throw him out
the door anyway, and then he grunted and pointed toward the inflatable couch by the ferns and miniature palm trees. "Wait there."

Travis shrugged, and walked back to the chairs. Outwardly he
tried to look nonchalant, but inside, his heart was pounding so hard
he was surprised it didn't show through the light cotton shirt he was
wearing beneath his windbreaker. If the guard had made him wait
outside or even next to the front desk while he called upstairs, his
plan would have been shot down before it even got started. Part of
him wished that he had. It would have been easier to just turn around
and walk back out the door. To be able to say, "Well I gave it my best
shot, but it just didn't work out."

As he dropped onto the couch, he slipped off his pack and
lowered it to the gray and red carpet, careful to position it so that
the unzipped opening at the top was facing toward the nearest in-
ground planter. From the corner of his eye, he checked the desk,
not surprised to find the guard watching him with an unwavering
glare as he spoke into the phone. He began counting silently to
twenty, picturing the conversation that Keith Spencer would be
having with his Assistant.

Timing was critical now. If Travis waited too long, there would be
enough time to either have him brought up or sent away and he
would miss his chance, but if he moved too quickly, it might make
the guard more suspicious than he already was. Inside his jacket

pocket, he fingered the ringer control on his cellular phone. When he reached a count of twenty, he pushed the button, and then pretended to search his pockets for the source of the electronic ringing.

Taking the phone from his jacket, he snapped it open. There was no point in looking toward the guard now; either he was on his way over, or he was still stuck on the line, waiting for instructions from Mr. Spencer.

"Hello." Travis nodded his head as he pretended to speak to someone and then slid his jacket sleeve up and checked his watch.

"Oh, I had no idea. You did? Well of course, I'll be right there. Bye."

He closed the phone and returned it to his pocket. Finally he allowed himself to turn around and look at the guard, and was relieved to see that although he was watching him intently, he was still on the phone.

"That was my wife. I have to get home right away." He shrugged his shoulders and grinned sheepishly. "I guess you'll have to tell Mr. Spencer that I need to reschedule our meeting."

Without waiting for a response, Travis turned and reached down to pick up his pack, his body effectively blocking it from the guard's sight. Feeling incredibly exposed, he lifted the shoulder straps and tilted the bag's opening down toward the ferns until he felt something inside begin to move. There was a slight mechanical whirring, and then a fire-engine-red remote-controlled pickup truck rolled backward out of the top of the pack and into the planter. He nudged it back with his foot until it disappeared into the cover of the foliage.

As soon as he was sure the toy truck was hidden from sight, he turned and walked to the front door. Slinging his backpack over one arm, he looked across the lobby and saw that the guard had hung up the phone and was coming around the desk.

"Mr. Spencer says he has no appointment with you."

Travis shouldered one of the doors open as its electronic opener started to engage, and stepped quickly through it and out onto the walkway. Behind him he could hear the thud of running footsteps.

"Sorry, I must have looked at the wrong page in my planner," he called out above the Open Door voice coming from the doorframe. "I'll call you to reschedule. Soon."

As he jogged into the parking lot, he looked over his shoulder and saw the burly guard observing him uncertainly from the doorway.

Now he just had to hope that security or the cleaning crew didn't discover the truck before he came back that night.

* * *

Kneeling in the parking lot between a silver Mazda Miata and a white Chevy Blazer, Travis studied the lobby through a pair of high-powered binoculars. He had picked them up in a sporting goods store that afternoon along with a small flashlight and a Swiss army knife. At the last minute, he had also filled out the paper work to buy a handgun. Not that he thought he would really go through with the purchase, but if an emergency came up he might need to move quickly. While living in Utah, he had done his share of deer hunting, but the thought of firing at a person made him sick to his stomach.

Laying the binoculars down on the pack beside him, he raised up into a low crouch and surveyed the rest of the parking lot. His knees ached from pressing for hours against the sharp pieces of glass and gravel strewn across the asphalt, and they popped like muted fire-crackers as he stretched them. Even though it was nearly three in the morning, there were still more than a dozen cars in front of the building and twice that many around back. Clear evidence of the company's determination to press forward with their release date, despite the loss of two key members of their Assistant team.

He had arrived at midnight, first peering out from behind the thick green leaves of the oleanders, and finally, as things started to quiet down, moving up to his current position between the cars. Earlier there had been a constant stream of people coming in and out of the office, but since the janitorial crew left nearly twenty minutes ago, things had quieted down. He tucked the binoculars back into his pack and pulled out a small black plastic box with a pair of levers sticking out of the front and a retractable antenna on top.

For what seemed like the hundredth time that night, Travis wished the building's exterior wasn't so well lit. As an employee, he had appreciated the feeling of security the bright halogen lights provided, but now, leaving the safety of his dark hiding place for their penetrating glare, he felt as exposed as a bug under a magnifying glass. As it was, he had to be satisfied with pulling his cap down low over his forehead as he walked toward the doors. After extending the antenna on the control box, he thumbed the On switch, and saw the tiny power light glow green. He hoped that inside, on the remote-controlled truck, a similar light had just changed from red to green also. When he had tested it at home, there seemed to be more than enough range to reach this far.

As he reached the doors, he cupped one hand against the glass to cut the glare, and checked to make sure there was no one in sight inside the lobby. When he was sure it was empty, he briefly looked around one more time and then pushed the speed lever on the controller forward. He watched the ferns where he had hidden the truck, but nothing moved. He tried again, pushing the box against the glass to improve the range, but there was still no motion among the long green leaves.

It was over. He felt the despair of being beaten again. Someone had discovered the truck and carried it off. And even though he had been careful to wipe any of his fingerprints off it, how hard would it be for security to figure out who had left it in the lobby and why? For all he knew, maybe they had already figured it out. Couldn't they be crouching just out of sight inside the building waiting for him to try to break in? There could be someone circling around from the back of the building even as he waited.

He nearly bolted, fleeing back into the safety of the dark, but something told him to stop and give it one last try. Wasn't it at least possible that one of the truck's tires had gotten lodged against a fern or even the edge of the planter? He pulled the speed lever slightly back toward reverse while steering to the left, and then released the steering lever and jammed the speed all the way up to turbo. Inside the building, a red blur raced out of the bushes and disappeared behind the guard's desk so fast he almost missed it. Travis had already started to turn away from the door before his brain registered what he had seen.

Half afraid that he had just imagined the movement, he pulled the lever back to reverse, and then pumped his fist in the air as the bright red truck backed slowly out from behind the desk and came to a stop in the center of the lobby.

"You just earned yourself a wash and a new battery," he whispered as he steered the truck around the desk and toward the doors. Every time he had tried to come up with a plan for getting more information on Runt, he had been stumped by the same problem. There was no way he could think of to get any software application in through the company's firewall. If he could gain access to the internal network, he thought he could find a way to get from one workstation to another. But that would require getting into the building, and that was where all of his plans had fizzled.

He had no idea how to make a fake ID card to trigger open the doors, and even if he could slip in the back door behind an employee, anyone in the company would alert security as soon as they recognized him. He had briefly considered asking Ricky to help him, but he couldn't risk getting another friend involved in what he knew was a dangerous situation. It had been while he was running that he remembered seeing the electronic motion sensor on his first day in the office. It was designed to unlock the door for employees who were leaving the building after hours. Just because a person could set off the movement sensor, didn't mean that it would detect a six-inch-tall toy truck, but it was the only idea that he had been able to come up with.

As he guided the car deliberately back and forth in front of the entrance, his hands carefully maneuvering each of the control levers, he listened for the familiar click of the opener kicking in. He started nearly twenty feet away and crisscrossed his way nearer, bringing the car about six inches closer with each pass. On his eighteenth run, just as he was beginning to feel like it wouldn't work, he heard the sound he had been waiting for, and the familiar Open Door voice had never seemed more welcoming. He pushed through the doors and picked up the truck by its plastic cab before racing into the dim lobby. Although he was terrified of being discovered, he couldn't stop the broad grin that spread across his face any more than he could stop the music that kept running through his head.

"Bum, bum, ba dum-bum, bum, bum, ba dum-bum, da-da-dum, da-da-dum" he quietly hummed the "Mission Impossible" theme song under his breath as he slipped into the darkened restroom at the back of the lobby.

As the door swished shut behind him, Travis leaned back against the cool tile wall and caught his breath. The sharp smell of recently applied ammonia burned his sinuses and the back of his throat, but he covered his mouth with one hand and fought the urge to cough. The cleaning crew had turned off the lights, and since this bathroom was only used by visitors he felt confident that he could remain undisturbed for as long as he would need to. Still his hands trembled slightly as he turned off the power on the truck and controller and tucked them back into his pack.

Without the glowing lights of the toy, he was completely blind as he fished around inside his pack for the cold metal tube of the flashlight. He wasn't sure whether the bathroom lights would show through to the lobby or not, but there was no point in taking any more risks than he had to. Switching on the flashlight, he used its narrow beam to locate his pocketknife. Then clipping the penlight to the front of his jacket so that it formed a tight white circle of light on the floor, he carried his pack into the nearest stall and set it down next to him.

Up until tonight, he hadn't actually broken the law, but if he got caught now it would be for breaking and entering at the very least. *I can still turn back,* he thought. *No one even needs to know I was here.* It might very well be his last chance to turn back, but if he quit now he would never be able to look himself in the eye. He had made the decision to go for this and, regardless of the consequences, he was going to see it through.

Getting into the building was only the first step in getting access to a computer he could use to break into the network. After nine P.M. all of the office doors locked, completely sealing off the lobby from the rest of the building. But Ricky had unknowingly given him the clue he needed to move anywhere around the building without being seen, at least on the first floor. Using the screwdriver blade of his knife, he tried to loosen up one of the tiles of the bathroom floor. The thick wax that had been applied to the floor for years was caked into the cracks between each of the tiles, but he was finally able to scrape it away using the sharper cutting blade of the knife.

Inserting the screwdriver back into the crack, he pried at the tile until it popped open, revealing the crawl space below. He lowered his pack into the shadows and then climbed in himself, being sure to orient himself in the same direction as the hallway that ran next to the restroom. He unclipped the light from his jacket and held it in his teeth as he pulled a sheet of graph paper from his pocket. That afternoon, he had used a pencil and ruler to chart the approximate dimensions of the rooms and hallways now above him to the best of his memory.

Mentally counting each movement of his hands, he began crawling forward, the flashlight in his mouth casting strange shapes in front of him. Practicing on his kitchen floor the night before, he had estimated that he was able to cover about fifteen inches with each reach of his arm. Every time he counted to eight, he pulled out a pencil stub and marked off another square on the sheet of paper, signaling that he had covered ten more feet.

After twenty squares, he dropped the sheet of paper to the concrete floor and used the flashlight to illuminate the space around him. To his right, a row of thin copper pipes reflected the light back at him, and then disappeared into the blackness when he moved the beam away. About twenty feet straight ahead were what looked like stacks of slim storage boxes that had been hidden down there for who knew how many years. But neither of them provided the landmark he was searching for.

Looking back the way he had come, he found that the opening had disappeared in the darkness. It was impossible to visually estimate how far he had crawled. He would have to rely on his homemade map and rough measurements. Referring back to the sheet, he decided that he had probably veered too far to the right. Turning to the left, he began moving hesitantly forward running his hands carefully over the cool concrete. He counted off another twenty feet, and was starting to worry that he might have overshot his target completely, before his right hand came down on what he had been searching for—a strand of long, blue cable.

He played the beam of light along its length until it joined a series of other cables and disappeared into the tiles above. He could picture how they emerged from the floor and snaked their way to the various computers spread throughout the testing lab. In the rest of the building the network cables were fished through the ceiling and down the walls, but the lab had so many interconnected computers that it was easier to just run the cables beneath them in the crawl space. Moving forward until he was directly below one of the holes that had been drilled through the floor tiles, Travis switched off his flashlight and stared up at the scattered light that filtered down through the thick strand of wires.

The very reasons that made the lab the easiest place to install his Assistant also made it the most dangerous for Travis to sneak into. The lab's computers were used by more than a dozen testers, making screen-saver passwords unfeasible. The PCs were linked to all of the company servers and often had network administrator rights, giving them complete read/write access to dozens of other systems. That access would allow him to install software on nearly any computer. However, that also meant that it would not be surprising to find people in the lab at any hour of the day or night. Often one or more members of the testing team carried a pager that notified them of a system crash requiring them to come into the office immediately to reset the computer at fault.

He had considered trying to return to his own system with the hope that his passwords had been left unchanged, but he had given up on that plan almost immediately, realizing that as soon as they had fired him they would have seized his computer to search for any incriminating evidence of his supposed espionage. And even if they had left his passwords intact, he would still have to hack into the rest of the network and risk some IS manager spotting his entry and tracing any files that he had installed.

No, the lab was definitely the heart of the company, and if he was going to infiltrate their systems he might as well do it right. It also brought him a perverse sense of pleasure to know that he was breaking into Runt's territory. After having his own privacy invaded so many times, it was nice to be the invader that night instead of the invaded.

Lifting his head as close to the opening as he could get it, he covered his other ear and listened for voices. At first, all he could hear was the hum of the cooling fans in the systems above him, and then a voice he didn't recognize shouted almost directly above him.

"Anyone start running twenty-two yet?"

In the distance he could hear a muted response, but he was unable to make out the words.

"Can't anyone read around here? The schedule shows that twenty-two and twenty-three should have been run two hours ago."

It sounded to Travis like the person at the other end of the room said something about *breakers*. And then he realized that it must have been *break room*, when the closer voice said, "Yeah, I could go for a soda myself." The sound of footsteps moved away from him and was followed by loud laughter that was cut off as the door swung shut.

As soon as he heard the door bang closed, Travis shoved up on the tile. As he had hoped, the tile came up easily, as though it had been removed often by people servicing the computers. Lifting it just high enough so that he could raise his eyes a few inches above the floor, he scanned the room for any signs of movement. For a moment, he thought the lab had been completely rearranged since he had last seen it—nothing was where he remembered it. He was disoriented until he realized he was on the opposite side of the room from where he had expected to be. He had miscalculated the distance he was covering by at least a dozen feet, bringing him out beneath the Macintosh computers instead of the PCs that he needed to install his file on. Leaving his pack on the floor in the darkness, he took out a CD and popped back up for one last quick look around.

He couldn't see around the corner where Runt's office was located, but the rest of the lab was empty for the moment. He quickly pulled himself up out of the floor and scrambled across to the PCs on the other side of the room. Most of the screens had gone into sleep mode, flashing geodesic shapes or constantly changing fractal patterns. Walking quickly from one PC to another, he tapped each of their space bars to awaken them, all the while listening for voices or footsteps coming from the other side of the door. He knew that if he heard them at all, it would probably be too late. The odds of him getting across the room and back down into the hole before the door opened were slim at best.

Halfway down the row of monitors, he found what he was looking for—a computer that had been logged onto the network with an administrator password. He clicked on the Network Neighborhood icon and was gratified to see that he had access to a handful of directories on Runt's personal computer, including the one where new Assistants were stored. He quickly inserted the CD into the computer and began uploading it. After a month of passing files across to testing, he had the routine down cold. There was a small chance that Runt might wonder why a new Assistant had come without any notification, but he hoped that things were in enough turmoil with the looming deadline that he wouldn't bother to check on it.

Once the Assistant was installed on Runt's computer, it would automatically blend in with the other Assistants installed there, and begin secretly indexing and downloading all of his files. Using the computer's microphone and video camera, it would also record any conversations that Runt had within his office. All of this information would then be transferred over the Internet back to Travis. Before he got back home, the Assistant should already be transferring files to the array of hard drives he had set up in his spare bedroom.

As he watched the status of the files being copied from computer to computer, he thought again about the video he had of Runt stealing files from his computer. If only he had been able to make out the face of the person standing just off screen, he could install his Assistant on their computer too, doubling his chances of getting the information he needed to prove his innocence. Closing his eyes, he tried to connect the fuzzy partial image with the voice that he had heard whispering above him the night he fell asleep under the floor, but he kept drawing a blank.

Travis was so intent on his thoughts that he didn't hear the sound of squeaking chair wheels coming from inside Runt's office. It wasn't until he heard Runt's voice that he started from his reverie.

"Hey, any of you guys wanna go grab a shake?"

Travis barely had time to drop out of his chair and slide under the table before he saw Runt's big leather boots stomp around the corner, and he knew instantly that he had been a hair too slow.

"Hey, what's going on?" Travis tensed his body as Runt came running across the room. As he watched the big man race toward him, he realized how stupid he had been. He had never planned what he might do if he got caught, and he could only imagine what Runt would do now that he had him alone. He could never out-muscle him, and even if he did manage to get past him somehow, the police would be waiting at his apartment when he got back.

Feeling trapped, he searched for some kind of weapon but there was nothing in reach. Even his backpack with his pocketknife was still back in the crawlspace. With Runt only a few feet away, Travis desperately grabbed the legs of the rolling chair in front of him and prepared to ram it forward into the knees that were now at his eye level. He would run for the door and deal with the police when he got there . . . if he got there.

Steeling his arms to piston forward, Travis gritted his teeth in anticipation of the contact. Then, just before he sprang, Runt passed by him to stop at one of the other computers Travis had checked on his way across the room.

"Which one of those clowns stopped the test cycle?" Runt muttered, and above his head Travis could hear the sound of Runt typing on the keyboard he had just been using.

Was it possible that Runt hadn't seen him? Breathing harshly, Travis kept his grip on the chair, watching the head of testing standing less than an arm's length away. Sure that he was being toyed with, he kept expecting at any moment to see Runt's face dip beneath the edge of the table, his eyes black and lifeless. He could almost hear his voice growling, "Now you're mine." But instead, Runt turned, slammed open the lab door, and bellowed for the other testers as he left the room.

Travis was so relieved that for a moment he sat frozen in place like a rabbit that has just felt the hawk's iron talons brush lightly above its fur. Then his paralysis broke and he rushed madly across the room, barely remembering to go back for his CD before diving down into the hole and dragging the tile back into place.

Desperate to get away as quickly as possible, he scuttled blindly through the blackness. His flashlight had somehow been lost in his panicked dash to get back out of sight, and with no sense of direction or distance, Travis felt his fear turning quickly to panic as he spent what seemed like an eternity searching desperately for the way out. It was only through sheer luck that he crawled headfirst into the copper pipes he had seen earlier and was able to follow them back to the bathroom, where he located the open hole by the strong disinfectant smell wafting through it.

Climbing up into the safety of the closed stall, he dragged himself into a corner and clutched his knees to his chest. The emotions he had managed to hold back for the last ninety minutes finally overtook him. His body shivered violently as he buried his face into the rough fabric of his pack and gasped helplessly.

He didn't know how long he sat huddled on the tile, his body shaking uncontrollably. But at last, he was able to get to his feet and stumble out the door and across the lobby. He could just make out the first rays of early-morning light glowing through the clouds. He didn't even think about checking to see if anyone was in sight until the doors swung open, and he saw that someone was standing on the walkway in front of him.

For a split second he mistook the broad shoulders and arms for Runt, then he realized the man was much too short.

"Ricky, I . . . " he stammered, unable to think of any explanation for his presence. But Ricky continued through the door without even turning his head.

"Never saw you," he whispered, and then disappeared into the building.

CHAPTER 11

The evidence had to be there somewhere. Hidden in the seemingly endless reams of pages silently spitting out of the laser printer, or on one of the hard drives that continued their sporadic humming and clicking as more information poured into them through the cable modem.

Somewhere in the gigabytes of data his Assistant was gathering from Runt's computer was the information that would help him prove his innocence, and, hopefully, Runt's guilt at the same time. But for every question he found a possible answer to, there were four that left him completely baffled. Who was Runt's inside partner? Why would they provide information to a competitor, when the imminent Open Door IPO was bound to make them hundreds of thousands, if not millions of dollars? Had the plan been to make him the scapegoat all along or was his involvement simply chance?

Travis grabbed another handful of sheets from the printer and began poring over them by the light of the two floor lamps that he had dragged in from the living room. Although it was almost one-thirty in the afternoon, the rest of the apartment was still dark. Only an occasional spear of afternoon sunlight emerged through the tightly closed blinds. After Lisa left, he had gone through the whole apartment, double-checking all the window locks and making sure that even the windows that were two stories above the parking lot were covered.

Searching for clues was a frustratingly slow process. Most of the pages contained nothing more than simple interoffice messages (*10 am meeting with all marketing staff*) or the endless rounds of off-color jokes and stories that had become the electronic junk mail of the 90s. Yet he read them all with equal thoroughness, occasionally using a yellow marker to highlight an e-mail address to check on, or a line of text that seemed important, then placing those pages in a small pile to his left. The rest he absently discarded to his right, where they drifted to the floor somewhere in the vicinity of a sloping mound of paper that lay nearly six feet across.

In front of him, disjointed images flashed across the screen of the seventeen-inch monitor while the accompanying sound squawked from a pair of speakers set to either side of it. Each of the images showed the distinctive fish-eye perspective of the video cameras that all the Open Door employees had attached to the top of their computer monitors. It had been a simple matter to have his Assistant sense any sounds above a certain threshold and begin record mode. The real problem was filtering the valuable information from the junk. It was like watching an eighteen-hour movie edited by a madman.

Some of the clips were only three seconds long, the minimum record time he had set in his program, triggered by a cough or a single word. Others stretched out for thirty minutes or more—a telephone call, or one especially annoying stretch where Runt continually whistled the Pink Panther theme off key for nearly forty minutes. He had been tempted to turn off the speakers or hit Fast Forward, but there was always the chance he might miss something important. And even if he didn't, his mind would convince him that he had, until he forced himself to listen to the whole thing over again. So he suffered through it as he continued to sift through the stacks of e-mails and documents that were piled up on the desk around him.

He was highlighting a new e-mail address to add to his list when the computer sounds were interrupted by the sharp crack of someone banging on his front door. The pen marked a jagged yellow lightning bolt off the edge of the page as he spun around in his chair and stared with wide, panicked eyes into the dark hallway. In the thirty-six hours since he had broken into the Open Door building, he had been constantly on edge, fearing just this moment. All it would take was one person to notice the extra-heavy traffic on the network, or for Runt to grow suspicious of the new Assistant that had seemingly appeared from nowhere. They would be able to follow the data trail right to his door. He didn't know whether he was more afraid that it would be the police or that it wouldn't. He could just as easily envision ending up at the bottom of a remote ravine, as Rob had.

His first thought was to hide under the desk until whoever it was went away. But what if they didn't go away? What if the next sound was metal jiggling against metal in the front lock, or a screwdriver blade prying at the window next to him? He couldn't stand to curl trembling beneath the desk, not knowing whether at any minute someone might come charging into the room.

Raising himself to his feet, he scattered the pages he held onto the desktop and tiptoed as silently as he could across the carpeted floor and into the hallway. Just as he reached the living room, the pounding returned and for a moment it was all he could do to keep from bolting back into the bedroom.

From outside the door a voice called out, "Hello. Anyone home?"

Well, that ruled out the police. From his television experience, they always shouted things like, "Open up. Police," just seconds before they knocked down the door. It didn't sound like Runt's voice either, but it could easily be one of the goons who had shot at him from the van. He raced into the kitchen to search for something he could use as a weapon; there was a baseball bat somewhere, but he didn't have time to search for it. His eyes stopped on the knife drawer and he pulled out a sharp, six-inch blade. He thought that Lisa had called it a chef's knife. Remembering the gun that the man in the van had fired at him on the bike path, he felt nearly defenseless as he padded silently up to the door. He vowed to go through with buying a gun of his own if he managed to somehow escape.

"I saw his car parked out front," another voice said from outside.

The hand he held the knife with trembled visibly and he tried to force it to stop shaking as he leaned forward and placed his eye against the peephole. He felt positive they would somehow sense him watching them, and for a moment they both seemed to stare directly back at him. Their faces were just as he had imagined, hard and steely eyed. Looking down, he felt the back of his neck grow ice cold as he saw they were both carrying big black handguns.

Then, as if through a trick of lighting, the guns changed into books, and he saw that they were both wearing suits and ties. The faces that had seemed dangerous and sinister at first glance were really the familiar faces of Grizzly and what's-his-head, his home teachers. As relief washed over him, he let his body slump against the door and the knife blade knocked against the doorknob with a metallic clang.

"Travis?" Both men looked expectantly toward the door at the sound, and he knew that he would have to answer now or they would both know that he had been hiding from them.

He cracked the door open a few inches and looked out.

"Hi Travis. How are you doing? We missed you at church today."

"Hi Brother um . . . " he struggled, trying to remember the man who stood next to Grizzly.

"Adams." He shot a clean pink hand through the doorway, and instinctively Travis opened the door a little further and brought his arm forward to shake hands, before realizing that he was still holding the knife.

"I was just making myself a sandwich," he offered lamely, quickly switching the knife to his other had.

"Must have been a big one." Grizzly shook his hand, his eyes far too inquisitive for Travis's liking.

"So, what can I do for you?" Even more than he wanted to change the subject, he wanted to get back to searching through the night's files.

"Lisa told us last Sunday that today would be a good day to visit." Adams shifted from one foot to the other as though uncomfortable to be standing outside.

They seemed to be studying him, and Travis was belatedly aware that he hadn't showered or combed his hair for more than two days. Trying to peer into the darkened apartment over Travis's shoulder, Grizzly asked, "Is Lisa feeling all right?"

Sensing a chance for a quick exit, Travis pounced on it. "No, she's actually back home with her parents, recovering from a kidney infection. And I've been feeling a little sick myself."

As soon as he spoke the words, he recognized his mistake. Both men were immediately through the door uttering platitudes and ushering him toward the couch.

"I'm so sorry."

"We didn't know."

"When did this all happen?"

There was no way, short of physically pushing them back through the door, that he could keep them out now, and he found himself sitting on the couch with both of them perched on chairs across from him. But even as they offered to have someone bring in dinners, and asked for more information on Lisa's condition, Travis saw Grizzly's eyes dart toward the hall and the huge pile of paper visible through the open door. He could just make out the sounds of Runt's voice coming from the computer's speakers.

He had to get them out, before they started asking questions he wasn't prepared to answer. As much as he appreciated their concern—and he guessed he did owe Grizzly some gratitude for hooking him up with Mr. Merino—what he needed most right now was privacy. He wasn't about to have women bringing in crocks of soup and plastic containers of Jell-O at all hours of the day. Jumping to his feet, he walked to the end of the hall, where he closed the office door and turned back to face them.

"Thank you very much for all of your help. But right now I really just need to get some rest. So if you don't mind, I think that I'll just handle everything myself for a while." He walked to the front door and held it open, trying to hide his relief as they awkwardly scrambled to their feet and gathered up their scriptures.

"I'll be sure and call you if anything further comes up." He shook each of their hands as they passed by on their way out the door.

Seeming to regain his composure, Grizzly paused in the doorway. "Everything work out all right with that referral I gave you?"

"Just fine. Thanks." Travis nodded and gently pushed the door against him.

"Are you sure there's nothing else we can do for you?" Grizzly seemed determined to make the visit last as long as possible. But just then the phone started to ring, saving Travis from any further answers.

"That's probably Lisa now. I've got to go," Travis said, and finally managed to push the door all the way closed, turning the deadbolt as soon as it clicked shut.

"Hello." Travis picked up the phone, hoping that it was Lisa finally returning his calls.

At first, the voice on the other end of the line was so quiet that he started to hang up, thinking that no one was there. But then, beneath a slight static hissing, he thought he recognized someone whispering his name.

"Who is this?" he asked reluctantly, thinking it was another threat.

"Travis. I need to talk to you."

"Holly?" He didn't know who he had been expecting, but it definitely had not been Open Door's VP of Marketing.

"Something's going on here and I need your help." In the background, Travis could hear the sound of traffic and realized that Holly must be calling from her cell phone.

"Help with what?" Travis sensed a trap. Was this how she had gotten to Rob?

"We need to meet. I can't talk to you over the phone."

"Do you really think I'm that stupid? Tell your friends that your damsel in distress act might have worked on Rob, but I'm not falling for it."

Even above the traffic noise, her gasp was audible. "What do you know about Rob? Do you know something the police aren't saying?"

"This isn't going to work," Travis snapped, his surprise giving way to anger. "You wanted to trash the Assistant project, and now it looks like you've done it. I admit that I'm surprised even *you* would go so far as to sabotage Open Door to do it. But if you played any part in having Rob killed, I swear I'll see that you go to prison forever."

Holly's silence was broken by what sounded like a sob. "That *is* what happened, isn't it? When I saw it on the news, I was so scared that he had been killed. But I tried to convince myself that it couldn't have anything to do with . . . " Again it sounded like she was crying. She sounded so distraught that Travis was tempted to believe her. But couldn't she be faking this to arouse his sympathy?

"I'm sorry." She sounded a little more under control. "It's just that when I got that threatening phone call, I suddenly felt so overwhelmed. And you were the only person I thought I could trust."

"Threatening call?" Travis was stunned. Why would they threaten one of their own? Had she started something rolling only to watch it get out of control? "Look, Holly. Whatever you've done, the best thing is to just go to the police and tell them everything. You've got to stop this before anyone else gets hurt."

Suddenly Holly seemed to grasp the meaning of Travis's words.

"You think I did this?" She snorted a gust of hysterical laughter. "That this was some ploy to get rid of Rob's precious Assistants?"

"Isn't that why you called?" Travis felt a faint stirring of doubt. If she was acting, she should get an Academy Award.

"I called because someone left a message on my home phone telling me to keep my nose out of things that were none of my affair or I would end up like Rob. At first I thought it was some kind of sick joke. I didn't even know what they were talking about. But then I realized that someone was worried about the questions I had been asking about you and Rob. I was just trying to find out what was going on, and how it might affect the IPO. I never even connected your getting fired with Rob's death. Travis what is this all about?"

Travis hesitated before answering. If she was in on this with Runt, she could be pumping him for information, trying to figure out how much he actually knew. But what if she was telling the truth? Could his conscience bear it, if she turned up dead too? "Listen Holly, I'm not sure I know any more than you do. But if you really aren't part of this, get away from Open Door and stay away until after the IPO."

"Just like that? Walk out the door?" Holly sounded incredulous.

"Don't just walk, Holly. Run. There are some crazy people working there."

"That's easy for you to say, Travis. You don't have millions of dollars in stock options on the line."

Now it was Travis's turn to sound incredulous. "You'd risk your life for stock options?" But even as he asked the question, Travis felt it hitting way too close to home. Wasn't that awfully close to what he was doing?

"I guess so." Holly's voice seemed drained of all emotion. "I'm not sure you could ever understand. You're not that kind of guy. You're different."

"Maybe I'm not as different as you think," Travis said. "Well, at least be careful."

"I will. And thanks for the warning." Holly seemed on the verge of hanging up, before seeming to remember something.

"Travis. I think maybe you know more than you're letting on. And I really do believe that you got a bad deal here. Anyway, I don't know if it will help you or not, but that night when Rob came to talk to me—the night before he . . . disappeared—he said one other thing to me. I was trying to figure out what it meant, but now I'm afraid to look into it any further."

"I understand," Travis said.

"Well I don't know whether you can use it or not. But Rob said he was going to look into how many stock options certain employees had been granted. Does that mean anything to you?"

Travis wondered. Was there a chance Runt hadn't been granted as many shares as the other employees? He didn't know why that would be the case, but he would look into it.

"I'm really not sure," he said. "But I'll check on it."

"Good luck," she breathed, and the line went dead.

Returning to his computer, Travis dropped into the chair and scrubbed his eyelids with the palms of his hands. He closed his eyes, longing to be back at the ranch with his wife. In the last three days, he had slept less than six hours and he could feel the fatigue catching up with him. What he really needed was a long vacation somewhere far away from everything stressful. He pictured himself standing thigh deep in the cool rushing water of the Provo River, studying the current for the familiar ripple of a trout rising to feed. Lisa was lounging on the bank, doing one of her crossword puzzles. He moved his fly rod back and forth, letting out more and more line as the fly arced further and further out.

It was all a matter of vision, he thought. Two anglers could use the same pole, the same line, even the same fly, and yet have completely different results. The fisherman who comes home empty-handed most nights sees the river as a single body of water. He casts his line randomly into the current, occasionally lucking across a trout, but as often as not spending the entire day watching as his lure floats fruitlessly past the best spots.

But the successful fisherman sees beyond what the naked eye can tell him. He views the river as a series of eddies and currents, a puzzle with its own personality and characteristics. By reading the river, even one that he has never seen before, an angler can instantly tell where the fish are most likely to be hiding. It is necessary to think like a fish. Where is the food coming from? Where is the shelter to provide protection from predators?

Was it possible that he was doing the same thing with all the information flowing past his eyes? Was he allowing himself to be so preoccupied with the sheer mass of data that he was missing the clues that were right in front of him?

His mind went back to the final e-mail he had received from Rob, announcing his decision to leave the company. He knew that it had to be a forgery, and he was reasonably sure that Runt wasn't clever enough to pull it off. The person who sent the message was more than likely the same person who had told Runt what files to copy. But who could have gotten access to the e-mail system and known about the meeting Rob had scheduled with Peter's team for that morning? He ran through a number of possibilities in his mind, but no one seemed to have the combination of technical expertise and inside knowledge as well as an obvious motive.

Something kept nagging at his mind about the message. Some vital piece of information seemed to float just out of his reach, tugging at his memory and then disappearing just as it started to come into focus, like a bit of melody that he couldn't quite remember the words to.

"Assistant, find e-mail. From Rob Detweiler. To All. Subject, keyword, good-bye." He waited while the trout on the screen checked a watch that had appeared on one of its fins. After almost a minute, the e-mail message appeared on his screen.

Something about the message was wrong but he couldn't seem to pin it down.

After serious consideration, I have come to the conclusion that the company and I would be better served by my leaving. I am sure that Peter will be able to cover everything at my 8:30 meeting. I am sorry for the abruptness.

But that wasn't right, was it? Hadn't the meeting been scheduled for eight? He clearly remembered Rob telling him to go home early, that they would meet at eight. Flipping through his planner, he saw the meeting penciled in for eight A.M. and he remembered how the other developers had all joked about Rob sleeping in. It was a fairly minor mistake, and yet everything else had been so carefully orchestrated that it seemed glaring by comparison. Why would someone get the time wrong by half an hour? Unless . . . he sat forward so quickly that he banged his hip on the side of the desk.

It was Peter who had pointed out the only person who would have a reason to get the meeting time wrong. On the first day Travis met him, he had laughed at Rob's attempt to get David Lee to the interview on time. *He even wrote a filter that intercepts all his e-mails and moves the time on his appointments to half an hour later*, he had said.

And that meant that if Rob had sent out a message to the other VPs detailing his planned schedule as they had agreed only hours earlier to do, David Lee would have read eight instead of eight-thirty. So when he sent out the bogus final e-mail from Rob he would have had a legitimate reason for making that mistake. David Lee was one of the few people in the company who was technical enough to break into the network e-mail system, and high enough on the company totem pole to convince the president that Travis was a traitor.

Now that he was thinking clearly, he realized that another clue had slipped by him. Popping in the CD he had recorded of Runt stealing his files, he clicked the Play button. At first all he saw was Runt typing on the keyboard. But then after he had completed downloading the first set of files, he picked up a pen and checked off something in the notebook he was holding. Travis froze the picture and zoomed in. It could have been a coincidence, and he understood why he had overlooked it before. But now that he knew what he was looking for, he was certain it was one of the notebooks David Lee was constantly poring over. He had to be the unknown insider working with Runt.

Travis's fingers blurred across the keys as he opened up a new e-mail. He hadn't found any way to breach the Open Door firewall, and he wasn't about to try breaking back into the building; but in the hope that he might come up with another suspect and need to copy the Assistant to other machines, he had installed what was known in the industry as a backdoor. Using an alias account that he had set up, he sent an e-mail to Runt's address. To Runt, it would look like a junk message sent as part of a mass mailing. The subject was innocuous enough. "Earn thousands in your spare time." He would probably delete it without even reading it. But as soon as it was received, the series of letters and numbers at the bottom of the message would set off a command embedded within the Assistant framework that would cause it to install a copy of itself on David

Lee's computer. It could only work if Runt had been given access to one of Lee's drives, but from what he had just learned, Travis didn't think there would be much of a problem.

* * *

Travis was in the shower when the phone began ringing. He thought it might be Mr. Merino calling to remind him of their nine-thirty appointment. Travis had called him as soon as he realized that David Lee was Runt's partner. He had expected that on a Sunday he would get the attorney's answering service, but apparently Mr. Merino worked Silicon Valley hours as well, because he picked up on the second ring.

Travis had explained his suspicions without mentioning any names. He would save that for a face-to-face meeting. Mr. Merino was anxious to meet, and they had settled on nine-thirty the next morning. Wrapping a towel around his waist, Travis raced across the bedroom and picked up the phone before his machine could get it.

"Mr. Merino?"

"I warned you to stay out of this." It was the cold, computer-generated voice he had heard on his Open Door voice mail, and Travis jerked back from the phone as if he had just laid a poisonous serpent against his face. "At least Rob went quickly, but I'm going to enjoy watching you suffer."

"Who is this?" Travis tried to sound unafraid, but his voice trembled nonetheless.

There was a short pause, and then the voice said, "Just think of me as the Enforcer Assistant. You don't get any more warnings, Travis. Your wife may be gone, but if you talk to anyone else, she'll be a widow."

"You can't . . . " Travis started, but the line went dead before he could finish whatever he was going to say. Dropping the phone to the floor, he backed away from it and then spun around to look behind him as if whoever was behind the threatening voice was already in his apartment.

"You can't scare me," he said, and then laughed weakly at how terrified his own voice sounded. He had hoped Runt would forget about him after he was fired. But whether he knew about Travis's conversation the day before with Holly, or was trying to keep Merino from helping him, Runt obviously hadn't forgotten him. But he was so close. There was no way he could stop now.

He needed some kind of protection, and a kitchen knife wasn't going to do it. Rummaging through the top drawer of the nightstand, he pulled out the papers he had filled out at the gun shop. It wasn't like he was actually going to shoot someone. Just the sight of a gun should be enough to dissuade anyone who might threaten him. If it came down to that, he would probably run before he would actually fire a gun at a human being anyway, but he wouldn't allow himself to be threatened anymore.

It won't come to that. It won't come to that. It was the mantra that he repeated over and over in his head as he tucked the papers into his pocket along with his keys. He would have just enough time to stop by the gun shop before he went to meet with the attorney.

* * *

Mr. Merino's office was just as Travis remembered it, cluttered enough to give the impression that he had plenty of business, without seeming disorganized. It was a few minutes after nine-thirty Monday morning. Traffic had slowed him down a little more than he had expected, but Mr. Merino didn't seem to mind.

"Thanks for taking the time to meet with me on such short notice." Travis laid his file folder on the attorney's desk.

"No problem," Merino said, first examining the folder's front and back and then lifting it experimentally before opening it. "Hmm, this is quite a bit of information. What do you have here, two hundred pages?"

"About two hundred and fifty." Travis rubbed his hands together nervously.

"Do you mind me asking how you came by this?"

"I have what you might call a friend on the inside." Travis said.

"That wouldn't be Ricky, the programmer you told me about, would it?"

"No." Travis answered vehemently. "He is not involved in any of this."

Merino nodded and scribbled a note on his legal pad. "I can see that you would rather not discuss it, but I must warn you that if this ever goes to court the Judge will want to know how this information was obtained."

"I hope it never gets that far," Travis said. "I just want to prove that I'm innocent and let them see what's really going on right under their noses."

"Yes, well let's hope that's all it will take." Merino seemed to consider pressing the issue further and then tapped the thick green and yellow stripes that Travis had applied to the front of the folder with marking pens. "What's this?" he asked.

"It's just a coding system I use to keep track of my notes," Travis said.

"Um hmm. Very good." The attorney leaned further back in his chair and crossed his legs, adjusting the creases of his sharply pressed slacks with one hand as he flipped through the pages of the folder with the other.

After nearly ten minutes of what looked to Travis like almost random page flipping, Merino seemed to nearly lose his balance as he suddenly lurched forward across the desk and pointed the folder at him. "This David Lee. Do you have any actual proof that he is somehow involved in all of this?"

He seemed to be holding his breath, until Travis shook his head, then he dropped back into his chair with an audible exhalation of air.

"No, not yet. Why, do you think it's important?" Travis asked.

Merino laid the folder back onto the desk and tapped the cover pointedly with one finger. "Well, you can never be sure. But it would certainly seem like the involvement of a senior-level member of the company could help your story's credibility quite a bit."

Sketching a series of intersecting arrows on his pad, the attorney asked in an almost offhand manner, "Any idea when you think you might get some conclusive evidence on this David Lee?"

"I haven't gone through everything yet," Travis said. "But I'm hoping to find something in the next day or two."

Across the desk from him, Merino had picked up the pad again and was jotting notes that were shielded from Travis's view. "The next day or two, hmm? What type of proof do you expect to find, exactly?"

"I'm really not sure."

"But you are sure it's him and not one of the other VPs?"

"Pretty sure." Travis shrugged. "I could be wrong, but I'll let you know as soon as I find out anything more."

Merino pursed his lips and slid the pad into one of his desk drawers. "Yes, you do that." Standing up, he extended one hand. The tailored gray blazer he was wearing hiked up to reveal a stylish gold wristwatch as he shook Travis's hand. He walked him toward the door of his office.

"I'll have Kathleen check back with you in a few days, but if anything new comes up before then, you have my card."

"I do, and I will definitely call," Travis said. For a moment, he thought there was something else he had meant to ask, but if there was he couldn't remember it now, and so he continued out into the small lobby. He waited in front of the secretary's desk, as she ushered in the next appointment, and then she had him sign several documents the office had put together for him.

"Just the standard legal mumbo jumbo that says we are representing you in any actions filed against Open Door, et cetera, et cetera," she joked as he moved rapidly through each of the lines she had Xed.

She seemed to be moving around more easily on her sore knee, and her brace had been replaced by a thick, flesh-colored elastic bandage. Again Travis was struck by how muscular she looked for a secretary. With the exception of her knee, she seemed like she could be using the desk to do vaults off of, instead of sitting behind it.

"Oh, I like to go to the gym," she answered with an embarrassed shrug when he asked her about it. "It helps me take out my day's frustrations before driving through all the traffic. And besides, it's not like I've got a family to rush home to or anything."

"I should probably consider it myself," he said. "Where do you go?"

For just a moment her eyes widened and he was afraid he had embarrassed her again. Then she shook her head and smiled. "Actually it's a private club that my parents belong to."

He nodded. "I see. Well, I actually have a pretty nice gym that's in our apartment complex; I just need to find the time to go."

"Well there you go." She seemed almost relieved as he walked out the door, and he decided not to bring it up again. Sometimes people were really peculiar about certain subjects.

Stepping out onto the porch, he scanned the street in both directions before walking down to his car. Before opening the door, he checked to see that the red alarm light on the dashboard was still blinking, and then glanced briefly under the car before finally opening the door and getting in. Even after the pictures and the guys in the van, it still felt paranoid to check out his car every time he got in, but he couldn't help it.

Not that he would probably be able to tell the difference between a car bomb and a distributor cap, but he still found himself looking over his shoulder everywhere he went and grimacing slightly every time he started the car.

As he drove back to the apartment, he made a mental list of all the things he wanted to review that afternoon. Most important was financial incentives for both Runt and David. In his excitement over discovering David's involvement, he had forgotten to follow up on Holly's tip, and it still bothered him that anyone would jeopardize the kind of money that Runt and especially David, as a VP, would stand to make when the company went public.

Ahead of him, the stoplight turned yellow and he gunned the engine, hoping to beat the light, before realizing that the elderly couple in front of him was stopping. He jerked his foot off the gas pedal and pumped the brake nearly to the floor, feeling the antilock brakes engage as the heavy SUV screeched to a stop only inches from the back bumper of the dark green Cadillac.

On the passenger's side, something heavy slid out from under the seat and banged against the front of the floorboard. For a moment he didn't recognize it, and the fear that was constantly bubbling just under the surface of his self-control tried to break loose and convince him that it actually was a bomb. Then he remembered what he had slid under the seat when he had stopped at the attorney's office, and he nearly bit his tongue thinking about how easily he could have blown his head off.

Like removing a red-hot coal from the embers with a pair of pincers, he reached gingerly forward and lifted the semi-automatic handgun up off the floor and put it into the glove compartment. Even with the orange safety showing, it still felt like handling a dangerous animal, and he unconsciously wiped his hand on the leg of his jeans as he pulled forward into traffic. But he had bought it, and regardless of how he might feel about handguns personally, he was determined to protect himself if anyone came after him again.

As he signaled right to get onto the freeway, he remembered the other thing he was going to ask Mr. Merino, and he abruptly pulled back across traffic and into the left-hand turn lane, nearly colliding with a young blond woman in a silver BMW, who blared her horn and made an obscene gesture as she sped away.

Making a U-turn, he headed back toward the law office. He had wanted to check on the legality of carrying a handgun in his car. Regardless of what the law said, he was going to take it with him everywhere. But he would have to find a better hiding place than the glove box, if any cop who pulled him over for a driving violation could arrest him for having a gun tucked in with his registration.

As he turned back onto the street of quaint older houses, now all remodeled into expensive offices and salons, he saw that Mr. Merino was standing on the front porch of his building, talking to a tall man in a dark leather jacket. It must have been someone who had just arrived, because he was sure the man who had entered the office as he was leaving hadn't had such long hair.

Seeing an open parking spot across the street, he flipped a quick U-turn and pulled into the space. In his rearview mirror he saw the man take something from the attorney. As he opened the driver's side door and began to step out, the man turned and walked down the steps. Travis froze in the act of getting out of the car as he recognized who the man in the leather jacket was. Even from this distance it was impossible to miss the scraggly beard of his home teacher.

Pulling the door closed, he dropped low in his seat and watched as Grizzly walked up the street in his direction. It didn't mean anything. It was just a coincidence of timing. Grizzly had been the one who referred him to Mr. Merino, so of course he must use him as well. He should get out of the car and say "Hi." How stupid would it look if Grizzly continued this far and saw him ducked down in his seat like some kind of guilty kid who has just stolen a candy bar from the local Quick Stop?

He had nearly convinced himself to get out, his hand reaching for the door lever, when Grizzly turned to get into his car and switched the object he had been carrying to his other hand as he fished into his pocket for his keys.

Travis's breath caught in his throat as he recognized the markings on the off-white folder—the green and yellow stripes that he had marked himself only the night before at his kitchen table. The folder that he had just given Mr. Merino, his attorney, and that Grizzly now tossed cavalierly onto the seat of his car before climbing in and pulling the door closed after him.

Clapping his hands to the front of his mouth, to keep himself from screaming, Travis dropped below the window and out of sight as Grizzly's battered sedan rolled past. Grizzly was in on it too. He should never have trusted him. He had known that something was wrong from the beginning, had told Lisa that he was too nosey. But she was so sure that because he was their home teacher they could trust him. And because of her trust, Travis had overlooked his doubts.

"No, no, NO." He banged his head over and over against the side of the door and for a moment everything seemed to go slightly gray. It felt like the spring of some huge steel trap had suddenly snapped shut, crushing his throat in its vicious jaws, so that he could barely breath.

What had he done? Everything he had discovered was laid out in those papers. It wouldn't take more than a day to figure out how he'd gotten them. And now they were being hand delivered to the people who had killed Rob and his wife and threatened to do the same to him, by his own home teacher.

If he couldn't trust the people in his own church, who could he trust? Around him the wall of cars and buildings seemed to be closing in like eager hands. Jamming the keys forward, he ground the ignition for nearly ten seconds before realizing that the car was running. He forced the shifter into drive and gunned the accelerator, the metal of his front bumper pinging off the car in front of him as he fishtailed out into the street. Behind him the electronic wailing of the other car's alarm disappeared as he chose turns at random, trying desperately to elude the people he was sure were behind him.

If he had seen himself in the mirror, he wouldn't have recognized the pale white face with the dark-circled eyes staring back at him. But his eyes never left the road as he raced maniacally from one street to another. Muttering almost inaudibly, and certainly unconsciously, "No one, trust no one, trust no one."

He had no idea how much time had passed before he found himself parked in a gravel lot behind a long low bank of warehouses. His face was pressed to the steering wheel, both arms curled tightly above his head. His eyes felt hot and sore and his lips tasted salty with dried tears when he ran his tongue across them. Although the car was still running, he hadn't bothered to turn on the air conditioning, and the afternoon sun had turned the Jeep's interior into a greenhouse.

Rolling down the windows, he sighed with relief as a light breeze blew across his hot skin. He had never felt more alone in his life. There was no one he felt that he could turn to now. The only people he could trust were the same people he was afraid of endangering. As he struggled to come up with any kind of coherent plan, he heard the words of his father-in-law who now seemed worlds away. "When you've gone through enough good times and bad times with someone, you kind of get on a first-name basis."

Could he pray? He knew that was what Lisa would do. But she'd always had more faith than he did. He had felt like he needed to rely on his own strength. But if it was true that *faith without works* was dead, couldn't it also be true that *works without faith* were equally dead? He knew that he hadn't been very spiritual lately, concentrating so hard on work that church had seemed like just another distraction. But now, unsure of whether anyone would even listen to him, he bowed his head and hesitantly began to speak.

"Heavenly Father, I . . . " he faltered for a moment and then continued on quickly. "I know I haven't been a very good Mormon lately, and probably not even a very good husband, but I don't know where else to turn. I think I've really messed things up and I hope that Lisa can forgive me and that You can too."

His mind searched for the right words. How could he ask God to help him when he wasn't even sure what he needed? Finally remembering the words he had heard Lisa's younger brothers and sisters sing in Primary, he bowed his head again and closed his prayer.

"Please help me to choose the right, and please help Lisa to know how much I love her. Amen."

* * *

From the journal of Lisa Edwards

Monday, May 10

I have to do something now. I know there is no way that my parents would let me go to Travis, but for the last few days I have been getting stronger and stronger promptings that he needs me. Then just a few minutes ago, it was like he was right by my side calling me. I don't know how, but in some way I am going to help him, no matter what it takes.

CHAPTER 12

Slamming the apartment door shut behind him, Travis engaged both the passage lock and dead bolt with shaking fingers and then, after scanning the room for a moment, dragged a kitchen chair through the hallway and forced it beneath the knob.

In the kitchen, the slanting rays of late afternoon sun leaked through a crack at the bottom of the blinds and illuminated the shriveled plants in the paper cups that stood along the sill. He was surprised to see that the clock next to the sink showed that it was nearly five. It was hard to believe how much time had passed.

Reaching under the back edge of his T-shirt, he found the rough-textured handgrip of the pistol and slid it out of the waistband of his jeans. He considered the orange safety switch before thumbing it tentatively to the off position, and then began searching through each of the rooms.

Continuing into the master bedroom, he saw that the softly beeping answering machine showed two new messages since he had left that morning. He almost pushed the Erase button, sure they would be more threats or worse, but it would be stupid and dangerous to ignore any source of information. The only thing he had going for him now was that he knew they were on to him and they still thought he was in the dark.

Pushing the safety on the gun back into the on position, he laid it on the nightstand and pressed the glowing red Play button on the machine.

"Travis?" He dropped down onto the bed at the sound of Lisa's voice. She hadn't spoken more than a dozen words to him, despite his phoning her every day, since she left.

"I was really hoping that you would be there." Her voice sounded husky like she had just finished crying or was trying not to start. "I'm sorry that I've been ignoring you, but I was really mad. Actually I'm still mad, but I've been getting the strongest feeling that you are in trouble. Are you in trouble, Travis?"

She paused for a moment as though expecting him to respond and then rushed through the rest of her message. "The thing is, that I really think that I should be out there with you. I'm not supposed to fly I know, but maybe I could get an exception, or I could rent a car or even take the bus. I know Mom and Dad wouldn't agree. But I'm feeling a lot better now, and I need to be there with you, and whether you'll admit it or not, you need me there. So please call me as soon as you get this. I love you and I'll help you find a way out of this. So bye. Call me!" There was a click and then a single electronic beep as the number on the machine changed to a one.

Picking up the phone, he started to dial and then set it back down again. What could he say? Yes, he was in trouble, but having her here would only make it worse. What he needed to do was get through this and then never leave her again. He continued to stare at the phone a moment longer, his jaw muscles working, before giving up and pushing the Play button on the answering machine again.

"Hi Travis, this is Sherrie Benson, Lisa's visiting teacher. I just heard about Lisa and I was wondering if you needed anything. I'm going to be out most of the day, but if you need any help with meals or keeping the place up, call and I'll have someone in the Relief Society get on it in three wags of a dead lamb's tail. Which come to think of it might not seem all that fast, but please do call if you need anything. Oh, and also, can you give me Lisa's number in Utah? I'd like to check and see how she's feeling. Thanks. My number is 555-4878."

He couldn't help smiling a little. The rest of the world might be falling to pieces, but the Relief Society would always be right behind to provide dessert. Come to think of it though, there might be one thing she could help him with. Watching the tape rewind in the machine, he picked up the phone and dialed her number.

After four rings, her machine picked up. "Hi this is Sherrie Benson. I'm away from the *line*, but if you want to *draw* on my resources you really *art* to leave a *graphic* message before I stop being punny."

At the tone, he hesitated, not sure exactly how to word his question to a machine. "Hi, this is Travis Edwards and I was just calling to . . . " he was interrupted by the click of the phone picking up.

"Travis?" Sherrie asked, her voice exuberant and upbeat as usual.

"Yeah, I just got your message," Travis said.

"Wait a minute and let me turn off the machine." She set down the phone with a clunk, and then after a few seconds came back on the line. "How is everything going? Is Lisa feeling any better? Do you need anything?" Her questions tumbled out, one after another.

"I just heard from her and she's feeling much better." He gave her the number of Lisa's parents and assured her that he was managing just fine on his own.

"There is one thing you could help me out with though." He tried to sound casual. "I need to talk to Grizzly and I don't have his work number. You don't by any chance know where he works do you?"

Her laughter on the other end of the line was completely unexpected, until he realized what he had just said. "Grizzly. That's a new one. But I think Dave Halloran is the only person in the ward who fits that name to a tee."

"Oh, it's just a nickname that Lisa and I . . . " he stammered to a halt.

"Somehow I think he'd get a kick out of it," she laughed. "But where he works . . . I know he's a programmer of some kind, but he changes jobs quite a bit." She paused for a minute as if thinking.

"It seems to me that a few months ago he moved to a new company. Some sort of Internet thing." Travis felt his heart leap into his throat and he both dreaded and expected what he heard next. "Does NetSailor sound right?"

He struggled to speak above a whisper. "Yeah, that sounds familiar all right. Thanks Sherrie, I'll give him a call." He let the phone drop back into its cradle, his head spinning with questions. It was all too convenient. What were the odds that he would just happen to move into the same ward as someone who worked for the competitor that was stealing his company's files? Less than zero.

But if it wasn't a coincidence, how could they possibly have influenced where he would move? Grizzly had been in the ward long before Travis ever heard of the job at Open Door, and the only reason he had even moved into the ward was because of some offer that the company included in its—

He jumped up from the bed and ran into the kitchen, where he pulled open the drawer where Lisa stored all of their bills and other important papers. Pulling the drawer out and off its tracks, he dumped its contents out onto the table and began pawing through the stack of envelopes and papers. It had been in the relocation packet that Open Door mailed out. A bright yellow coupon stapled to the front of the apartment brochure. He found it tucked under the user's manual for their microwave oven.

"Save $400 off of our published rate!" Carrying it back into the bedroom, he picked up the phone and dialed the front office of the apartment complex.

"It's a great day at the Valley View Apartments. How can I help you?" a young-sounding woman's voice answered.

"Hello, I'm thinking about renting an apartment and I wondered if you could tell me what your rates are for a two bedroom, two bath?" Travis asked.

"It depends on the location, but the basic rate is $1200 plus security and first and last month's rent," she rattled off.

That matched what the brochure said. "I also have a coupon for a discount of $400 per month," he said.

"I'm sorry, you must be confusing us with another complex. We don't offer any discounts. As it is, we have a waiting list of nearly thirty names right now."

Travis turned the coupon over, looking for the expiration date or offer limitations that were at the bottom of every other coupon he had ever seen, and wondered why he hadn't noticed their absence earlier. "Are you sure? I think it's some sort of corporate offer from Open Door."

"I'm sorry sir, we really don't offer any discounts, corporate or otherwise. But if you'd like me to add your name to the list, I'd be happy to."

"No, that's OK." He started to hang up and then thought of one more question. "Your waiting list. How long have you had it?"

"Since the day we opened. This is a very popular complex."

"So if I'd wanted to rent an apartment with you say two or three months ago, how long would I have had to wait?"

"A bare minimum of ninety days."

"No matter what?"

"No matter what."

"Thank you. Good-bye." He gently hung up the phone. It didn't make any sense. Did they have someone in Open Door's Human Resources department and the apartment complex? Why go to all this trouble just to get Travis to move into this particular apartment complex?

Picking up the phone again, he dialed a number that he knew by heart and after entering the proper extension was surprised at how good it was to hear the sound of Ricky's voice.

"Hey Ricky, I know I shouldn't be calling you there, but I need an answer quickly and you're the only person I can talk to," Travis said.

"Fire away," Ricky said, as though nothing at all had changed.

"When you came to work for Open Door, they transferred you up from L.A. right?"

"Almost a year ago to the day," Ricky said.

"Were there any special offers in your relocation package?" Travis asked.

"What relocation package?"

"You know, the one with all the information about apartments and schools, from the HR . . . " Travis's voice slowly died as realization dawned on him.

"I've never seen any kind of relocation packet, and as far as I know, Open Door has never had one." Ricky paused for a moment and then continued. "Are you all right Travis? I can leave this stuff and be at your place in ten minutes if you need help."

"No, but thanks. I'll call you if I need anything." He could barely feel the phone in his hand as he hung it up. His whole body seemed to be going numb. Pushing all of the papers off onto the floor, he lowered his head to the smooth, cool tabletop and tried to think.

It had all been a setup from the beginning. The special offer had been a trap to ensure he would move into Grizzly's ward, and he had stepped right into it.

Grizzly, David, Runt, and who knew how many others. They had known from the very beginning that he was coming. He had to try to think from their perspective. Obviously NetSailor had been afraid that Open Door was going to steal their thunder by going public first and had somehow gotten Runt and David to give them the Assistant files. No, *give* was the wrong word. There was far too much money involved, and a big chunk of it must be going directly into the pockets of those two.

He understood why Open Door had been so anxious to hire him. In just a little over a month, he had been able to give their Assistants the necessary infrastructure to turn them from mere shells into useful Assistants. But why would David and Runt go to all the trouble of stealing files he would have given Runt anyway? Why risk making him suspicious, unless there was something they couldn't get without breaking into his computer. The only files he wouldn't have sent were the actual source code files.

Sitting up slowly, he massaged his temples with his fingertips. The only reason he could imagine for stealing his source code files would be if NetSailor was going to try and claim they had written the original code themselves. It would be next to impossible to prove, considering all the records that Open Door must have of the application development cycle. But it could certainly muddy the waters enough to . . . He went to the calendar on the kitchen wall and counted the days until the square outlined in bold red.

Just a few days until the day Open Door went public. If NetSailor released their stolen Assistants first, and then claimed that Open Door had stolen *their* code, it could be devastating enough to force Open Door to delay their IPO. And that would allow NetSailor to go public first, giving them enough of an edge to drive their own stock prices through the roof.

It seemed almost beyond belief that any company would risk its entire reputation for a difference of only a week or two, and yet this world of dot coms was completely unlike anything he had ever seen. Ordinary business plans were thrown out the window to create six-month wonders. People talked about retiring in their twenties and he had overheard some coworkers talking about mere millionaires with disdain. You hadn't really made it until you had "jet money," enough stock to buy your own jet.

But the question still remained. Why would two members of senior management risk their own stock options for the benefit of another company? Walking in to check on the computer, he was relieved to see that, for the moment at least, the Assistants on Runt's and David's computers were still sending information. He knew it wouldn't be long before the flow of data was cut off abruptly. He could send another coded e-mail that would instruct the program to delete itself and as much of its back trail as possible, but he didn't want to kill the courier until he absolutely had to. The more information he could get before they pulled the plug, the better.

"Assistant, find all files with keywords stock, incentive, or options in directories Runt and Lee. Route to printer." The computer's hard drive began to buzz, and the printer whirred to life. He walked to the printer and began flipping through the sheets as they emerged. On the third page, he found what he was looking for. The title read, "Letter of Acceptance for David Lee."

Halfway down, his eyes stopped on the words "Zero Stock Options." It seemed impossible to believe. How could a VP have no stock options when even the part-timers had them? It wasn't until he saw the increased base salary and cash bonuses further down the page that he understood. Reading through the terms, he shook his head and smiled. "You shortsighted idiot. You traded away all of your stock options for cash. I guess you didn't really believe they could go all the way."

It was beginning to make sense now. Once David realized that he had given up millions in stock for what probably amounted to less than fifty thousand dollars, it had been too late to do anything about it. He might even have gone back to Spencer and tried to work out a deal, but in the end he had opted to sell out the company for the competition's stock instead. That was what Rob had caught onto in the HERETIC meeting. David had talked about pricing Beemers, but somehow Rob had known that he had given up his options. Rob must have gone to talk to him about it, and David realized that he had blown his cover.

That still didn't explain why Runt had gone along with it, but Travis suspected that greed was probably the operative word. Lee needed an insider to help him get the files, and it appeared that the offer had been good enough to buy Runt. Now that he knew how and why, he just needed to get some hard proof. The first thing to look for was any trail of their file transfers they might have left behind. He was pretty sure they would have sent them electronically. They wouldn't want to chance someone seeing them physically passing off a disk or CD.

Sitting down in front of the keyboard, he spoke to his computer. "Assistant, search all file transfers. Size, two megabytes or larger."

In less than a minute, text filled the screen. Travis scrolled through three pages of information, but none of the transfers matched the files he was looking for. It was probably too much to hope for anyway. David and Runt would be crazy to send their files out through the company firewall. Any mail that was sent out over the company network would leave a permanent record that would be available to anyone who knew where to look. But David and Runt had gone back into the lab the night he had been under the floor, which seemed to indicate they were using company computers to transfer the files.

Was there any way they could have sent the files from the testing lab without going through the network? "Only if they used a modem," he muttered under his breath. And then the reality of what he had just said hit him. They had dozens of modems to test the speed of the site over different connections. It would have been a piece of cake to dial out on one of the analog phone lines to an anonymous Internet account, without ever passing through the company firewall.

"Assistant, search for dial-up accounts." The hard drive whirred momentarily and then a half-dozen lines of text appeared on the screen.

"Assistant, search all dial-up accounts for all e-mail attachments sent. Size, two megabytes or larger." On the screen, the trout seemed to shrug and a high-pitched male voice said "Sorry, no results found."

Of course, that would just be too easy. They would surely delete all records of any e-mail as soon as it was sent. And for that matter, there was no way to even know that these were anything other than perfectly ordinary accounts used for testing purposes. On the other hand, it was the only possibility that he could think of at the moment.

"Assistant, search dial-up accounts for all e-mail messages sent and deleted." An envelope icon appeared on the screen next to a line of text that read "From: Bluto, To: Popeye, Subject: Spinach."

"Popeye works for NetSailor," Travis said, smiling grimly. "Runt just can't resist a bad pun."

Clicking the icon, he read the single sentence that the message contained.

"Final delivery Monday, 10:00 PM PST"

minutes, they discussed business plans and product specifications until they were interrupted by a petite redheaded nurse carrying a half-dozen clipboards.

"Travis Edwards?"

"Yes." They both looked up from a sheet of hospital stationery they had been scribbling notes on.

"Your wife sent me to look for you," she smiled. "She was afraid you might have been abducted by aliens."

Embarrassed at how much time had passed, Ricky apologized and wheeled Travis back toward his room. "I guess with everything that's happened, she wants to keep you kind of close."

"I guess so," Travis grinned.

When they got back to the room, the visiting teachers were gone and the nurses had taken the baby back to the nursery.

"So what were you two talking about all that time?" Lisa asked, as Ricky helped Travis back into bed.

Ricky and Travis exchanged guilty glances. "Oh you know, just work stuff," Travis said.

"Uh huh." Lisa didn't look like she was buying it for a minute. "This work stuff wouldn't involve keeping my new baby here in California would it?"

"Oh well, it . . . "

"Not that . . . "

They both ended in a guilty silence. And Ricky shifted his feet uncomfortably. "Listen, I really have to be going. But it was great to see you both." Ricky waved, and backed out the door.

Turning toward Lisa, Travis laughed nervously. "You know I would never do anything that would take you away from Utah without . . . " His words died away as he realized how they sounded.

"You know, I think I've heard that somewhere before," Lisa laughed. And then with a wink she added, "But what makes you think I wouldn't want my baby to stay here for a while longer?"

* * *

That night, hours after the lights had gone out, Travis was still unable to fall asleep. "Lisa, are you awake?"

"Yes." Her voice was warm and comforting in the darkness.

"Last night when I was running from Runt, my leg hurt so bad that I didn't think I could make it."

"I'm not surprised. The doctors were amazed that you were able to stand on it at all. They say you are going to need months of physical therapy."

"But then, just when I felt like I had to quit, I closed my eyes and you were there."

"I know," she said confidently.

"How could you know?" he asked.

"When the agents radioed to Grizzly that you were being chased by Runt on foot, I knew you would have no problem outrunning him. And yet I kept having a very strong feeling that you were in bad trouble. There was nothing I could do for you, but I knew you needed me there." She paused for so long that he almost asked if she was all right, but then she continued, her voice soft and husky.

"I closed my eyes and I prayed as hard as I could that you would be safe. And then it was like Heavenly Father put your hands in mine and I held on as tight as I could. I kept telling you that you could make it, and squeezing your hands, praying that you would be all right. Finally I felt your hands sliding away from me, but by then I knew you were OK."

Travis lay in the dark quietly thinking about what she had said, and then whispered, "He really does answer our prayers, doesn't He?"

"Yes, He does," she whispered back.

"I know we can't kneel together, but do you think we could say a prayer now?" Travis asked. And from across the room, Lisa's answer was immediate.

"I'd like that."

Bowing his head as best he could from the confines of the hospital bed, Travis poured out his thankfulness for their miraculous rescue, for Annie's safe birth, and for bringing them all safely back together. *It feels wonderful,* he thought, *to be praying to Heavenly Father when I'm not in desperate need of help.* When he finally concluded his prayer, he could hear Lisa quietly echoing his "Amen" from her bed.

"I love you," he called softly to her through the darkness.

He could hear the smile in her voice as she whispered back, "I love you too."

EPILOGUE

The white water swirled and eddied down the canyon, slowing whenever it had to detour around rocks or brush against the bank, and then rushing ahead over the drops in the riverbed. In one of the slower spots between a spear of mica-flecked granite and a sandy stretch of soil, a healthy young trout waited just beneath the surface, fanning its tail slowly back and forth to hold itself in place against the force of the current. Its discriminating eyes followed the twigs and other bit of detritus that floated above it, searching for the insects and larvae that made up most of its meals.

A few feet upriver an especially attractive bit of gray and red fluff dropped lightly onto the water and floated toward the trout. Confident that this was the meal it had been searching for, it raised its head up to the surface until its tail and dorsal fin actually protruded out of the water. Timing its rise so that fish met insect only inches from its hiding place, the trout snapped its strong jaws closed and dove beneath the water again.

Too late, it realized its mistake. The hook bit sharply into the roof of the fish's bony mouth as a length of nearly invisible nylon leader pulled sharply against its sensitive lips. Frantically lunging from left to right, leaping out of the water and then diving as deeply as the line would allow, it tried, to no avail, to shake loose the hook.

Slowly but consistently, giving a few feet, only to pull that much harder a moment later, the line inexorably pulled the trout forward until at last, weakened enough that it could barely resist, it was lifted to the glittering surface and up into the deadly atmosphere that would eventually kill it.

Travis reached his hand down into the icy-cold mountain water and lifted the trout up to where Lisa, sitting on the grassy bank, could see it. Laying her crossword puzzle book down next to her side, she clapped enthusiastically.

"Hooray, hooray."

Behind him, something slapped playfully at his ear, and a tiny high-pitched voiced mimicked, "'ray, 'ray."

Craning his head around behind him, he could see Annie's doll-like face wreathed in black curls. Leaning forward in her papoose carrier, she ran one sticky finger over the lens of his sunglasses, leaving a dark smear behind.

"Monkey," he laughed, and reached back with his free hand to tickle her under her chin, sending her into gales of infectious giggling.

Then, careful not to injure the gills, he lowered the fish back into the water and expertly removed the hook. The instant it tasted freedom, the trout darted back into the current and disappeared. Watching its glistening surface race through the water, Travis smiled. Let it grow bigger and hopefully wiser.

Adjusting his line so that the sharp fly wouldn't catch on anything, he dropped his sunglasses into his creel and waded toward shore. From the picnic ground, just out of sight beyond the trees, he could make out the aroma of grilling hamburgers and hotdogs. Just then Lisa's mother called out to everyone.

"Kids, lunch is ready! Come and get it before it's gone." He smiled, knowing there was always twice as much food as there were people.

Reaching the bank, he unhooked the papoose carrier and handed it carefully up to his wife. Annie giggled again, enjoying the ride, and reached her hands out toward Lisa.

Free of the backpack, Travis grabbed a strong root with one of his hands and hoisted himself out of the water. The rubber waders made him feel twice as heavy, and although he was down to only one physical therapy session a month, his left leg was still weak. The therapist said that it might never be as strong as it once was, but he wasn't so sure.

Leaving waders and creel by the bank, he took Lisa's hand as they walked back to join the others. It was nice to be able to take a few days off and fly out to visit the family. The past few months had been crazy getting investors lined up for their new company, but he was confident that Ricky could hold down the fort while he was away.

The offer from Open Door had been a good one, and there had been very little haggling on either part. Travis was happy to be rid of them and they were just as happy to have him agree to keep silent. There would still be the trials, of course. They seemed to drag on forever. But he would face those as they came. Runt and one of the other defendants had already pled guilty.

Reaching the picnic tables, he plopped Annie onto one knee and watched her tiny rosebud lips open as Lisa fed her a piece of deep-red watermelon. The juices ran down her chin and dripped onto her jumper as she munched happily.

It would have been nice to move back to Utah, he reflected, and he thought that eventually they would. But right now the opportunities were in Silicon Valley. That was where the best of the best gathered to prove who had the hottest code and the most imaginative ideas. It was where brainpower and silicon combined in one of the most exciting competitions ever.

And if there was one thing he had learned, it was that he and Lisa were both competitors.

Jeffrey was born in Oakland, California, and spent most of his youth in the greater Bay Area before it was known as the Silicon Valley. He served a mission for The Church of Jesus Christ of Latter-day Saints in the Utah Salt Lake City North Mission. He met his wife, Jennifer, in an Institute class, and they were married four months later in the Oakland Temple. They currently reside in San Jose and have four wonderful children with whom they enjoy reading, games, computers, and outdoor activities.

Having worked for several Utah County-based companies as well as two San Jose dot-coms, Jeffrey has personally experienced the culture shock of moving from one community to the other, and the rapid ups and downs of the Internet world. An avid runner, Jeffrey developed much of the plot for his novel while running up and down the Provo Canyon bike path depicted in this book. He has been involved in the creation and distribution of many of the technologies used in *Cutting Edge*.

Jeffrey welcomes readers' comments. You can write to him in care of Covenant Communications, P.O. Box 416, American Fork, Utah, 84003-0416, or at his e-mail address: jsavage@jeffreysavage.com.

BENEATH

the

SURFACE

The phone woke Hannah Dennison who had fallen asleep on the floor, her chin resting on an open book. Years later she would remember that phone call—and the discovery of the body in Lake Shiloh—as the end of her childhood and the false shelter of her own innocence. The second ring caused Hannah to lift her head slightly and stare at the page of Shakespeare framed by her elbows and arms, one forearm stacked on top of the other—it was the balcony scene of *Romeo and Juliet.* She used the cuff of her sweatshirt to rub off the little grease smudge her chin had left on the page. Her waist-long hair spread like tendrils of wild ivy over her plush bedroom carpet. During the third ring, Hannah unfolded herself from her tortured position. Her legs had been stretched out into Chinese splits in an unbroken line from her hips; her torso pressed flat on the floor above them. Madame Karanaeva had recommended that all her advanced ballet students sit in this position for fifteen minutes each day to perfect their turnouts and keep their muscles flexible. Hannah squinted to see the time on her clock radio. *Midnight.* She had held the painful position for more than three hours.

On the fourth ring, Hannah stood, testing her weight on her wobbly, overflexed muscles, and tottered over to the phone by her bed. On the fifth ring, wincing and moaning, Hannah picked up the receiver.

"Hannah? You okay?" came a gruff male voice from the phone. "It's Dale Farley."

"Yeah, Chief, just . . . suffering for my art," she replied, sitting gingerly on the edge of her bed, biting into the knuckle of her thumb.

"Your folks out of town again?"

Hannah looked at her clock again and realized that a phone call after midnight rarely brought good news. Suddenly she knew exactly why Dale Farley had called. "Have you got Gabe at the station, Chief?" She grimaced again, this time from having to deal with the antics of her twelve-year-old brother whom she had last observed sleeping soundly in his bedroom down the hall.

"Fourth time this summer, Hannah. Every time your parents go to one of them Christian pep rallies, Gabe seems to think he can do as he pleases. You need to call your Aunt Kate or get Jared or someone to bring you down to the station." Jared was Hannah's next-door neighbor who was old enough to drive. Aunt Kate lived across town.

"Can't you just send Gabe home in a squad car like you did last time?"

"I'm not going to do that, Hannah. I'm filing paper work on him for his own good. First step toward a juvie record, Han. He's too young to be hanging out down here on that college campus. You know how it gets over Labor Day weekend with all them college students coming back."

"So exactly what crime has Gabe committed, Chief?" she asked, protectiveness bristling up through her annoyance.

"I haven't actually caught him doing anything other than breaking curfew, but it's just a matter of time till I figure out what he's up to. We want to keep Gabe out of serious trouble, Hannah, so let's get your folks in on this and nip this midnight wandering thing in the bud."

Hannah was touched by the genuine worry she heard in Dale Farley's voice. The Chief had been a member of her father's church for as long as she could remember; most of his patrolmen were members too. In a concerted effort, they had kept Gabe's mischief off the police blotter, and the Dennison family name had remained unsullied all summer long.

Her father's church functioned as the center of the social and religious life in the small town of Griggsberg. His non-denominational house of worship called The Church on the Hill stood on the high end of Bennigan's Bluff; the stained-glass figure of Christ could be seen from anywhere in town. The church was the loom on which the threads of all their lives were anchored, then woven into a tidy, predictable pattern. *Loom*. That was a good word. In addition to providing its foundation, the church loomed over the town like a watchful presence.

Behind the forty-foot-high bluff snaked a good-sized river called the Little Blue. Between the Bluff and the town, a glistening lake curved like a kidney bean, meeting the river at both ends of the lake. Before it had accidentally flooded years before, the lake basin had once been a dusty limestone quarry. After the quarry flooded, forming the lake, Midwest Christian College had moved its campus from downtown Kansas City to Griggsberg. The shiny new college campus and the magnificent church above it had transformed Griggsberg into a bustling, prosperous college town.

Hannah had fallen silent as she considered how she would get down the Bluff to the police station to claim her brother without the whole town finding out he was in jail. "Okay, Chief, I'll throw on some clothes and find a way down there." She hung up the phone and massaged her calf muscles through the large holes of her favorite dingy-white, wooly leg warmers. Scattered on the floor by her bed were the five Shakespearean plays she had been reading over the summer for her honors English class. The test was on Tuesday, the first day of school. *Maybe Gabe will settle down once school starts up again,* she thought wearily as she stacked her books.

Without changing her grungy San Francisco Ballet sweatshirt that she always wore to bed, Hannah stepped into a navy blue pleated skirt and buttoned it at her slender waist. She couldn't find her Doc Martens in her cluttered room, so she grabbed her leather dance slippers with the black elastic bands from her dance bag. She snugged these on, then wove her unruly ash blonde hair into a single messy braid, secured it with the inky rubber band from the morning newspaper, and tossed it over her shoulder. From the glass dish on top of her father's dresser, Hannah picked up a large ring of keys and found the one to his Ford Taurus. No sense in bothering anyone at this hour. Although Hannah was still two months shy of her sixteenth birthday, she'd been driving the family car for more than a year whenever her parents left on one of their frequent trips to speak and sing at church conferences, to participate in political rallies, or to appear on Christian television shows. *How else can I get bags of groceries up the steep roads of the Bluff?* she always thought to herself whenever she took the car. *Do they expect me to make a nuisance of myself whenever I need to haul anything home or get Gabe and me where we need to go?* She wasn't going to let a few pesky laws keep her from doing what she needed to do. Over the last year, Hannah had developed a secret pride in her ability to run a home and look after her brother during the frequent absences of the adults who lived there. She thought of these self-taught skills as her personal contribution to the family ministry. Knowing how to survive and get things done had freed up her talented, charismatic parents so they could go out and save the world.

Without turning the headlights on, Hannah backed the Taurus out of the garage and headed down the hill. *No sense in waking the neighbors.* In the rearview mirror, she caught sight of Gabe's wide-open bedroom window on the second floor of the house. One of his royal-blue curtains with the rows of red and yellow superman logos flapped in the breeze like a wagging tongue. She noticed for the first time how close the branches of the elm tree had grown to her brother's window, and made a mental note to get the saw out and chop them down. *Time to bust Superman out of jail,* thought Hannah bitterly as she rumbled over the wooden floorboards of the covered bridge. She switched on the headlights and drove toward the police station.